ALAN BRAYNE was born in the Black Country, and currently works in Indonesia where he has taught English since 1996. *Jakarta Shadows* is his first novel.

Jakarta Shadows

Alan Brayne

TINDAL STREET PRESS

First published in 2002 by
Tindal Street Press Ltd
217 The Custard Factory, Gibb Street, Birmingham, B9 4AA
www.tindalstreet.org.uk

Copy Editor: Penny Rendall
Typesetting: Tindal Street Press Ltd

A CIP catalogue reference for this book is available from
the British Library.

ISBN 0 9535895 8 7

Printed and bound in Great Britain by
Biddles Ltd, Woodbridge Park Estate, Guildford.

To my mother and father

1

I don't know much about paradise, but I am sure of one thing. It won't last. As soon as you're nice and mellow, Satan will make his entrance. My Satan took the form of a guy aged around thirty, with greasy hair, who launched himself into the seat next to mine. He wore a stained white shirt, the buttons of which bulged at the gut to reveal hairy rolls of flesh. He was formidably drunk.

Arrivederci paradise. Not that the bar at the Hotel Platinum would have been many people's vision of the Elysian fields. It was a characterless hole that might have been anywhere on the globe, the kind of dried-up space you'd find in an airport departure lounge. Drab furniture, a mix of uninspiring cuisine. Satellite TV gaped mindlessly in the corner. None of the customers seemed to be watching it. None of the customers seemed to be alive.

It suited me fine. So, the bar staff oozed resentment and the clients had eyes like dead fish, but the Platinum was just perfect that night, when all I wanted to do was drink myself to oblivion. In the Platinum bar, no one expected me to be polite or to make genteel conversation. I was a suit and tie like the rest of them, with a face like a frozen clock. Paradise enough for me.

'So, how long ya been here, pal?' Satan asked, in an accent that managed to grate even though it was colourless. A phoney, transatlantic drawl that was a parody of New

York American. It could have been custom made for the Hotel Platinum.

I glanced at the heavy flesh slumped in the chair next to mine, too close for comfort. Something behind the eyes made my skin crawl.

'In Jakarta?'

'Yeah. In Jakarta.'

'A year.'

'Figures,' he said, with a sneer, and took a swig of his liquor.

'Figures?'

'You got that look. Like you're there for the taking.'

I gave a short, edgy laugh. I wasn't sure what signals I was giving off, nervousness or aggression, but I needn't have concerned myself. He hadn't the slightest interest.

'I guess you like this dump of a city?'

'It's OK.'

He snorted. 'Wait a while, pal. You just wait a while.'

I wanted to tell him to piss off. Tonight was my dose of self-pity and this slimeball seemed set to spoil it. But I'm English to the tip of my little finger and could never be less than polite. I found myself asking him how long he'd been living in Indonesia.

The question seemed to throw him off balance. 'Too long, pal. Who the fuck cares?' I wasn't sure if he was just too drunk to remember or he didn't want to tell me.

'Jakarta is the armpit of south-east Asia,' he announced, in an exultant croak. 'And believe me, south-east Asia has a hell of a lot of armpits. Bangkok, Pattaya, Manila – I smelt them all.'

I watched him lean back and laugh, delighted with himself. The story of my life. Long hours in bars. Inconsequential conversations, as often as not with people I didn't even like.

'So, what d'ya do here in Jakarta?' he asked.

'I work for an NGO. You?'

'Oh, this and that.'

For the first time I regarded him closely. To my surprise, I was looking at someone who'd probably been handsome once. But the years hadn't been that kind to him, and I doubted if he'd been kind to himself. His body bore all the signs of a lifetime of dissipation – lank hair, sallow skin, flabby extra weight that didn't suit him one bit. Dark good looks rapidly gone to seed.

He leant over to place a sweaty palm on my forearm. I gulped down a mouthful of gin to disguise my shiver.

'NGO, eh? Important guy.' The contempt was palpable. 'So what d'ya like about this damn fine city? The culture?'

'OK, I know it's ugly. I know it's polluted.'

'You're not kidding, pal. This place is the pits.'

'The people are the most important thing for me. I love the Indonesian people.'

He snorted again, more vigorously. I ran my previous sentence back through my head. It sounded patronizing as hell. I deserved the snort.

'I guess you figure they're friendly. Sure they are.' He gestured in the direction of the bar. 'They just love us white guys. *Bules*.' He stretched the final diphthong in the word – *boolaaayz*. '*Bules* have fistfuls of dollars. You don't know anything.'

I gazed absently at the bubbles clinging to the lemon in my gin and tonic. His arrogance was all the more annoying for the fact that it disturbed me.

'You come here with your guidebooks and the natives give you a grin and chime, "Hello mister." Oh, and you get so excited because they want to be your soulmate.' He fell back into his chair and scratched his gut. 'They're taking you for a ride, buddy. You'll find out the first time one of them shits on you.'

'Sounds a pretty bad place,' I said. 'Why are you here?'

He rubbed his thumb and index finger together to signal money. 'Why are any of us here, pal?'

What a bind it is to be brought up English, with an etiquette manual lodged inside your skull. A little voice telling you to mind your Ps and Qs and make sure you've washed behind your ears. I scrabbled around for an excuse to get out of his company. Lacking inspiration, I stared up at the TV screen. Some fitness freak in a purple leotard was leaping up and down and beaming a fake-tan smile.

I'd missed my moment and Satan sprang back to life, having found his second wind. He leant across and attempted a confidential whisper. A megaphone might have helped.

'Shall I tell you about Indonesians? About what really lies underneath those phoney smiles and that religious shit? Filthy lucre, pal. You got it and they'll lick your derrière. Lick it nice and shiny and thank you, sir, for the privilege.' He took out his wallet and flashed a wad of notes in front of my nose. 'That's what gets these guys hot and excited. Offer them enough and they'll sell you their own children. If you don't believe me, I've seen it.'

The DJ put on a recording of 'Fly Me to the Moon' set to a disco beat. A portly white gent in a Hawaiian shirt dragged a waitress onto the dance floor and started gyrating.

'And you want to know the irony? We're drawn to it, like flies to shit.'

He lifted his glass with a dramatic flourish, like a speaker about to make a toast, but forgot his pearls of wisdom once the glass hit mid-air. He cut a bizarre figure, this trash spitting venom. I guess you could say he was pathetic, slouched there, stewed in booze, scarcely able to form words. But for all that, there was something demonic about him, a hatred and a power that chilled me inside. It didn't seem possible that a human heart could harbour such loathing; it had to stem from some malevolent force beyond him.

'You drink real slow,' he slurred, as he struggled to focus on my face.

'So what's the hurry?'

He shrugged his shoulders. 'You up for another?'

'Not yet.'

'Not yet, eh? *Belum*. Just listen to yourself, pal. You've gone native.'

His head nodded and his eyelids flickered, and I thought for one happy moment he was about to fall asleep on me. No such luck. He sprang back up like a demented jack-in-the-box, bawling across at a waitress with a fresh burst of energy.

'Hey, *mbak*! Bacardi! *Satu lagi, besar!* Pronto!'

The waitress approached, with tentative steps, edging over to my side of the table before leaning across to wipe the surface clean. She placed a fresh beermat on the wood and, on top of the mat, a large, misty glass of Bacardi stuffed with ice.

'Not bad, uh?' Satan grinned, baring his upper teeth. 'Face is kind of average, I guess, but a fuckable ass.' I couldn't tell if she understood what he'd said. If she did, she hid it well. 'How about it? Fancy her for the night? I'm sure it can be arranged.'

I felt my face flush. 'She does her job OK,' I stammered, and hated myself for sounding like such a prig.

He flashed a sarcastic glance in my direction. 'Or maybe the waiter's more to your taste. I guess he's cute enough, if you're into that kind of thing.' He leant across, gripped hold of my knee and slipped me a grin. 'Go on, pal – spoil yourself. This is Jakarta, the Garden of Earthly Delights.' He leant back to luxuriate in his Wildean wit. 'As sketched by Hieronymus Bosch.'

A gust of air from the door blew his smell in my direction

and I caught a whiff of aftershave and body odour. His eyes were fizzing with pleasure; he was enjoying the frisson of power he felt from my obvious unease. I squeezed tighter into my chair to edge further away from him.

'You can get whatever you want here, pal,' he said, with a twist of the lip. 'If you've got the balls to take it.'

I picked up my glass. Two cubes of half-melted ice clanked in the bottom.

Satan's face grew serious, with the profound look that a drunkard gets when he's trying to remember something. He held his finger in the air, poised like a conductor's baton, as if he were about to say something highly meaningful.

'I have to piss.'

As he swayed back and forth and struggled to his feet, I thought he might pass out on me. He couldn't be far from oblivion, that was sure. As for me, it seemed I'd have to wait longer for the joys of nothingness. The pleasure of his company had sobered me up, as viciously as freezing water. The world was sharp once more and angular, the place I'd spent the evening working hard to escape. I'd lost that soft-focus feeling I loved so much.

He staggered towards the door, up the tiny flight of steps, each one tastefully dotted with a line of orange fairy lights. This time, for sure, I wouldn't need a second chance. As soon as the door swung shut behind him, I was out of there, as fast as my legs could carry me.

The face behind the wheel belonged to a true Jakarta taxi driver. Tetchy and sullen. My efforts at conversation had produced nothing but indistinct grunts and a refusal to meet my eye. I gave up and leant back in my seat. He seemed relieved, and spent the rest of the journey muttering to himself under his breath.

His foul mood didn't seem to be aimed at me in particular, but at life, Jakarta and the universe. I watched whatever was eating him inside screw up his face. It beat me completely. Sure, I could understand why taxi drivers got ratty during the day, when Jakarta congeals into gridlock and their job must be hell. But it was late at night, the road was clear and he was about to earn a few painless *rupiah*.

All the same, he seemed determined to nurture his festering mood, as he scowled at the darkness ahead. A car lurched into the fast lane in front of us, without indicating – standard practice in Jakarta, day or night. '*Monyet!*' my driver spat, slamming his fist on the horn, before overtaking the car on the inside.

I stared out at Ciputat Raya. Except for the charred remains of burnt-out buildings, it was looking almost normal again after the riots. Sometimes I loved this city. God only knew why, since it was hot and filthy, and totally bereft of charm or culture. But whatever else it lacked, the city sure had energy. The buzz of millions of people struggling to eke out a living. In a country gripped by economic crisis, where an empty gut beckoned at the end of each day, all the world was open for business, twenty-four hours.

A gang of young men hung around a bus shelter. One of them howled like a dog and plucked a badly tuned guitar. At night, when the air smelt clean and the little lights glowed in the *warungs*, it was almost easy to wipe out Jakarta's ugliness.

I lived in a luxury complex in the south of the city, a place designed to make its residents forget they'd said farewell to western suburbia. Even the newspaper ads that the developers put out, featuring Teutonic families in Wimbledon whites, bore a clear subliminal message: brown faces need not apply. The security guards on the gate made their usual cursory glance as my taxi slipped through. They were far too busy on more important matters, such as gambling. The taxi driver stared sniffily at my tip, said

13

nothing and pulled away. The sticky night air enveloped me and sweat trickled down my face as I fumbled with the padlock on the gate.

My house was pretty much standard for a *bule* manager in Jakarta – a glamorous white shell built in a style which might be politely described as quasi-American. It could have provided the setting for an upmarket soap. I entered through the front door into the barren grandeur of the huge, bare living space and a yoke of depression fell upon me. It felt as if nobody lived there. I'd been in Jakarta more than a year now and still I hadn't got around to buying any stuff to make this place feel more like a home. I trudged up to the bedroom, switched on the AC and slumped on the bed.

The guy from the Platinum loomed large in my mind. I repeated our conversation over and over, except this time I was really smart and said all the witty things I should have said in the first place. I was feeling pretty pissed off with myself – I'd acquiesced in his racist ranting and now I was trying to absolve myself when it was all too late. Even his memory made me feel dirty somehow. Something about that slimeball had really got under my skin.

The clock by the bed read 2:47. I heard a sound in the darkness, perhaps a rat in the roof above me. I sat up in silence, holding my breath, listening for where the sound came from. I tried the bedside lamp. It gave the usual click, but the room stayed pitch black. I waited for my eyes to adjust, then edged towards the door and turned on the main light.

In the sudden glare of the bulb, I stared down at my feet and the stark white tiles, which gleamed like a public toilet. Cockroaches, too many to count, scurried across the tiles in search of darkness, like creatures gone mad.

A click, and the clock advanced to 2:48. I felt something twitch on my left arm. A cockroach crouched, malignant, on my pale skin, its antennae licking the air from side to side. A moment later, it was scuttling up my arm towards my neck.

The light went out. The door edged open. In the shadows of the doorway hunched the figure from the Platinum. He'd come to get me and I couldn't escape.

I screamed and woke up with a start. Sweat poured down my face: a cold, sticky sweat that was beginning to dry and leave an oily film on my skin. I gradually became aware of rattling at the front gate. Barely awake, I struggled to discipline my mind, as the dream sucked it back down like a whirlpool. Was someone rattling the gate, or was I still dreaming? How much of last night had really happened and how much had been a dream? My bedroom had become some place I'd never seen before. A haunted zone. The evil presence from my dream hovered in the corner, in the murky dusk between fantasy and reality, to drag me back.

The rattling at the gate grew more insistent. The clock by the bed read 3:16. I staggered to the wardrobe and wrapped a sarong around my waist. Outside the air was cool and I stared blearily into the night. A middle-aged Indonesian man, immaculately dressed in a navy blue jacket and tie, stared back at me from the darkness.

'Mr Young?'

'Yes.'

'Mr Graham Young?'

'Yes.'

'Suprianto from the Jakarta police. Will you come with me, please, sir?'

'I'm sorry?'

'Will you come with me, please?'

I knew at once that the dream was over. I was wide awake.

2

Suprianto's black BMW floated like a hearse along the empty city streets. It drew to a halt outside a Padang restaurant. The building was all in darkness, except for a small room at the back.

The table at which I sat was bare; the other three had plain paper tablecloths and were laid for dinner, western style. Strange enough at four in the morning and in any case not customary – Padang restaurants never use tablecloths and the cutlery stands in a holder in the centre of the table.

'I want to make our conversation friendly, Mr Young.' He spoke his English with a quaint accent, lending equal stress to every syllable, a mite too meticulously. Echoes of the BBC World Service. It sounded as if he'd learnt it a century ago.

'How do I know you're a policeman?'

'I already show you my card.' He produced a piece of ID from his jacket pocket. It included a photograph, a name, a number. I looked at it and pretended I knew what I was looking for.

'I think there's been some mistake.'

'There is no mistake.'

A tap at the door. An elderly man entered, bearing a tray with a teapot, two cups, two spoons, a jug of milk, a bowl of sugar and a little heap of paper serviettes. He set the tray down on the table.

'Tea,' Suprianto beamed, with pride. 'I know English people like to drink tea.'

'I'd like to know what this is all about.'

'Please, help yourself, Mr Young.' Progress seemed unlikely until I did, so I poured the yellow liquid into my cup. He edged the little milk jug closer towards me. 'I believe English people like milk with their tea.'

It tasted as foul as it looked. 'Not for me, thank you.'

He seemed quite crestfallen. 'Western people. Always you want to get straight to the point.'

'It's the middle of the night. I'd appreciate it.'

The benign smile left his face as if someone had pulled out the plug. 'Did you go last night to Hotel Platinum?'

'You know I did or you wouldn't ask me.' We exchanged frosty stares. 'Is drinking in the Platinum an arrestable offence?'

He placed a serviette beneath his cup and poured himself tea. 'I came to this restaurant, Mr Young, because I did not want to make this interview so formal. I do not like to question you, but I have my duty. But I understand that you are western people. Perhaps you prefer the police station.'

The clock on the wall crunched out the seconds one by one. Watching dawn break in a Jakarta police station sounded less than inviting. 'I was at the Platinum last night from seven till about eleven.'

'Thank you, Mr Young.' He piled sugar into his tea. 'Did you have appointment?'

'Appointment?'

'To meet with someone.'

'No.'

'You are sure about this?'

'Of course I'm sure.'

'But you spoke to someone.'

'Yes, I spoke to someone.'

He nodded his head and sipped his tea. In the silence that

followed, the room seemed to shrink around me. On the white wall opposite, the plastic clock, a freebie from Bank BNI, continued to clunk out the seconds. The only other adornment in the room was a wooden plaque bearing an Islamic blessing in Arabic characters.

Most of my previous encounters with the Indonesian police had involved on-the-spot fines for fabricated motoring offences. Everybody avoided the police in Indonesia if they could. It was cheaper.

Suprianto held his cup poised high in the air. 'Please, Mr Young. Drink your tea. It will get cold.' Perhaps I'd need to rethink the Indonesian cop as bovine bully. This one seemed a smooth operator. He gave off an air of refinement – sensitivity, even. Not to mention guile.

I found myself talking to fill the silence. 'I got to the Platinum around seven o'clock. I had a quick snack, sat drinking on my own for a couple of hours. Around ten o'clock, maybe, this person came over and struck up a conversation.'

'Do you often drink alone?'

'It's been known to happen. It's called an alcohol problem.' I regretted my flippancy as soon as the words left my lips.

'Did you have a plan to meet with this person?'

'I've already told you, no.'

'But he came and made a conversation?'

'That's right.'

'Did you recognize him?'

'Should I have?'

'He spoke to you. This is not so usual for strangers in the west.'

'I certainly didn't encourage him. I wanted to be left alone. Look, what is all this? Is this man in some kind of trouble?'

The policeman gave a fleeting smile, before nodding in the

direction of the teapot. 'Please, Mr Young, your cup is empty.'

'Look, I didn't know this guy from Adam, OK? If you want to know the truth, he gave me the creeps.'

He took a serviette and mopped up a drop of tea that had spilt on the table. 'What is your position in Jakarta, Mr Young?'

'My position?'

'Your work.'

'I work for an NGO.'

'Ah yes, I remember. I read something in the newspaper.'

'So why ask me, if you know already?'

He poured more tea into his cup. 'And what is the purpose of your work?'

'In theory, I ensure that aid is getting through to the people it's intended for. A lot of it disappears in Indonesia.' I shifted position in the silence. 'I investigate irregularities.'

'A kind of detective, in fact?'

'I suppose so.'

'You must meet many influential people.'

I shook my head and smiled. 'Have you heard of the phrase "lip service"?'

He added more sugar to his cup. 'And you must also make enemies.'

'What's your point, Detective Suprianto?'

'I am only collecting the facts, Mr Young.' He sipped his tea. 'I have been a detective for many years. Like Hercule Poirot, yes?'

I stifled a smile at his woeful pronunciation. Haircool Parrot.

'He doesn't always believe people when they tell him things, because often they lie. Perhaps you know with this man and have appointment to make a deal.'

'It's drugs, isn't it?'

'This is something more evil than drugs, Mr Young.' The

finger on the clock juddered forward a few more seconds. 'Do you believe in evil?'

'Evil?'

He rose to his feet. 'How long have you been living in Jakarta?'

'Just over a year.'

'Then you know about Doctor White.'

I listened to my voice grow quiet and defensive, as if it were searching for some place to hide. 'I read the papers. I hear the gossip. The same as everyone else.'

The newspapers weren't saying very much. Every now and then, some bloodless strip of words giving the details of the latest corpse. But the city was quivering with rumours. Rumours that the young girls were sexually abused first, before they were sliced up with surgical precision. Dismembered. Rumours that Doctor White was a well-spoken *bule*.

'One year of my life, Mr Young. Doctor White is a clever man.'

'So what's this got to do with me?'

'You are also a clever man.'

'I wish to speak to the British Embassy.' My words rang out loud and clear as they echoed around the bare walls. They seemed quite ridiculous amid the decorum of china teacups. They sounded so English and pompous. 'I won't answer any more questions until I have a lawyer present.'

'I do not accuse you, Mr Young.'

'Then what are you doing?'

'The man you spoke with last night –'

His meaning struck home and I sucked in a mouthful of air. 'Doctor White?'

'Perhaps you do not believe me. But I already know what is true. My men have followed him for months.'

I wiped my brow and fidgeted on my chair. Fragments of last night's dream were slicing my mind like slivers of glass.

Suprianto began to pace around the room. 'Do you know Pekalongan, Mr Young?'

'I'm sorry?'

'Pekalongan. *Kota Batik*.'

'Only on the map. I've never been there.'

'I grew up near that place, on the north coast of Java. I used to watch the boats go to sea every day. Many hours later, they came home with fish. When the sea was calm, they let me go with them. Then I sat with the fishermen and I learnt how to wait.'

I found it hard to concentrate on his words. The presence from my dream had joined us in the room and my heart was pounding.

'Sometimes there was a very big fish, old and clever. Then we must wait a long time. We must put our net in the sea and wait. All day, perhaps. In the end, the clever fish will grow careless.'

'If you've followed this man for months, you must know I've got nothing to do with him.'

'I want to think so, Mr Young, because I like you.' He sat down opposite me once more. 'But I am a detective and I must consider everything. Perhaps you know Doctor White. You share same tastes.' His voice slowed down until it beat out each syllable like a metronome. 'Evil happens very secretly. Perhaps you are not so careless.'

'I'd never met this man before in my life,' I said.

He took a pack of Marlboro from his jacket pocket and offered me one.

'I swear it.'

'You don't smoke, Mr Young?'

He waited until I shook my head before withdrawing the pack. 'Good for health, yes? Indonesian people are not so discipline. Do you mind?' He read my silence as a signal of consent and removed a cigarette from the pack. 'I enjoy a cigarette very much when I drink tea.' He struck a match in slow motion, lit the cigarette in the same fastidious manner, lifted the tip to his lips and sucked in the smoke with a contented little sigh.

Halfway through his cigarette, the policeman rose to his feet. 'We must go now, Mr Young.'

'Go where?'

'To meet with Doctor White.'

'He won't be able to tell you anything about me.'

'Of course not. He is dead.'

I shivered beneath the fluorescent light. I'd only known a smell like this in hospitals. Sterile and astringent, puckering my nose and standing the hairs at the back of my neck on end. Another shiver pierced me as the sheet was lifted back. It was only the second time I'd seen a dead body.

The first had belonged to my father in his coffin. So long ago that I barely remember the funeral, but I'll never forget his skin that morning, shiny as wax, unreal, almost plastic. How different from the corpse beside me now, where there'd been no cosmetic attempt to prettify death. The body lay, fat and undignified, on a slab of concrete, and it was hard to imagine a shedding of tears for the soul that once inhabited it. The left-hand side of the face had been smashed in and the pale skin there was caked with purple.

The attendant studied my face intently. 'He dead, mister.'

'Uh?'

'Dead,' he repeated, lifting an arm and letting it slam back down on the concrete to prove his point. He grinned.

I composed myself in order to take in the corpse. Despite such a violent death, the body seemed scarcely changed: less strange to my eyes than the husk of my own father had been. The presence I'd met the night before still lingered there, as if there hadn't been time yet to exit the skin.

The attendant gave a giggle of nervous excitement. I guess he'd seen thousands of dead bodies in his life, but it wasn't every day he met a *bule* face to face. I was much more compelling than any cadaver. I moved and I spoke.

'How did he die?' I asked Suprianto, for no real reason.

The detective shook his head. The question was out off bounds.

The attendant leant over and stroked the curly black hairs on the dead man's lower arm. '*Bulu bulu*,' he said with a grin, revealing teeth in an advanced state of decay. He peered at his own skin, baby smooth, before turning his attention back to the hirsute corpse. '*Banyak sekali bulunya*.' From the corner of his eye, I caught him peeking at the hairs on my right arm. I could tell he wanted to check these out, to make sure they felt just the same. He glanced over at Suprianto and thought better of it.

My head reeled and I clung to the edge of the slab. The detective rattled out an order.

The attendant hurried over to open the door to the world outside. A rush of hot air hit me in the face. 'Mister! Mister!' he shouted, brandishing a fold-up chair in bright red plastic. He stood beside the chair, quaking with excitement, as he offered to help me into the seat. This might be his chance to touch a living *bule*.

But Suprianto took charge before I could move, and the attendant was forced to step reluctantly back. The policeman placed his hand on my shoulder and guided me into the seat, while the attendant watched from a respectful distance, shifting the weight of his body from foot to foot. How badly he longed to be an actor in this drama unfolding before him. He pleaded with Suprianto, gazing deep into his eyes, but the policeman ignored him and glanced away.

Beyond the strip of light that clung to the edge of the building, the night outside loomed black and impenetrable. Suprianto gave a nod in the direction of the attendant – it was time for him to return to his hermetic world of fluorescence and formaldehyde. The latter bluffed it out for the briefest of moments, pretending not to notice the detective's signal, before his courage failed him and he surrendered with a slump of the shoulders. 'Goodbye, mister,' he sighed, in the dejected tone of a child who must eat up his supper and be packed off to bed.

As the door creaked shut behind him, it seemed to suck in all the light and the dark night smothered me like clothes soaked in sweat. Suprianto positioned himself opposite my chair and took out another cigarette.

'Mr Young?'

I looked up and gave a tired nod.

'The dead man. Is this the man you talk with at Hotel Platinum?'

'Yes.'

'You are certain about this?'

'Yes.' Moths crashed into the light above my head as if they hoped to shatter their wings. 'I'm certain.'

He put a hand on my shoulder and helped me to my feet. 'You may go home now.' Whatever I'd been expecting to happen next, it wasn't this. 'You are very tired, I think. May I drive you to your house?'

'Please.'

'Tomorrow you must make a statement.'

'You don't believe me?'

'There is no reason to worry about this. It is only formality.' He produced a bundle of papers from his inside pocket. 'In Indonesia, there is always paperwork. After *reformasi*, even more. Everything must be clean now, and honest. There must be no *korupsi*.'

For the third time in as many hours, I sat in Suprianto's car staring out at a benighted city. For the third time since I arrived in Indonesia, I watched a city I didn't recognize. I recalled my very first taxi ride from Soekarno-Hatta airport to Ciputat, along the monotonous toll road, with the skyscrapers of the Golden Triangle business zone against the skyline. Then the shocking lurch into streets choked with cars, clogged with litter, thick with brown air. I remembered the night in May, soon after the riots, when I drove past the smoking ruins of Ramayana and Borobodur shopping malls, past the burnt-out shells of torched cars, past faces that were hostile or greedy or blank with shock. Danger in the air and fear you could smell. And now, for the third time, the city had become an alien place to me. Life was stirring – it was close to daybreak and the mosques were wailing their bleak dawn chorus. I was a foreigner in a land where I didn't belong.

I asked the detective to turn the AC on full, but still the sweat poured down my face. Inside me I yearned for rain. Not the deluge of a tropical rainstorm, but the melancholy drizzle of an English autumn, dissolving the world and making it soft. I felt implicated in some way, an accomplice to evil. I longed to take a shower.

Suprianto wound down the window and tossed a cigarette stub into the street. Dawn was washing the sky clean. A pale sky, like stone. Pondok Indah, Lebak Bulus, Ciputat Raya – soon I would be home. We arranged a time for me to make my statement. That afternoon, once I'd had a chance to rest. Suprianto reassured me again that it was just a formality, but there wasn't any warmth in his voice: he had done his duty. He drove silently away.

My place of residence towered in front of me against the bleached morning sky. I remembered how I had felt a year ago when I turned the key in this lock for the very first time. Inside me now, I had the same feeling.

3

Twenty-four hours later, sleepless, I watched another dawn creep over the complex. A thin, unformed morning, squeezed from the horizon like a difficult birth. The sky was the colour of bone, hardly any shade at all.

I stepped out of the door, beyond the front gate. The complex was twitching into life, like some specimen on a laboratory slab. Drivers busied themselves washing cars. A lone white face had emerged from one of the doorways, familiar to my eyes, though we'd never conversed. The passenger door snapped shut and the car pulled away.

Such a basic structure to our lives, one day. Sunrise to sunset. And the mess in between, the tangle of threads and scraps of cloth, somehow gets patched into a tapestry that seems to make sense. On a normal day, I'd be one of the actors in this breakfast scene, trussed up in my suit and tie. Today I found myself observing it, detached, and the old familiar patterns unravelled before my eyes. The picture became meaningless, like a city viewed from the air: lights flashing on and off in random windows.

The past twenty-four hours had taken no shape, had felt quite seamless. And somewhere in that blur of hours, Suprianto had come for his statement.

'It is only formality, Mr Young,' he repeated.

I was escorted in his car to the centre of town, slumped in

a seat so soft it felt like a pillow. A maze of dirty streets later, the rear door of the car was held open for me.

'Come this way, please.'

I stepped out of the car. This must be what it felt like to be a rock star or a president, cocooned in a virtual world of jets and limousines. Then released from the capsule abruptly, to an assault of flashing cameras and chattering faces, stepping down into places that were nothing but names. I stared up at a slab of Dickensian grey. We slipped through a side door and burrowed through a warren of musty corridors, by a line of empty rooms like soldiers to attention. The faces that flashed past me gave respectful greetings. '*Selamat sore.*' At least I knew what time of day it was.

'We are almost there now.'

We squeezed into a grim little lift which creaked and lurched up the building. More corridors and doors. Deferential bows greeted us as we passed: Suprianto was clearly an important figure in this clandestine anthill.

One last door was held open for me, different from the rest, in elegantly carved wood. 'Welcome to my office, Mr Young.'

The room smelt heady with books. Papers lay scattered in piles on a sturdy teak desk. I felt as if I had stepped into a professor's den at an Oxbridge college. Against the far wall, volumes stood in military order in huge glass cabinets.

'Please sit down. We must prepare our statement.'

I took my place in the leather chair, as instructed. The digital clock on the desk read 4:17. It seemed quite out of place in such a timeless room. The figures seemed meaningless, mere mathematics.

'Do not worry,' the detective smiled. 'It is acceptable in English.'

As we agreed each clause and sentence, he wrote them down in a meticulous hand. The final version stretched to slightly more than one page. Suprianto stood up and read the statement aloud, stopping from time to time to question a word and its implications, sometimes suggesting an alternative.

A knock on the door. A cup of coffee appeared on the desk, with milk and sugar and biscuits. A hand removed the carefully scripted lines.

Suprianto leant back in his chair and surveyed his empire. 'What do you think of my office, Mr Young?'

'It's fine.'

'I copied from a business magazine. A picture of an office in England. Because a detective's mind must be logical, like an English mind.'

He seemed disappointed when I didn't take up the conversation. He walked over to the window. 'Jakarta. It is an ugly city, yes? Every year it gets bigger, and nobody will stop and control it.'

The statement returned, typed up on two squares of paper, a top copy and a carbon. 'Please, Mr Young, you must read it first.' I tried to do as he asked, but I couldn't. Each word remained a strip of black characters, meaningless scratches, as if written in a foreign alphabet. The patterns didn't fit together.

'And now your signature.'

The street outside my house stretched ahead of me, without trees. They seemed such a long time ago now, those hours in Suprianto's office. On either side as I looked down the street in the pale morning light, neat little lawns, impossibly square. The gate of the house opposite slid open and I caught a glimpse of the white guy who lived there. I recalled what Suprianto had said the previous evening, when he brought me back from police headquarters. 'You are lucky to live here, Mr Young. This is a beautiful complex. It is so peaceful.'

For peaceful, read orderly, regulated. As clean as his shoes.

'But many Indonesian people do not like this, perhaps. It is too quiet,' he continued as he gazed up at the building. 'Perhaps you will come to my house one day. Meet with my wife and my family.'

I had assumed this was pointless small talk. I hoped never to see him again and I felt sure he knew this. 'That would be nice,' I replied. 'Thank you.'

'I can practise my English, perhaps. I have forgotten so much.'

The smell inside his car came back to me as I stared down the street. Leather and cigarettes. I hated this complex. I hated its air of desolation. It was meant to evoke an English village, some sleepy spot in the affluent Home Counties, yet it was how I imagined a nouveau riche estate might look on the outskirts of Los Angeles. White coffins for white people, while outside in the heat Hispanics toiled. Only here, in this complex, the skin drenched in sweat was Indo-Malay, a deeper shade of brown. And the bow of the head that obscured the brown eyes was more submissive.

I could never recall hearing music in the complex, nor even human voices. The place always seemed quite soundless, except for car doors opening and closing, engines revving up and pulling away. I certainly never heard laughter. I trudged along the street, kicking up dust. The feeling in my stomach scared me. I began to walk more quickly.

I took the path of sloping steps to the swimming pool and the smell of chlorine. The water was a rootless blue, rippling before my eyes, hypnotic. Loungers lay empty beneath red and white parasols.

No one could see me here, by the water's edge. I'd longed for this moment of isolation, ever since I left the bar at the Platinum. I knelt by the edge of the pool and gazed at the distorted reflection of a pebble that lay on the bottom. I concentrated and tried to make Doctor White's face appear in the shimmering blue mirror below me, but I could only conjure his smell. That mix of aftershave and body odour.

As the shock wore off, I felt a kind of disappointment. Body odour. Where was the suave man of mystery brushing the sleeve of his Armani jacket and mocking my suburban values in cut-crystal accent? How could Doctor White have been so obvious, so vile? I laughed out loud. How much better the movies did these things.

At last, thank God, I felt some sense of irony again. The irony that got me through life, that I'd lost completely since I'd stepped out of the Platinum. I launched both my arms in the pool and tossed waves of cold water high into the air, splashing it over my face and my body. I felt clean again.

'Hey, neighbour!' a voice called out, as I opened my gate.

It was the white guy from the house opposite. I'd seen him hundreds of times, but I couldn't remember exchanging a single word. His face appeared, fixed in a rigid grin, in the gap between the two halves of the huge grey gates.

'Did you see the piece on CNN?' he asked.

'I don't watch CNN.'

'They did a piece about the political situation here. I tell you, we're not being given all the facts.'

'No?'

'You bet your life we're not. Have you any idea how many people really died in May?' The grin didn't budge.

'I couldn't say.'

'More than these geeks are letting on, that's for sure.'

'CNN can be a bit sensationalist at times.'

'I guess you figure the BBC has more class, uh?' For a fleeting moment, the grin fell away. 'What the hell, I'm not about to argue with you, buddy.' He rewound his face to its previous expression of warmth. 'We both take a free press for granted, that's why we're different from these guys here. I got no time for all this censorship.'

'Things are opening up a bit now.'

'Sure they are.' His tone of voice made it clear that he thought my suggestion was insane. He pointed to my driveway and, presumably, to the lack of any car there. 'I noticed you're not going to work today.'

'No.'

'I guess you heard, then.'

'Heard what?'

'About the riots.'

'Have there been more riots?'

'Didn't you hear? Yesterday.'

'Where?'

'In the north of the city. Near Pluit.'

'I didn't see anything on the local news.'

He raised his eyebrows. 'There wouldn't be, would there?'

'So where'd you hear about it? CNN?'

'A colleague rang. I'm wondering if it's safe to go to work.'

'And where did he get it from?'

'Someone phoned and told him.'

'It's probably just another rumour. You know how they're flying about right now.'

Irritation crept into his voice. 'It's called a phone tree. You know? Each guy informs the next guy? Keeps him up to date. You should join one, buddy.'

'Did you watch CNN this morning?'

'A few minutes ago.'

'So? Was there anything about it?'

'Not yet. Hell, I'm only trying to warn you!'

'Thanks. I'll keep my ears open.'

He made a conscious attempt to mellow his voice once more. 'We got to stick together at a time like this. This place is pretty volatile right now. I was only wondering if you'd heard anything.'

So now I knew why he'd spoken, after all those mornings of silence. 'No, I haven't,' I said, rather coldly. 'I'm sorry.'

'Oh, OK. Well, you take care now, uh?'

'Sure.'

'Have a nice day.' The grin widened to expose a row of shiny teeth. The grey gate pulled shut.

The silence in the complex was complete again. I thought about the white guy opposite and realized just how scared everyone was. Except for me. Even as I'd watched the news footage of the riots in May, I'd stayed aloof from it all, as if they were happening in a distant country. I had no idea why, since I was nobody's vision of a hero. It was something about Jakarta, perhaps. In a virtual city, you can't get hurt.

I listened to the click of my key in the lock. I guessed it was the conversation I'd just had, but I felt a hint of menace as the door swung shut behind me. Walls can protect, but they can trap just as easily. I heard voices from the kitchen.

My gardener and my maid were squabbling, as usual. They fell silent when I entered the room. I could tell from their eyes that my recent behaviour was making them edgy – they weren't sure what to expect from me. I couldn't bear them around me for another whole day, so I gave the maid the day off and told her to go home. She eyed me suspiciously and continued to wash up the plates.

'Don't worry, Enti, I'll do that. You just go home.'

She went to speak but said nothing, before reluctantly drying her hands. I opened the fridge door. Just over one bottle of gin left, but I was almost out of tonic. I gave my gardener some money and sent him to the supermarket. He could make sure Enti got home safely at the same time.

Alone in my study with the bottle at my side, I squatted on the floor next to the wooden cabinet. Inside, immaculately stacked in three neat piles, was every copy of the *Jakarta Post* since the day I arrived in Indonesia. This anal retentiveness had nothing to do with me. It was Enti's work, and she seemed so proud of maintaining this collection that I'd never had the heart to throw them out. I supposed her last white boss had liked things done this way, so she'd figured it must be what every *bule* wanted.

I turned the first pile upside down and worked my way from the bottom. The earliest copy, my first day in Jakarta. I began to comb each issue for items about Doctor White. Two weeks following my arrival, I found the first possible piece. 'Body Found on Beach' was the bland headline for an article that described the remains of a young girl washed up by the waves. I opened the desk drawer and took out a pair of scissors. Snip snip snip.

Three weeks later, I found a second item – front-page news this time. A young female body, floating in a river, in the north of the city. I couldn't be certain that Doctor White was involved. The item was somewhat coy and didn't describe the corpse in sufficient detail to make a confident decision. Lots of people die in Indonesia, for lots of reasons, and sometimes in horrible ways. In these early days, too, no one had suspected a pattern, so the item made no reference to the previous killing. I read it carefully through several times before deciding I could include it. I took a swig of gin and picked up my scissors.

Over the next few months, cuttings appeared more regularly for my ghoulish scrapbook. Even so, I felt I still needed to scour each one thoroughly. So many lives end abruptly, at another person's hand. The proof was in the detail. If the victim was male, I ruled it out. The body had to be that of a young girl, there needed to be signs of previous sexual assault and the remains had to be mutilated. If these criteria were not completely satisfied, I moved on to the next page and my scissors stayed on the desk, shining.

March 18, an important day. The very first piece to connect the killings. No name was attached at this point, nor speculation about motive – just the tantalizing suggestion that the murders might form part of a pattern. I cut this out more carefully and took a long, slow drink of my gin.

Then May came and the riots filled the papers. For two long months, not a single item that met my stringent requirements. I flicked through the pages with gathering impatience. At last, on the very first day of July, two girls killed on the same night, found bleeding to death in alleyways in south Jakarta. And for the first time the newspaper said it. 'Doctor White'. Framed in quotation marks, but still they said it. Shivers ran up and down my spine as I sliced out the article with shaking fingers.

Before me, on the shiny surface of the desk, lay forty scraps of paper, probably more. I set them out scrupulously in chronological order beneath the X-ray of the table lamp. Night was falling outside. This was a secret task I had embarked on, so I drew the curtains. Eight or nine hours now, sifting through newsprint. Factual reports of murders, shots of grieving families, speculation about Doctor White, who and why.

I was beginning to feel drunk at last. It had taken so long. Not happy drunk, or sad drunk, or aggressive drunk. Just numb drunk.

I needed to fit the articles into some sort of master pattern. There had to be some logic to all of this – at least some kind of structure. I wanted to creep up on Doctor White so I could glimpse his shadow amongst these scraps of paper. But the longer I stared at the rectangles of print and the harder I focused on each word, the more elusive he became. Was there really a creature of flesh and blood behind these black markings, or was I seeking a phantom? Were these murders connected, or were they just random acts of violence in a fractured city?

Suddenly I felt sick. I knew that soon I would either throw up or pass out. Darkness seeped through my mind like a patch of blood on white gauze. At last, the moment I'd longed for, since before this crazy nightmare ever began. Oblivion. Delicious oblivion.

4

I awoke to dazzling sunlight and the sound of a man selling vegetables as he tapped his stick on the gates of the houses. Scraps of newspaper littered the desk and lay strewn like confetti on the floor. I remembered the previous day and waited for the hangover to hit. I felt as fresh as a daisy.

I breezed into the kitchen and poured water into the percolator. Enti was cleaning the stove.

'Good morning, Enti. Isn't it a beautiful day?'

She looked perplexed, but said nothing. Once I was busy making coffee, she took her chance to slip into the study and started to tidy the newspapers back into piles. Cup in hand, I went back to find her leaning over the desk, peering curiously at the squares of cut-up newsprint.

'Don't worry, Enti. I'll do that.'

I bounced over to the desk and started to hum some mindless pop tune. Her eyes screwed up with suspicion. My cheerfulness seemed to unsettle her even more than my brooding silence of the previous two days.

'How about some breakfast, Enti? I'm starving.'

Perhaps I merely imagined the knowing look in her eye. But for a moment I felt ashamed of the scraps of cut-up newsprint that lay scattered across the floor. As soon as she left, I gathered them into a pile and slipped them into the drawer, along with the scissors.

I walked back into the kitchen, to the smell of bacon and toast, continuing to hum my banal little melody. Enti made a show of fierce concentration as she leant over the stove, determinedly frying bacon, but she couldn't quite control the nervous glances that peeked from the corner of her eye. I suppose if you're a maid, erratic changes in your boss's behaviour might herald the sack.

I spread the french windows open and breathed in the morning. Too early still for Jakarta's usual stink. A sun like the eye of a daisy, a hint of frangipani in the air.

I couldn't deny the ex-pat lifestyle had its advantages. Such as sitting at the table on my terrace while Enti lovingly attended to my every whim. My inexplicable joviality persisted, with not a glimpse of a hangover to dull it. Precisely the opposite – my senses seemed on fire. The burnt aroma of coffee swirled around my mouth and the bacon tasted just as good as it smelt.

I stared into the garden. Tidy and well organized, like the rest of the complex. The grey walls at the rear were lined with shards of glass – a warning to burglars. As the sun bore down, without any breeze, the space began to feel like a prison cell. A handful of frangipani petals sprinkled the lawn, a fresh fall during the night. They hinted at a beauty and a freedom that lay elsewhere.

A gaggle of *becaks* stood in line at the complex gate, the drivers' faces hidden as they snoozed under canvas tops.

'Transport, mister?' Agus leant forward in his becak and flashed me a grin.

'*Selamat pagi, Agus. Apa kabar?*'

'*Baik baik saja, tuan.*'

He stood up and gestured towards his empty pedicab. Agus was the perfect tonic to launch my day, because he always seemed genuinely pleased to see me. I asked him to name his price to Ciputat Raya.

'*Wah! Jauh, tuan! Dan panas!*' His brown eyes twinkled as he wiped his brow with his hand. '*Tiga ribu.*'

'Three thousand!' I shrieked. My gasp of horror was a joke, of course. Agus laughed out loud. Even such a small transaction should be an entertaining dance of twists and turns. After much waving of arms and beating of chests, we agreed on a figure of two thousand.

The trip through the pitted road to Ciputat Raya was short and painful as I bumped up and down on the hard wooden seat. No longer in his first flush of youth, Agus panted as he cycled in the burning sun. We made small talk as we journeyed along. How was he? Fine, but his daughter was sick and he was worried about her. At that moment, I was far more worried about him. He was gasping for breath and sweat poured down his clenched red face.

We hit the fumes of the main road and the inevitable traffic jam. I took out my wallet and paid him. Three thousand after all. I got the feeling he had always known I'd cough up this amount.

He beamed a broad smile, instantly revitalized. 'Goodbye, *tuan*,' he chirped, as he turned his *becak* around and headed back to the complex.

If you're one of those danger freaks who needs a regular fix of adrenaline, there's no need to waste your money trekking in the jungles of Borneo – just catch a bus in Jakarta. They're driven by gleeful maniacs, every last one. Crazy guys who chortle at the sight of an oncoming truck driver with the same mad gleam in his eye. My bus hurtled down the road, narrowly missing a taxi, before causing a van to swerve violently to the left. The driver whooped with delight. He was enjoying himself. I whooped, too. I was free for the day and in the mood for some Jakartan culture.

Forget the tourist guides. Forget Borobodur and Prambanan. Forget gamelan music, batik shirts and *wayang* shadow puppets. If you're looking for the real thing, genuine Jakartan culture as it's lived today, there's only one place to head for: the shopping mall.

Pondok Indah Mal towered before me in all its glory, a cathedral to consumerism. The signs on the walls outside shrieked the delights to be sampled within – McDonald's, Dunkin' Donuts, Sizzler, Wendy's, Pizza Hut – an oasis of Americana in an eastern wilderness. The mall had survived the May riots despite overlooking some of the most desolate slums in the whole of the city. As I stood on the footbridge and stared at the building in the sunshine, I fancied it looked more imperious than ever, strengthened by its recent ordeal.

To reach the mall, my bus had scorched through one of the city's most exclusive residential areas. Metro Pondok Indah was a broad boulevard lined with palm trees, redolent of Miami or Los Angeles rather than grimy Jakarta. Set back from the road, vast houses of astonishing vulgarity rose from the ground, shapeless slabs of concrete painted white, replete with Art Deco fripperies, mock-Grecian columns and Evita Perón balconies which nobody used. There's one golden rule in Jakarta – if you've got it, baby, flaunt it!

The mall was buzzing with Jakarta's rich and would-be rich. If the country was mired in an economic crisis, it seemed no one had stopped to tell these guys. Or maybe they were all indulging in Jakarta's favourite pastime – window-shopping. Ah, the mysterious east! I walked past the Body Shop and Marks & Spencer to the foot of the escalators.

'Good morning, sir.' A woman in a golden sarong gave me a leaflet. 'You want to come to my restaurant?'

'Maybe later.' Indonesian for 'no'.

A businesswoman with shoulder pads that belonged on an American footballer blocked the escalator while she gabbled into her handphone. Two sulky young girls waited behind, too shy or too proud to push past. Draped against a railing, a brown Adonis in cut-off shorts and Rayban shades practised his pose of ennui. A second Adonis peered over the balcony at the floor below, where a group of stylists from Rudi Hadisuwarno – *the* place to have your hair done in South Jakarta – camped it up outside the salon door. Pale and harassed, an ex-pat family whizzed past.

'Good morning, sir. Do you have a moment?'

I spotted the leaflet in his hand. 'Maybe later.'

Two Indonesian ladies dripping with jewellery, weighed down with bags and the burden of endless shopping gazed vaguely around with the bored, glazed eyes of lizards in the sun. Not much life there, but plenty of lifestyle.

Another leaflet later, I rode the escalator to the top floor. A young man in T-shirt and jeans joined me on my step and beamed me a smile. 'Where are you from, sir?'

'England,' I stated, factually, careful not to return the smile. I wasn't in the mood to be a guinea pig for his English. Not very friendly, I know, but sometimes *bules* need to make space for themselves in Jakarta, if they're not to be eaten alive.

I slipped past Bang Slamet restaurant, but not without a leaflet for my collection. A big smile from the waiter there, a handsome young man in a red and black costume which was meant to be traditional Madurese. At least the swarm of teenage boys hanging around outside Cinema 21 ignored me. Looking almost identical in their crumpled white shirts and grey school trousers, they smoked cigarettes and flirted with passing girls.

Pondok Indah Mal – PIM to those in the know – wasn't just a collection of retail outlets, but a modern-day piazza – a place to see and be seen, meet friends, gossip and chat, escape from the humidity and heat. If the joint wasn't quite jumping, it was wiggling a toe or two.

A slap on the back left me gasping for breath.

'Hey, Graham! Long time no see!'

'Oh. Hi, George.'

'Not working today?'

'I've got a two-week break between contracts.'

'So you're staying on, then?'

'Looks like it. I've signed on the dotted line for another year.'

'Rather you than me.'

'What do you mean?'

'You haven't heard, then? I'm leaving.'

'What?'

'Thursday afternoon. Got a moment?'

'Sure. How about Ooh La La?'

Sad to say, Café Ooh La La failed to live up to the promise of its frivolous name. Despite the Gallic pretensions of a couple of Cézanne posters on the wall, it was hard to imagine Jean-Paul Sartre fitfully sucking Gitanes in one of the corners. We picked up plastic trays and waited in a queue to get served at the counter. How positively Left Bank.

'Why are you leaving?' I asked.

'Company's pulling out of Indonesia.'

'Altogether?'

'Can't blame them, can you? I wouldn't invest my money in this dump.'

Almond croissants and quiche lorraine. OK, so it wasn't Montmartre, but at least it wasn't rice again. The gastronomically challenged ex-pats of Jakarta are grateful for what they can get.

I asked the boy behind the counter for some hot garlic bread. 'So where are they sending you?'

George shook his head. 'I'm surplus to company requirements, old boy. Available to the highest bidder as from Friday.'

'Oh.' I gave a lame smile. 'I'm sorry, George.'

'There's no need to be. I can't wait to get out of this place.'

The garlic bread appeared, steaming as the boy spread open the foil. He placed my coffee and snacks on the red plastic tray and we shuffled along to join a second queue to pay the cashier.

'So what made you decide to stay on?' George asked.

'I don't know. Inertia, I guess.'

'Aren't you worried about this place?'

'The politics, you mean?'

He nodded. The cashier scowled and pointed to a figure on the computerized screen.

I went for my wallet. George held up his hand. 'No, let me, Graham. I can't use this Mickey Mouse money anywhere else.'

'You don't have change?' the cashier glowered.

George gave her the kind of withering look I'd love to be able to deliver to surly shop staff. It had the controlled resolve of a customer who would go straight to the manager and calmly complain. The cashier's attitude changed instantly to grudging respect.

'I'm not so worried,' I said, as I picked up my tray. 'Things seem to have settled down now Soeharto's gone.'

'Don't kid yourself, Graham.'

We sat at a table overlooking the main road. The air in the sky was the colour of cigarette stains. To our left, the vast white mansions of Metro Pondok Indah jutted out of the concrete like tombstones. Within walking distance to our right, a huddle of shacks built from cardboard and corrugated iron.

'Don't you think there's a real desire for change here?' I asked him.

'I'm sure there is, old boy. But not among the people who matter.'

I fingered my coffee spoon. Tucking into an almond croissant, gazing down at a dual carriageway humming with cars, it was hard to believe that this was a country in crisis. George tore open his sachet of sugar and stirred it into his coffee. 'All this talk about *reformasi*, it's window-dressing, Graham. Soeharto and his cronies haven't gone. They're just lying low for a while.'

The traffic below had ground to a halt and a long line of cars belched fumes into the air. Business as usual. Just like before the May riots.

'You don't know how relieved I'll be to get out of here,' he said.

'History moves on, George.'

'Not here, it doesn't. It's not just a few rotten apples. The country functions on corruption. You must know that better than anyone, in your job.'

'I've got no illusions about my job, George. It's a game. I have to turn a blind eye to most of the stuff that goes on. The trick is keeping everyone happy.'

I gazed around the Ooh La La. Apart from a blond-haired family who looked as if they should be leaping down an Austrian mountainside, George and I were the only *bules* seated there. I watched the well-heeled Jakartans nibbling at their patisserie like extras on a film set.

'Have you seen today's *Jakarta Post*?' he asked.

'Sorry?'

'Today's *Jakarta Post*. Have you seen it?' I shook my head. 'Try this for a little light reading.' He opened his briefcase and threw a copy onto the table with a thud. 'They gang-raped a nine-year-old girl. Then they mutilated her genitals. The poor little thing died later in a hospital in Singapore.'

I skimmed through the headlines. A committee had just announced the findings of its report into the May riots and most of the front page was taken up with tales of alleged atrocities. More than a hundred Chinese women had been raped. At the foot of the page, the piece about the little girl.

'Now tell me this isn't a sick country.'

'That kind of thing happens everywhere when law and order breaks down.' I listened to the words as they left my lips. How callous they sounded.

'But at least in other places they'd be caught, Graham. And punished.' He gnawed at his cinnamon toast without enthusiasm. 'Not here. You can buy anything in this country if you're rich enough.'

'Yes, well, I guess that's the way of the world.'

He let out a little laugh and shook his head. 'You're a strange man, Graham.'

'Strange?' I smiled.

'I don't mean – what I mean is, you fit in so well here.'

'I suppose I do.'

'How do you manage it? I've never been able to pull off that trick.'

'I guess I've always been a bit of a chameleon. Put me some place new and I soon change colour.'

'You don't know how lucky you are. I've never really adapted.'

I looked him over in his jacket and tie. More or less the same age as me, but so much older somehow. Sensible. Respectable. Even out of work he dressed like a manager.

'We're very different people, you and I,' he said, stabbing out his cigarette.

He couldn't have been more right. We were chalk and cheese. Professional contacts, not friends. Yet here in Jakarta we shared something, despite all our differences. We were united as ex-pats, by the birthplace in our passports. By our white skin.

'It's the greed I find hardest to take, Graham,' he said, with feeling. 'They look at you coming and all they see is some easy dosh. As if you're nothing but a wallet. I'm not a rich man.'

'Oh, come off it, George.' I pointed towards the tin shacks. 'We're up there with Rockefeller compared to the guys who live over there. Can you even begin to imagine living like that?'

Four Indonesian suits arrived at the next table, visibly wealthy. Much too important to queue for their food like everyone else, they sat down and summoned a waiter. As soon as he arrived, they ignored him completely and began to discuss their latest business ventures.

'I'm scared for my family, Graham. This is no place for a wife and kids.'

'I guess not,' I replied, my attention distracted by the plight of the waiter at the next table. Not sure whether to take the suits' order and serve them, or to ask them to go up to the counter.

'We needed an armed escort in May, to get us to the airport. They crammed us into this vehicle built like a tank.' The suits were in full flow by now, showing off to each other, firing questions at the waiter about the food. Did the pesto contain real basil? And virgin olive oil? 'We had soldiers with machine guns to protect us. The mobs were stopping the cars on the toll road and demanding money. If you didn't give them any, they dragged you out and torched your car.'

The waiter, who earned a pittance and had probably been given no training, stumbled in his efforts to come up with answers. I felt really sorry for the guy. This was his role in the scene – a symbol of the great uneducated, the lower orders who banged on the gates of Jakarta's rich and filled them with secret foreboding. For all their swagger, there was a self-consciousness about the suits as they boasted, a fear that they might be found out, that even they might be plunged into the same abyss.

'It could have been my wife who was raped. It could have been my little girl who died in Singapore.'

'It's a lot easier for me, I can see that. I'm only responsible for myself.'

'Don't you ever want to go back?' he asked.

'To England?' I shook my head and smiled.

'It's the little things I miss. Like drinking water from the tap. Taking a walk in the park.' His eyes glistened. 'You'll never guess what I miss most of all, Graham.'

'The cricket?'

The suits next door had upped the ante. The conversation had shifted to descriptions of their business trips to London and Rome. I could make out a smattering of English words, embroidering their chatter like sequins.

At least my joke about cricket raised some kind of smile. 'I've missed rules, Graham. I was always the first to complain about them back home, but at least you know where you stand there.'

'There are rules here, too. They're just different.'

'Well, there's one rule, for sure. Money. If you've got it, you can do what you like.'

'We have no cause to complain, George.' He looked at me as if completely perplexed by my meaning. 'Your house has a swimming pool, for Christ's sake! There's no way we could afford this lifestyle in England.'

He sat up square and straight, with a defensive raise of the chin. 'I don't deny the advantages of the life here.'

'Too right. We're not innocent in all this. We're part of the corruption here. We'll break the rules when it suits us by flashing our money around.'

'Money isn't everything, Graham.'

'It helps.'

He took another cigarette from his pack. 'Do you mind?'

'Why are most of us here, if not for the money?' I asked. 'Not for the culture, that's for sure. The closest we get to that is eating overpriced *nasi goreng* in the Shangri-la.'

Once he was dragging on his cigarette, George seemed a trifle more cheerful. He pointed through the window to a dilapidated orange bus leaving a trail of black smoke in its wake. 'I suppose that's one good thing about this place,' he said. 'The air out there is killing me anyway, so I might as well smoke.'

By now, the four suits were having four separate conversations on four separate mobiles. Jakarta could be such a ridiculous city. One thing I loved about living there was how often it made me laugh out loud.

George produced a handkerchief and pretended to blow his nose. 'I can't wait for Thursday to arrive.'

I'd never seen him like this before. He was usually so English. So desiccated. He gazed out of the window. I looked around the café. We were suddenly overcome by embarrassment.

The handkerchief was tucked away, George seemed back in full control of himself and we struggled on for a few more minutes, jabbering about nothing in particular. The nice safe things that English people always talk about. Until George plucked up the courage to say what we both wanted to say.

'Oh well, better get going, I suppose. Heading my way?'

I knew what I ought to reply. 'I think I might stay and have another coffee.'

'Right. Well.' He stood up and shook my hand. A firm business-like grip. 'All the best, Graham.'

'All the best, George. Safe journey home.'

I watched him stride through the café into the mall. You could tell he didn't fit in, even from the way he walked. It seemed to be one of the ironies of ex-pat life, certainly in Jakarta, that so many of the people who lived it were totally unsuited to it. So they cliqued together with their own kind in a fantasy England that perhaps existed fifty years ago. No one I knew back in England was remotely like these anachronisms. Maybe there was a factory somewhere in Surrey where they were already cloning the next generation of these time-warped misfits.

My eyes followed George as he disappeared down the escalator. For a moment I almost envied him. He had something he believed in. Blighty. Cricket pitches and warm beer. But it was only for a moment and I soon got my senses back. Cricket? Well, I believed if you had a fairly sinful life, you might be booked for the hellfire and brimstone. But if you were especially wicked, like you cooked children alive or voted Conservative, then you were condemned to the Oval for eternity. And as for beer, warm or cold, I'd long since given it up for the more visceral pleasures of gin.

I swept a quick glance around Café Ooh La La. How well groomed everyone looked, how flawlessly manicured and insincere. It was hard work to like this city sometimes. But if I belonged anywhere on this earth, perhaps this city was where I belonged, this half-breed metropolis which was neither east nor west, this void where cultures clashed and wiped each other out. On the other side of the window, in the polluted streets below, cars crawled along an anonymous stretch of concrete. I opened the *Jakarta Post* and it felt far more natural to me than spreading open the *Times*.

5

I thought about the nine-year-old girl. The scruffy kids who sold newspapers and bottles of water at the side of the road, some of them as young as five or six. Who'd bother if one of those kids went missing? I thought about the man without arms or legs who begged under the flyover on Jalan Arteri, a few grimy coins in his battered tin bowl. All these people who had such unbearable lives.

I thought about my own kids. I didn't do that often these days. I wondered how they were getting on. They were fine, I felt sure – my ex-wife was a good mother and she'd fight like a tiger to protect them. If there were ever a serious problem, she'd write to me. Anyway, maybe they had a substitute daddy by now. I hoped so. It was no more than my ex-wife deserved.

I'd been so lost in my thoughts that I hadn't noticed the flow of cars dry up on the street below. Suddenly, on the other side of the sheet of glass, the concrete stretched, deserted, in both directions. Not even a stray dog. I felt a shiver down my spine as I stared out at the wasteland below: all the filth and the cars that made Jakarta so ugly at the same time made it real.

I heard a sound in the distance that I couldn't distinguish, faint at first. It slowly grew louder. From the mindless blue of a cloudless sky, a military helicopter appeared, chopping the air with its blades. It came to hover above the car park.

'Oh God, it's true!' a female voice called out, in a North American accent.

Everyone in the café – customers, waiters, cashiers – dashed across to look out of the window.

A door slid open in the base of the helicopter, from where a rope ladder was suspended until it hung just a few feet off the ground. A soldier clambered down and leapt the last few feet to hit the concrete. He landed with bended knees before springing up straight, body stiff, rifle in hand. His mouth howled open, but the roar was muffled by the vast sheet of glass, like a silent scream. He froze and stared ahead, finger on trigger.

The woman's companion placed his arm around her shoulder.

'I told you!' she shrieked.

'It'll be all right, honey.'

'I told you we should have gotten out while we could!'

The man turned to face me. 'Has the whole city gone up again?'

'I'm sorry?'

'Is it happening everywhere, like last time?'

'I don't know anything. I'm sorry.'

Bodies jostled each other for a view at the window as a steady stream of soldiers spilled from the chopper, each one producing a perfect copy of the first man's manoeuvre. Soon a cordon of figures in military uniform stood sentry on the mall perimeter, the tips of their rifles aimed at the deserted street.

'There were riots in Karawaci yesterday,' the American man said.

'I heard in Pluit.'

'It's everywhere, isn't it? The whole goddamned city's up in flames again.'

The final soldier emerged from the bowels of the helicopter to take up position on the rim of the car park. A dozen stone bodies faced outwards, without moving, like gargoyles guarding the walls of a cathedral.

'I can't stand it here any more!' the woman screamed. She burst into tears.

Her partner lingered at her side, extremely uncomfortable. He seemed unable to cope with such naked emotion. Not certain what to do, whether to hold her more tightly or to let her go, he stared aggressively around, as if looking for someone to blame.

'I want to go back home!' she sobbed.

'We will. I promise, darling.'

'You've said that before. All you care about is money.'

An Indonesian man with flecks of silver in his hair stepped forward and tried to comfort her. She brushed him away with her hand and stood biting her lip to choke back the tears.

'Please, don't be afraid,' the man said. 'It is only –' He turned to his wife for help. '*Latihan. Apa latihan?*'

'Exercises,' his wife translated, wrapping her arm around the woman's shoulders and guiding her to a seat. 'Don't worry, my dear. It's only the army doing some exercises.'

'Are you sure?'

'Of course. It isn't real. Look, the streets are empty.'

The Indonesian lady took a tissue from one of the tables and placed it in the trembling hand. 'You mustn't cry. They are here to protect us.'

Having disgorged its final gargoyle, the helicopter hovered in mid-air like an angry wasp. The gusts of wind from its blades whipped up scraps of paper and sent them swirling around the car park. The soldiers stood, statuesque, on the edge of the mall, distanced from each other with mathematical precision, looking elegant in their jungle-green fatigues and scarlet berets.

'There you are,' the American hissed at his partner. 'It's the military doing a few exercises. That's all.'

She wiped her eyes with the back of her hand, embarrassed. He turned his face away from her and stared through the glass. The seconds ticked by. She unfolded the crumpled tissue in her palm and blew her nose.

Suddenly, as if a button had been pushed to rewind a video, the men replayed their exercise in reverse. The rope ladder shuddered as a sequence of heavy boots landed on the bottom rung. Like insects into a secret nest, the dark-green creatures scuttled back into the helicopter. The hatch in the bottom slid shut, the whir of the blades grew fiercer and the buzzing machine took off into the cloudless sky.

The American man, apparently satisfied that the war games were over, abandoned his post at the window and signalled for his partner to follow him. For a moment her resentment showed; her stare was a little too hard and a little too long. Then she wiped her face with her hand and dutifully followed.

As a *bule* in Jakarta, you get used to being watched, even shadowed. It's not unusual to pick up a follower who trails nervously behind, trying to meet your eye and pluck up the courage to speak. Then the questions rattle out with desperate intensity. Predictable stuff about Man U or the latest boy band, interspersed with pieces of obscure vocabulary and even more obscure grammar. Condolences for Diana, as if you and she had been close chums who often shared champers at Ascot. And ultimately, perhaps, the big one – was there really free sex in the west?

These two were different. It was something about the eyes.

The mall soon reverted to normal after the buzz of the military exercise. Muzak wafted through the loudspeakers, the bodies milled around and all the shoppers softly melted back into their usual trance. It was chilling in a way, how quickly everyone seemed able to wipe out the memory of the soldiers, as if they'd never been there and their rifles had been merely toys. You mustn't cry: they're here to protect us.

None of it seemed quite real to me, but I joined in anyway – window-shopping, along with the rest of them. My loyal shadows stayed close as I browsed from store to store. Dressed in T-shirts and jeans, they seemed ordinary enough, apart from something predatory in their eyes. I finally took the escalator to the ground floor and seated myself at a table outside Café Capri, looking through glass doors at the bamboo swaying outside. A waitress shuffled up and took my order for coffee and ice-cream. My shadows leant against the wall by the telephones and lit cigarettes. I remained under surveillance.

'Strawberry, yes?' the waitress chimed with desperate cheerfulness on returning to my table. She wore a white blouse and a smart black skirt, with a badge on her chest that read 'Training'.

'You don't have chocolate ice-cream?' Only her eyes moved, squinting nervously – her smile seemed tattooed on her lips. '*Coklat habis?*' She gave a panicky little giggle. I changed tack. 'What other flavours have you got?'

She cast a plaintive glance in the direction of the waiter. He was busy grooming his hair in the reflection of the cappuccino machine and pretended not to notice.

'Do you have vanilla?' Another nervous giggle. 'Coffee? Raspberry ripple?'

'Strawberry, yes?'

'Is that all there is? Is everything else *habis*?'

I hadn't the heart to go on. The poor girl seemed in such a state I figured she must be new and was terrified that I might complain. *Bules* love to complain. Whatever her reason, she was as determined to be the herald of glad tidings as the angel on a Christmas card. She cranked her smile wider in a last-ditch effort to appease me.

I conceded defeat. 'OK, forget the ice-cream. I'll just have a coffee.' She stood rigid and digested my request. '*Minta tolong, satu kopi, ya? Yang hitam*.' She gaped at me as if I'd spoken Armenian before fleeing to the safety of the kitchen.

'May we join you?'

I looked up. During my monologue with the waitress, the shadows had moved closer to my table and lingered a few feet away.

I folded my arms across my chest. 'If you wish.'

The taller one, clearly much more confident, chose the chair next to mine. His companion hesitated before seating himself opposite me.

'Where are you from?' the confident one asked.

'England.'

'I thought so.' He held out his hand for me to shake. 'Your clothes look very English.' I had no idea if he realized that the English aren't renowned for their sartorial elegance. 'My name's Susanto. But you can call me Santo if you like. My little name.'

'Graham.'

'Hi, Graham. Forgive my friend, he doesn't speak English at all.' They exchanged a few brisk sentences in a language I didn't know, presumably Javanese. 'His name is Wawan.'

'Pleased to meet you, Wawan.'

'Sorry, mister. I only speak little little English.'

I must have heard this phrase a thousand times in Indonesia, accompanied by laughing eyes and a timid grin. But these eyes didn't laugh. They brooded with suspicion. And, if I wasn't mistaken, something much worse. These eyes loathed me.

'He was lazy at school,' Santo quickly explained. 'Always fishing or chasing girls.'

An uneasy silence followed. I shuffled uncomfortably in my seat and glanced at the world outside. Clouds had started to clog up the spotless blue sky. 'Your English is excellent,' I ventured.

'I've been studying in Australia for three years.' He leant forward in his seat to examine me. 'You pick it up.'

I stared awkwardly back. He was slim to the point of emaciated, with delicate features and bony hands. His intelligent eyes darted back and forth behind tinted glasses, always searching for new things to alight on. Wawan was shorter and squatter, with darker skin and heavier features. He seemed glum and ill at ease, fiddling with the Cellophane on his cigarette pack. He had none of Santo's panache. They made an unlikely couple.

'Did you enjoy the cabaret?' Santo asked, with a sneer.

'Cabaret?'

'The soldiers showing off their toys.'

'Is that all it was?'

'Of course. What else?' He broke into laughter and placed a hand on my arm. 'A message to all the rich people who come here. Your money is safe and you can carry on shopping. There will be no revolution on the streets of Pondok Indah.'

I found his directness quite shocking. Even after the fall of Soeharto and all the animated talk of *reformasi*, few Indonesians would dare to speak quite so openly.

'You didn't buy anything yet?' he asked, glancing at my feet for shopping bags.

'I'm not really looking.'

'Just passing time, I guess? Same with me, Graham. One cassette. That's all.' He held up *Fat of the Land* by the Prodigy. 'PIM is really so boring. Before the riots there used to be a place called Aquarius. Maybe four hundred metres over there. Did you know it?' I nodded. 'Coolest place in town for music. But it got burnt down.'

The waitress crept up to the table like a condemned prisoner at dawn. On the tray in her hands, I spotted coffee, sugar, milk, plus a bumper-size dish of strawberry ice-cream. She tried hard to summon up her most alluring smile, but in her anxious state it collapsed, until it was no more than a tremor of her bottom lip. I spooned strawberry ice-cream into my mouth and did my best to look delighted.

Santo and Wawan both ordered Cokes. Chatting in Indonesian to two eligible young *cowok*, the waitress transformed from grub to butterfly before my eyes. It was quite some metamorphosis. The fingers that had been so anxious a moment ago now flicked through her hair with seductive ease, while her nervous little giggle had blossomed into a temptress's smile. The mood at the table changed completely. Even Wawan showed signs of life as the three of them teased each other and flirted.

For a moment I became invisible. It was a wonderful feeling.

'I want to pay now,' Santo stressed. '*Aku mau bayar sekarang.*' After checking to make sure that I was watching, he placed his money on the wooden tray. The waitress swept her fingers through her hair and sashayed back to the kitchen.

'What kind of music do you like, Graham?' Santo asked, as he removed the sleeve-notes from his cassette case.

'Jazz.'

'That's cool.' He read the notes as he spoke. 'I'm into alternative music. Are you into that at all?'

'I don't know much about the latest music, I'm afraid. I'm a bit of a fuddy-duddy.'

'Fuddy-duddy.' He tittered as he tried to mimic my accent.

'Old-fashioned.'

'Yes, I understand,' he said, with a touch of pique. He repeated the word several times under his breath, committing it to his memory. 'Don't knock your generation, Graham. Lots of the stuff you guys did was really cool. Like Iggy Pop. Do you know Iggy Pop?'

'Only a little.'

'I am the passenger!' he howled, more Moggy than Iggy.

'Classic rock, Graham. People who make music for art, not for money.'

'Don't you like Indonesian music?' I asked, taking my chance to show off in return. '*Dangdut?*'

'*Dangdut!*' Santo leapt up and performed a parody of the dance that goes with *dangdut* music. 'Wawan likes *dangdut.*' He laughed, pointing a finger at the sulky face. The glare he got in return persuaded him to sit back down and chat to his friend for a while in Javanese.

I tried to understand what they were saying – I got the feeling they were disputing something. Wawan eventually looked up at me and switched on a frigid smile.

'How about *keroncong?*' I persisted, keen to keep the musical conversation bubbling in order to hide my unease.

I had anticipated an even louder howl of dismay. I got a dismissive snort instead. '*Keroncong* is for old people.'

He flashed me the kind of look that under-25s the world over reserve for men with middle-aged spread. Meanwhile, Wawan gratefully returned his attention to his cigarette pack.

'But seriously, Graham, you guys did some great stuff,' Santo went on. 'The Sex Pistols. The Velvet Underground. I mean, some of that music was pretty way out. Don't you like any of that stuff?'

'Not my cup of tea.' I was delighted to see I'd unearthed one more gap in his English vocabulary. 'It's an idiom,' I explained. 'It means not my taste.' He crumpled his sleeve-notes back into their case. I got the strong impression that he hated not being perfect.

The waitress glided back, balancing a tray on her right palm. She placed two glasses of Coke on the table, misted over and clinking with ice. The tray bore a handful of small coins.

'Where did you get to hear this kind of music?' I asked. 'Australia?'

56

'Of course,' he snapped, in a tone which implied that my question was incredibly stupid.

'Did you like living there?'

'Why not?' He held up the cassette case for my benefit. 'They call this kind of music techno,' he explained, painstakingly, as if I had a rocking chair and an ear trumpet. 'That's what's cool about the west. There are so many kinds of music. Not just the Boyzone trash they listen to here.' He gestured that the waitress could take the change. It was an offhand gesture: he was bored with the flirtation already. 'Indonesian people are like sheep, Graham.'

He paused and leant back in his chair, cupping his hands behind his head. I got the feeling he wanted me to appreciate his fine grasp of English idiom. 'Like sheep,' he repeated, just in case I'd missed it the first time around.

I ignored him and sipped my coffee, determined not to feed his ego by giving any kind of response.

'Everyone likes the same things here, the shit they churn out on MTV. If it's not the latest big hit from the west, my people don't want to know.'

'We have MTV as well, you know.'

'Yeah, but nobody who's really cool ever watches it. It's for kids.' He whispered in my ear, with a disconcerting intimacy, 'I like western people, Graham. You're willing to stand out and be different.'

I drank some coffee as an excuse to edge myself away. 'You should see my neighbours,' I said. 'You'd soon change your mind.'

He seemed irritated that I'd rubbished his concept of the broad-minded westerner. 'So, why are you in Jakarta?' he suddenly asked.

The change of tone in his voice was so abrupt that I bolted upright in my seat. 'I work here.'

'What kind of work?'

'Why do you want to know?'

'I'm just interested. This is a pretty mixed-up city. People come here for lots of reasons.'

I glanced over at Wawan, still fumbling with the Cellophane on his cigarette pack, and then back at Santo. 'Have you two been following me?' I asked.

'Do I look like a policeman?' He pointed to his T-shirt with a calculated bonhomie. It was brilliant red and bore the slogan '*Reformasi!*' 'Or maybe I'm a *provokator* who got dropped from the military helicopter?'

My silence spelt out that I wasn't going to play this game.

He rapidly changed tack, reaching over to place his hand on mine. 'OK, so I'm sorry. Yes, we've been following you. We wanted to practise our English.' A lie so obvious I was surprised he'd made it.

'Your English is perfect and you know it.'

'I get bored, Graham. With Indonesian people, I mean. I know what they're going to say before they speak. I like to be surprised.'

I leant forward to sip my coffee, stared him in the eye and raised my eyebrows slightly.

Once again he flicked on a different mood. 'Are you normally such a suspicious guy, Graham?'

'I'm careful.'

'I guess it pays to be. Indonesia is pretty unstable right now.' A nasty edge had crept into the voice. 'Don't worry, I'm not going to ask you for money. That's what Indonesians always do with *bules*, isn't it?'

I stared silently out of the window at a darkening sky. There'd be a storm soon.

'Where do you study in Australia?' I asked, to break the silence.

'Sydney.'

'I've never been there. Is it nice?'

'It's OK.'

'Do you miss Indonesia?'

'It's my country. Of course I miss it. Do you miss England?'

'Not much.'

'I admire many things about the west, Graham. Your music. Your style. But I have my religion and it's not respected there. Western people are always so arrogant.'

Once again his outspokenness shocked me. The Javanese weren't supposed to do this kind of thing. They were supposed to be polite and submissive, and smile endlessly.

'You still think we're stupid because our skin is brown. You still think you're a lot more cultured than us.' I poured the last of my coffee to disguise my nervousness. 'Like that woman. Pauline Hanson. I used to watch her on TV in Australia and marvel at how cultured you white guys are.'

His lips curled upwards and he burst into high-pitched laughter. There was a twinkle in his eye – he'd been winding me up.

I laughed, too; with relief, mostly. And a kind of grudging admiration. He was a class act, this Santo. A smart guy.

'You shouldn't judge all white people by the standards of Pauline Hanson,' I eventually said.

'She only speaks what is true, Graham. Yes, she is stupid, and yes, she is ugly, but at least she's honest. She speaks what everyone thinks but will never say.'

'No, she doesn't, Santo. She doesn't represent anyone except for a few screwed-up fascists. Her whole platform is based on –'

A thunderous crash shattered the calm of the mall. A second crash followed, as the fist of a middle-aged man smashed for a second time on the glass entrance door. If it caused him pain, his face didn't register it. He had the eyes of a zombie, a creature possessed.

Inside the mall, everyone stood frozen. On the other side of the sheet of glass, it had started to rain.

The madman burst through the entrance, ranting at someone. At God, perhaps, for the muscles bulged on his neck as his huge eyes stared upwards. A security guard who tried to stand in his way got swatted aside like an irritating insect.

I laughed. I don't know why. Maybe a kind of shock. Because the whole thing seemed so incongruous amid the glossy opulence of Pondok Indah Mal.

The man lurched onwards, crashing into a shopper, scattering the contents of her bags across the floor. The security guard pounced into action and made a bolder attempt to apprehend him. The madman swung around and lashed out with a knife. The security guard pounced no further. With the traditional valour of his proud profession, he gave a sharp squeal of pain and scampered away.

Again I laughed. But I didn't laugh for long, because the crazy was heading my way. The line to God was engaged and he was ranting at me.

He scattered the chairs in his path across the floor. The table went flying. He spat in my face and lashed out with the blade. In his frenzy he missed. He slashed once more and missed a second time. A third slice through the air and my right arm was spurting blood.

I tumbled from my chair and went sprawling across the floor, helpless as he towered above me. I waited for the knife to come again. But the demons who possessed him lost their grip for just one moment and he paused. A fraction of a second, I didn't know why. Perhaps my helplessness had disarmed him. A moment, long enough for someone to try to grab him from behind. In the confusion that followed, the knife fell from his hand. It landed next to my face with a hollow clang.

Stripped of his knife, my attacker froze. As if it had contained all his power and without it he was impotent, like a discarded *wayang* puppet. I heard voices yelling. Santo and Wawan. Santo pushed his face close up to the man's, remonstrating furiously, while Wawan held him tightly from behind. They knew him. Even in all my confusion, I could tell that they knew him.

My blood spread across the white floor. Pain shot up my arm. I became aware I was still in danger and tried to stagger to my feet.

I looked around at the faces who had gathered and stood there watching. A circle of mouths gripped by an unnatural hush. The silence was finally shattered when my assailant broke into uncontrollable sobs. A stranger from the crowd held out his hand. I wasn't going to make it. My mind struggled furiously to stay afloat, but the whirlpool of darkness was much too strong and was sucking it down, beneath the surface of a turbulent sea.

6

I struggled to keep afloat on the black waves, flailing my way back to consciousness. A circle of faces swirled before my eyes. Masks I'd never seen. A mask that I did know blurred into focus. Detective Suprianto.

Two security guards hauled me to my feet and dragged me out of the mall. I could sense Suprianto, like a long, evening shadow, following behind. My body was yanked to the right, along the side of the building, and then through the tradesmen's entrance back inside. Past the prayer room and some toilets, into a dingy cell of a room, where a line of silent video screens ceaselessly flickered. Clips from around the mall in washed-out blue. The people captured on the screens seemed closer to insects.

My blood stained the white shirts of the guards a startling red. A hand laid a towel on a chair before they sat me down. A second hand switched on a desk fan. The air that blasted my face was too hot and too sticky to provide relief.

A big-boned woman marched through the doorway. One glance at the wound, and she clutched my arm at the elbow, dipped a wad of cotton wool in a bowl of water and swilled the cut. From somewhere appeared a battered first-aid box that looked as if it had seen service in the First World War. Hidden in its depths, though, lay enough pills and potions to keep a small hospital running. The woman scratched at the contents like a crab digging up sand.

My head still reeled. It was sickeningly hot in this windowless cell. At last the woman located the tube she wanted. She squeezed a blob of ointment onto her index finger, a rust colour that warned of iodine. She plastered it over the open wound.

I let out a yelp of pain. She peered at me over the top of her gold-framed spectacles and snapped a few words in Indonesian. Suprianto stood impassively at my side. I hadn't noticed him enter the room.

'You must go to hospital, Mr Young,' he translated, miming the action of sewing to show that I needed stitches.

Cleansed of dried-up blood, my wound looked embarrassingly trivial. My nurse eyed me coolly through her spectacles. Already she was binding my arm in a strip of white gauze. She barked out an instruction.

Panic ensued. The scissors were lost and there seemed no way to cut the strip of gauze. At last a baby-faced guard stepped forward, produced a knife from his belt and sliced through the cloth with due ceremony, like a VIP unveiling a plaque.

'You are very lucky, Mr Young,' Suprianto whispered. 'A crazy man attacked you.'

'He wasn't crazy.'

He avoided my gaze by busying himself with the contents of the first-aid box, sorting the tubes and bottles into rows.

'Of course he was crazy. He attacked you, with knife.'

The hero of the day, the young guard held his knife in the air, like a champion lifting his trophy. I winced as the bandage was wrenched tighter around my wound.

'Do not worry, Mr Young. The man is at the police station now.'

Something moved in the corner of my eye and I glanced down at the floor – in time to catch sight of a cockroach disappearing into the darkness under my chair.

'Who is he?'

'A crazy man.' He put his hand to his forehead and held it at a forty-five degree angle – the Indonesian signal for insanity.

'No. He wasn't crazy.'

A nod from Suprianto and I was yanked to my feet. A guard dragged me along more corridors to the drizzle of the outside world and the car park. My head was still spinning, I still felt sick. A surly driver lay with his feet on the dashboard of Suprianto's car, reading a newspaper. He watched, vaguely interested, as the guard struggled to help me into the back seat, then returned to his paper with a shrug.

Suprianto emerged from the building and the driver's face popped up above the newsprint, perky as a pet dog. He shot to attention and leapt from the car. The detective indicated that he would join me on the back seat; the driver trotted round and held the door open for him, fulsome as a bellboy at a swish hotel. I saw the look in Suprianto's eyes. He wasn't fooled for a moment.

Bullets of rain began to pummel the windscreen. The BMW pulled away.

'There is so much rain this week, Mr Young. Perhaps the rainy season will come more early this year.'

The freshness of the rain was clearing my head and I began to remember the things that had happened before I got sucked into the whirlpool. As if he somehow sensed my change of mood, Suprianto hurried to fill the silence before I spoke.

'The hospital is not so far. Five minutes perhaps.'

'Who were the young men?' I asked.

His face went as stiff as one of the wooden masks that adorn the stalls on Jalan Surabaya. 'You do not need to worry. Hospital Pondok Indah is very good.'

'I was talking to two young men. Who were they?' The car crept forward in a line of sluggish traffic. 'They knew the man who attacked me.'

Suprianto stared out at the street, although the rain beat down so hard that the windows were almost opaque, like liquid walls.

'I don't know, Mr Young. I didn't see any young men.'

I felt a stab of pain in my arm. 'They knew the man who attacked me. They were talking to him.'

He continued to avoid my eyes. 'They left when my men arrived, perhaps. Many Indonesians do not like police.'

'Before I passed out. They were shouting.' I waited for a response. I would have waited for a long time. 'Arguing.'

'You are confused, Mr Young. You have shock.'

The car hit a hole in the road, impossible to spot in the teeming rain. I lurched forward in my seat.

'You must try to relax,' he advised me. 'It is better if you do not speak.'

The BMW ground to a halt, stranded in the rain in one of Jakarta's traffic jams. The windscreen wipers screeched, the rain lashed down and I became aware of another sound, from the other side of the window.

I peered through the rain to make out a shape in the middle of the road just ahead of us. The black car inched forward. I could see that the shape was the body of a dog and the sound I could hear was its howling.

I wound down the window to halfway. Rain spat spitefully in my face. I saw a little white dog in the middle of the road, screaming with pain. A car had run him over and his back legs were crushed to a pulp. Around his body, a pool of water, stained bright red.

With the window open, the high-pitched screams became unbearable. A little white dog, scarcely more than a puppy, almost certain to die. It would kiss him with relief, the arrival of death. Death and silence. I was almost sure I didn't believe in a God. But if there was a God, these screams should reach up to heaven and make Him weep. They should make Him ashamed.

The rain continued to spatter my face, refreshing and bitter. The driver wound down his window and stared dumbly out. He pointed a finger at the dog and laughed out loud. A stupid laugh, as callous as concrete, coarser than the call of any wild animal. There was nothing as base as this in the jungle, this self-satisfied brutality. Suprianto glanced across at my face and must have seen the shock I was feeling. He snapped at the driver to pull shut his window.

'You will get wet, Mr Young.'

Why couldn't he die quickly, this poor little dog? Why couldn't this howling stop? It slashed me open like a surgeon's knife. I wanted to close the window, maybe then I could block out what I'd seen. But it was fascinating, too, to watch something die. Something innocent, a creature that didn't deserve such pain.

'Close your window, Mr Young. Please. You will get wet.'

Then a mercy killing came, like a doctor with a lethal injection. A car accelerated past us, aiming for a gap in the middle of the road, and struck the puppy full on. The creature got tossed in the air like a glove puppet, before landing on the concrete with a muffled thud. Only the sound of the rain now. The body of the dog lay in the middle of the road, like a piece of white sack.

It had gone. Whatever this thing called life was. Whether it was some mysterious force which transcended the physical, or merely a cocktail of chemicals fizzing around the brain. It had gone for ever.

I remembered my father's corpse on that cold March morning. The emptiness I stared into that day, something more dead than mere stones. I thought again of the limbless beggar under the flyover at Jalan Arteri. Pain, then oblivion.

I rolled up the window. Another stab of pain in my arm.

Suprianto noticed me wince and placed a consoling hand on my shoulder. 'I am sorry you must wait. In Jakarta, there is always traffic jam when it rains.'

The car edged forward a further twenty metres. The dog's corpse lay behind us now. I looked out of the back window. I felt hexed, suffused in some malign magic. An insane feeling. Not rational at all. But my heartbeat was racing.

'Mr Young?'

I felt it was behind me somewhere, the presence from my dream. Stalking me. These are the ramblings of a madman, I told myself – you have to get a grip on them. God knows where they'll lead you if you don't.

'Mr Young? Tell me again about the two young men.' I forced myself to concentrate on his voice. 'The two young men you saw,' he repeated. 'Perhaps you have some information to help us.'

'I've told you already.'

'What did they talk about when they make conversation?'

'Music. Australia.'

I struggled to make myself heard above the pounding of the rain on the car roof. Suprianto could afford his kindness. I felt like I was falling to pieces and the detective was in total control.

'Did they tell you their names?'

'Santo. Wawan.'

'I am sorry, Mr Young,' he said, with a little smile, as he dragged in his cigarette smoke. 'I did not see this Santo and Wawan. Later you can give us description.'

We pulled up outside the entrance to the hospital. The driver, keen to impress now his boss was on hand, bolted over to my door to hold it open. I ignored his ingratiating smile. A gang of drenched children appeared through the curtain of the rain, each boy plying an umbrella. Suprianto chose one he liked and held it above our heads as I followed him up the steps to the glass doors.

'I know with the doctors here, Mr Young. They helped my wife when she was sick.'

The gauze around my arm was caked with blood. No longer bright red, but a heavier shade, hints of purple and brown. The rain gushed in tiny whirlpools at my feet. The driver slammed his door shut and signalled right, to pull into the car park.

'Hepatitis. It is very dangerous.'

Hospitals spook me. They are always so silent and sterile, places where you go to die. This was my first time inside an Indonesian one. It could hardly have been more different from what I expected. The noise was exhausting. Entire families seemed to have camped out in reception and brought all their worldly possessions along. Their chatter set my head spinning again. But it was comforting, too, in a way. At least this place wasn't bleak. I couldn't smell death here, beneath a synthetic cleanliness.

Suprianto took hold of my shoulders and guided me into a chair. I stared down at the floor. 'What's happening to me?' I murmured.

He said nothing and strolled over to the receptionist. A few moments later, he marched back with a spring in his step. 'Only five minutes more, Mr Young. I have spoken to the young lady. She is my friend.'

Jumping the queue, an art form in Indonesia. A tiny part of a bigger corruption called KKN. *Korupsi, kolusi, nepotisme.* The subject on everyone's lips since the fall of Soeharto.

Children ran round and round the row of chairs, playing some kind of game. Nobody seemed to notice them apart from me. On the chair opposite mine, a woman was weeping softly into a handkerchief.

'Detective Suprianto?' I made sure I had his attention. 'Can I ask you some questions?'

His body stiffened. 'I am here to help you, Mr Young.'

'Please tell me what's going on.'

He took a Marlboro from his pack and went to light it,

before letting out a guilty little laugh. 'Of course, it is not allowed here.'

'I don't think you're telling me everything.' He tapped his cigarette on the pack several times and raised his eyebrows. 'Please – I want to know. Don't try to protect me. Not knowing is the worst thing of all.'

'What do you want to know, Mr Young?'

'About the man who attacked me. About the two young men.'

'I have already explained this. I do not know with these young men.'

'I think perhaps you do.'

'Why should I know with them?'

'There are too many coincidences.'

He tapped the cigarette once more. 'I'm sorry, I do not understand this word.' There was a pause, a test of nerve while we waited for each other to speak. It was no contest. He could keep this up for ever.

'A coincidence is like an accident.'

'An accident,' he repeated, tapping his cigarette to the rhythm of the word.

'When two things happen at the same time just by chance.'

His face dissolved into a model of perfect innocence. 'I was shopping, Mr Young.'

'Shopping.'

The receptionist caught my eye and flashed a huge smile to reassure me it would be my turn soon. I was running out of time.

'I'm scared,' I said, too shaken up to be embarrassed by such an admission. 'Something is happening that I can't understand.'

I was surprised to see the stiff face soften and the cigarette drumming come to a halt. He pulled up a chair and sat down at my side.

'Please trust me and tell me the truth,' I said. 'Are your men still following me?'

He produced a handkerchief from his pocket and wiped the sweat from his forehead. This was all very difficult for him.

'Do you think I might have links with Doctor White?'

He glanced over to the receptionist, willing her to call my name. 'I already tell you, Mr Young. I believe you are innocent.'

'But your men are still following me, aren't they?'

He said nothing, but the look in his eyes answered my question. The cigarette was slipped back into the pack and he pulled his chair up closer.

'I did not want to worry you, Mr Young.'

'Worry me?'

'Perhaps you are in danger.'

'What kind of danger?'

'I cannot tell you. It is complicated. I do not know everything myself.'

'What do you know?'

Two boys were playing soldiers. One of them dashed behind my chair to take cover, while his friend, an army commando, stalked him through the jungle.

'My country is in – how do you say? – in transition, yes? Indonesia is very dangerous at this moment. You must understand. This is not like England, where everything is stable. Where your history is already five hundred years old.'

The boy with an invisible rifle stood in front of me and stared straight at my eyes. He made the rattle of a machine gun and pretended to shoot me dead.

'What kind of danger?'

A bright young nurse bounced before me, effervescing. 'Mr Graham?' She was spankingly turned out, with skin as smooth as a mannequin.

Suprianto leapt up and answered on my behalf. 'This is Mr Graham.'

'The doctor is ready now,' the mannequin chirruped. I looked into her eyes and saw a different story. Beneath the faultlessly lacquered exterior, she was weary and harassed.

Suprianto held his hand out for me to shake. 'Forgive me, Mr Young, I must leave now.'

'What?'

'I am very busy today. But you are fine now.'

'This is a joke, isn't it?'

'I know with the doctor here. He is very good.'

'You can't tell me I'm in danger and then just vanish.'

'The doctor is ready now,' the nurse repeated, in a faltering voice. Cracks had appeared in her confidence, like crazing in porcelain. She stared at me, then at Suprianto, not knowing what to do next.

'You must be careful for a while,' the policeman advised. 'My driver will stay here and take you home.'

'Why? So you can keep a better eye on me?'

He chose not to respond to my barb, but stared gravely into my eyes. 'I suggest that you stay in your house where you are safe. For one week.'

'I can't do that. I'm going away.'

'Oh.' For once he wasn't quick enough erecting the screen and his real emotion showed. Surprise. It was good to learn he was vulnerable after all. It was good to learn there were things he didn't know about me.

'I'm due to fly to Bali tomorrow,' I explained. 'On holiday.'

'Bali!' He beamed with delight at the news.

'Are you saying it's not safe to go?'

'Of course it's safe! Yes, of course! Oh, you are very safe in Bali, Mr Young. My driver will take you to airport.' He leant across to whisper in my ear. 'Balinese girls are very beautiful, yes?'

And suddenly he'd gone, with a speed I'd never seen him show before. I gaped at the nurse by my side. She seemed deflated, a glass of sparkling wine which had lost its fizz.

A toddler knelt by my feet and tugged at my trouser leg. I went to shoo him away and felt a twinge of pain in my arm. 'I know,' I mumbled. 'I'm sorry. The doctor's waiting for me.'

She pepped herself up for one last big smile. With a wiggle of the hips, she glided forward, gesturing that I should follow. The children swarmed around me, continuing to shout and play soldiers. Without Suprianto, I felt exposed. I was a travelling stranger, and I hurried to the refuge of the doctor's room.

7

Bali, Paradise Island! Or so the brochures at the airport claim. The purists will argue it's crass and superficial and phoney, of course, as they clutch their *Lonely Planet*s and head off into the jungle in search of the authentic third-world experiences of dysentery and snakebite. As a pampered tourist lounging by the poolside, I find I can live with the ersatz. OK, so the culture comes in bite-size chunks and everything has a price. It still beats Great Yarmouth on a wet afternoon. And while there may be no such thing on Paradise Island as a free smile, Bali's about as cheap as paradise gets.

Cancel that last sentence. Paradise does not come cheap at Ketut's, a trendy bar in Ubud, boasting a long, expensive drinks menu and a clientele who can afford it. At night it's one of the hippest venues in town, with its blend of passing *bules* and locals keen to be seen. By daylight, though, Ketut's is often a sleepy spot, refreshing the occasional tourist who wanders in for a beer. It was a drowsy afternoon with the scent of jasmine on the breeze. I sat upstairs sipping gin and tonic, gazing idly at the people passing by on the street below. Another day, another bar.

Ubud is where Bali hawks its culture with upmarket swank. Unlike the glamour gals and beach boys who loiter on Kuta seafront, Ubud tourists aren't on the prowl for sunshine and sex. These earnest travellers are far more refined – their holy grail is the uplift of cultural experience. Not that the bodies who trudged past below looked as if they'd found it. They beat a weary path along the dusty street, their puffed-up, pink faces gripped with the grim determination of cultural tourists everywhere in their quest for authenticity. There were carvings to buy, galleries to explore, performances to witness, batik to collect, all in the enervating tropical heat. It's a tough job being a cultural tourist – give me a frolic on Kuta beach front every time.

An English couple in their late fifties, who looked as if they had never frolicked in their lives, sat glumly at a nearby table. Communication with the waitress was proving a problem. The husband was allergic to coconut, it seemed, but every effort on their part to explain this fact merely convinced the waitress further that they wanted to order it. Should I help out, I wondered, using my Indonesian? No, they were English: they'd only hate me for being a show-off.

'I don't know how it can be so difficult,' the wife hissed to the husband once the waitress was out of earshot. She caught me looking across at her and jutted out her chin. 'Are you German?' she asked, for no reason I could discern.

'English.'

'Oh.' She relaxed. 'We're from Halifax. Do you know it?'

'I'm afraid not.'

'You're from the south, I suppose. Are you alone?'

My heart sank. 'Yes.'

'I expect you're a businessman. Has your wife stayed back in England?'

'I'm divorced.'

'Oh.' Her voice must have shot up an octave. I doubted very much if she moved in social circles where divorce was virtually taken for granted.

'Well, we can't have you sitting on your own, can we?' she resolved, after a moment's deliberation. 'You must come over and join us.' She gestured towards an empty chair at their table. I lifted myself from my seat, resigned to the chore of polite conversation.

'I'm Marjorie and this is Harold.' She slid her horn-rimmed spectacles back up her nose with the palms of both hands. 'We don't bite, do we, Harold?'

He peered at me over the top of his bifocals.

'Graham.'

'You're from the south, aren't you?' I nodded. 'I thought so. You don't speak unless you're spoken to.' She lifted her teacup with dowager grace. 'We went to the south once. Bournemouth. I didn't like it.'

The waitress appeared at the top of the stairs with my next gin and tonic. Marjorie eyed its sparkle with disapproval. 'When did you arrive here?' she asked.

'I live here.'

'Oh. You live here.' She paused to digest this bizarre fact. 'I suppose that's very interesting.'

'Well, in Jakarta. The capital.'

'Harold and I have been here five days now,' she reported, with palpable regret.

'Don't you like it?'

She glanced around before confiding in a whisper, 'We're far from satisfied with the toilets.' I stifled my giggle with a mouthful of gin. 'The general standard of hygiene in this country leaves a lot to be desired. Harold's stomach hasn't been right since the plane landed.'

'I've been going three times a day,' he told me, gravely.

'I realize they may not have much money to spare,' she continued. 'But they should still show proper concern in the vital areas.' She pointed to the menu for Harold's benefit. 'The pizza should be safe enough, dear.'

I smiled to myself. Strangers in paradise: how on earth had they washed up in Ubud? A tsunami, perhaps, from Scarborough seafront.

'I expect it's all quite normal to you by now,' she said. 'The food and the mosquitoes.'

'I guess so.'

I studied them both. Aliens here in Ubud, yet put them in an English high street and they'd seem utterly drab. Most western tourists in Ubud, with the restrained good taste of their clothes and the perfect cut of their hair, exuded a rather French air, while the ones who didn't drip Gallic refinement tended to be leggy Scandinavian bombshells or bronzed Teutonic gods. Why on earth did I ever stay there, with my English dress sense and my middle-aged spread? I had to be some kind of masochist.

'I'm sorry to hear you're not enjoying it,' I said, as I tucked into the complimentary peanuts. At these prices, you made the most of the extras. 'I often come here for long weekends. To escape from Jakarta.' I held my gin and tonic high in the air, mischievously, to re-ignite her disapproval. 'It's a great place to relax.'

'I'm sure it's very nice. Once you get used to it.'

A clique of young Bohemians strutted in. Ubud's arty set. Shades and sarongs, stubble and tattoos. And that was just the women.

'We've never been to Asia before,' Marjorie informed me. 'We usually go to Portugal.'

'Indonesia must be quite a shock to the system, I guess.'

'Indeed.' She leant across and whispered, 'They just don't think like us, do they?'

I laughed. 'They certainly don't.'

Marjorie eyed one of the new arrivals up and down. A young woman with her hair in braids and a gold ring through her navel. A puff of air sighed from Marjorie's lips. She removed her spectacles to scan the menu. 'We were debating the chicken in Balinese sauce. Only I'm not convinced it's free of coconut.'

'I heard.'

'Harold's allergic, you see. Comes out in a rash.'

'Would you like me to check for you?'

'Oh, would you, please? That would be very kind.'

I tried in vain to get the attention of the waitress. She was far too busy with the latest arrivals, who had taken it on themselves to rearrange the furniture.

'Oh well,' Marjorie sighed, with stubborn cheerfulness. 'I'm sure our new hotel will be better.'

'You complained and got moved?'

'Oh dear me, no.' She seemed quite upset that I'd think such a thing. 'They take us somewhere else tomorrow. It's all part of the package deal. What's it called, Harold?' Before he could open his lips, she had answered her own question. 'Nusa Dua.'

Nusa Dua was a playground for the rich and would-be rich on the southernmost tip of the island. A manicured mausoleum of exclusive hotels and landscaped gardens. Hawaii, perhaps, or Florida. As authentically Balinese as Kentucky Fried Chicken.

'Very nice,' I teased. 'You'll have no trouble with the toilets there.'

She cast a dismissive look in my direction, as if my teasing were very juvenile. 'I expect you must be used to lower standards by now.'

Ouch! 'I'm sure you'll like it there,' I said, rather sheepishly, trying to worm my way back into favour. 'It wins all kinds of awards.'

The grimace relaxed. 'To be honest, we almost didn't come here at all. It was touch and go.' She raised her teacup with delicacy, as if entertaining the local reverend. 'After we watched all those riots on the television.'

The chimes of gamelan music drifted over from the café on the opposite side of the street. In the drowsy afternoon heat, softened by jasmine, riots seemed unimaginable.

'But the agent assured us it was quite safe here.'

I waved my arm to attract the waitress and winced with pain from the wound I'd received in Pondok Indah Mal.

Marjorie noted my discomfort. 'What happened?' she asked, pointing to my bandage. I could tell she'd been dying to ask this question since she first saw me.

I couldn't resist teasing her a little. 'Oh, nothing serious. I got a bit drunk and fell on some broken glass.'

'Oh.' She tried her very hardest not to give a reaction.

'Nothing really happened in Bali,' I continued. 'Riots-wise, I mean. They were mostly in Jakarta.'

'Where you live?' I nodded. 'So what did you do?'

'Sat tight at home. You were safe enough as long as you kept off the streets.'

'You stayed here?' she asked, with a raise of her eyebrows, clearly impressed by my unflappability. 'You're very brave.'

I laughed and shook my head. 'Not really.' At last I caught the attention of the waitress and beckoned her over. 'I'm no hero, believe me.'

Marjorie studied me carefully as I subjected the waitress to my half-cocked Indonesian. '*Ini pakai kelapa?*' I asked, pointing to the menu and the chicken in Balinese sauce. The waitress did her best to avoid giving an answer, but I'd lived in Indonesia long enough to know this game and I hung on with dogged persistence. I finally squeezed a reply from her lips. A guarantee – or the closest to a guarantee you'll ever get in Indonesia – that the Balinese chicken did not contain coconut.

'Well, we'd better try it then,' Marjorie said, with resolve rather than enthusiasm. 'But a pizza for you, I think, Harold.' She opened the menu and spelt out her order.

'And another gin and tonic, please,' I piped up.

Marjorie's disapproval seemed to have mellowed rather, into something closer to maternal concern. 'I imagine you must be under quite a lot of stress here.'

'Sure am!' I laughed, gesturing towards the bright blue sky. 'Having to cope with all this sunshine!'

She gave a little tut, not believing me for a moment. 'It can't be easy, I know, living so far from home.' She folded the menu shut. 'And with all the political problems they have here.'

I could tell how badly she wanted to discuss this. Probably her way of feeling she was still in control. 'They're no big deal,' I stated.

'No?'

'It's the little things that stress you out, actually. But riots?' I reached down into the bowl of freebies. 'Like shelling peanuts.'

'That's not how it looked on the BBC.'

'Well, TV exaggerates.'

'They were burning cars and looting shops. Why do people do such dreadful things?' I watched her fingers as they nervously stroked her cup.

'Poverty, mainly.'

'And how is rioting supposed to help anyone?'

'They don't know any other way here. All they've had is the Dutch and then two dictators.' I found myself glancing round as I spoke – old habits die hard. 'Speak out against Soeharto and they threw you in jail. Or left you floating face down in the river.'

The waitress edged towards us with a fretful look on her face. The chicken in Balinese sauce was *habis*.

'Finished,' I translated. 'Off the menu.'

Marjorie shook her head. 'That seems to happen a lot here.'

'Like I said, it's the little things that stress you out.'

She took off her spectacles and hung them around her neck. 'Well, it can't be easy for them,' she said, indulgently. 'What with having to speak a foreign language and everything.' She turned her attention once more to the menu. 'I think I'll just have a sandwich,' she said to the waitress, with a reassuring smile. 'Chicken and mayonnaise.'

She turned to face me. 'Radio 4 said they were attacking the Chinese,' she continued, firing on all cylinders by now. Marjorie was indomitable, in that self-effacing English way.

'They're often the target,' I said. 'People couldn't attack Soeharto, so they hit out at the Chinese instead.'

'Why?'

'In the past, they acted as middlemen between the Dutch and the native Malays. A lot of them got rich in the process.'

'So it's simply jealousy?'

'And resentment.' I leant forward and filled her cup for her. 'Do you mind if I ask you something?'

She nodded briefly.

'Why didn't you cancel and take your holiday somewhere else? Thailand or Malaysia?'

The spectacles went back on the nose. 'We don't defeat violence by running away from it.'

'You're not worried?'

'We talked it over, didn't we, Harold? They weren't going to make us change our plans. That's as good as giving in to them.'

The waitress returned with cutlery and napkins. I gave Marjorie a big smile. I could almost have kissed her, she was so ridiculously British. Perhaps it was only the gin.

'I've led such a quiet life, Graham. Nearly all of it a few streets from where I was born.' Once the waitress was out of sight, she picked up her fork and wiped it on her napkin. 'It must be hard for someone like you to understand, with your international lifestyle,' she continued. 'I always promised myself I'd see a bit of the world once I retired.'

'Even if you don't really enjoy it that much?'

'That's not the point. It does us good to see how some people suffer. Otherwise we forget how lucky we are. In England, I mean.'

'I'll drink to that,' I slurred, knocking back my gin. A cue for one last lingering look of disapproval, but followed swiftly this time by a forgiving smile, like an aunt who indulges a favourite rogue of a nephew.

The afternoon dissolved into twilight, as tends to happen in Ketut's once the G and Ts start flowing. Marjorie and Harold had long since departed in search of a chemist which stocked Harold's favoured indigestion cure. Dusk was falling and the waitress lit the candles on the tables. Geckos froze in the shadows, as still as death, to ambush the night's mosquitoes. The lilt of gamelan grew softer and more sensual in the evening breeze.

I took a ticket for the Barong dance from my pocket. Ubud Palace – 7.30 p.m. The tang of the lemon in my gin and tonic danced on my tongue, luring me to stay for more of the same. Another night, another bar. I chastised myself half-heartedly. I couldn't go on drinking like this for the rest of my life – I had to change. Maybe tomorrow.

The waitress rescued me from my momentary crisis of conscience. 'You have message, sir.'

'Message?'

She handed me a folded piece of paper. The outside was blank.

'Who from?'

She gave me a panicky smile. The upstairs bar was empty now, apart from four young men who wore sunglasses even though it was well into dusk. I figured they must be Italian.

The paper had been folded several times into a thick white square. I unwrapped it, fold by fold. The final unfolding revealed a dark red smudge. A fingerprint – a thumbprint – in blood.

My head shot up, like an animal startled by some sound in the jungle. The poses of the Italians seemed not to have moved. In the eaves, the geckos lurked, with pinpoint eyes.

Time had frozen in the candlelight.

'Who gave you this?' I snapped at the waitress. I glanced around and repeated myself, more calmly. 'Who gave you this?'

Her supervisor chose this moment to pop his head above the parapet of the stairs, like a prairie dog peeping from its hole. He stood there, proud gaze sweeping from side to side, inspecting his fiefdom.

'Who gave you this?' I asked, for a third time.

She repeated her nervous giggle. Noting me in conversation with a member of his staff, with a look of concern on my face, her supervisor instantly spotted a situation crying out for his expertise. He strode over to sort things out.

'Good evening, sir,' he smarmed. 'Is there a problem?' He switched on the kind of smile that invites a fist.

'Someone gave your waitress a message.'

'Yes, sir?'

'A message.'

He couldn't have had the faintest idea what I was talking about, of course, but was much too supercilious to admit this. Instead he reproduced the smile, something he'd learnt on a training course, condescending and obsequious at the same time. Not so much a prairie dog, more like a rat.

'A man give me this,' the waitress volunteered, much keener to assist now that her boss was on hand.

'*Bule* or Indonesian?'

She glanced at her superior to check if she should answer. He swallowed hard. The pressure was on. He had to do something, as befitted his loftier status, but hadn't a clue what to do. He chose to react to a complaint I'd never made.

'Was there a problem with your meal, sir?'

'What?'

'Or perhaps the service was too slow? I'm afraid we're rather short-staffed today.'

'Listen to me, will you? I'm not complaining. I'm just trying to find out who sent me this.'

He hadn't listened, and he sniffed the air like an anxious rodent. His hands had started to sweat. How badly he regretted setting foot on those stairs.

'A man give me. Indonesian people,' the waitress finally explained.

'Had you seen him before? *Pernah lihat dia?*'

She shook her head. '*Tidak pernah.*'

'You're sure the message was intended for me?' My voice was too rushed and she hadn't understood. 'You are sure there is no mistake?' I asked, more slowly.

Her boss, whose bemused face had been bobbing back and forth like a spectator at a tennis match, registered the magic word. 'Mistake'. His chance, at last, to spell out just who was in charge here. He turned on the waitress viciously, barking out his anger and stabbing his finger in the air. It was so cruel and so sudden that even the Italians forgot their sacred duty to look cool and broke off their conversation to stare across.

Tears welled up in the waitress's eyes. 'Look,' I said, thrusting the note under the rodent's nose. 'Someone gave this to your waitress. I'm just trying to find out who.'

He peered at the thumbprint in confusion, turned the piece of paper over to check the other side, pondered for a moment and then shrugged his shoulders. 'You have friend who make joke.'

'I have no friends in Ubud. I'm here alone.'

'You have friend who make joke,' he echoed, as if repeating it made it true. He raised his chin, challenging me to prove otherwise.

I enunciated each syllable like the worst type of Englishman abroad. 'I am here alone. I have no friends in Ubud. Will you please do me the politeness of listening to me?'

I noticed a smile flit across the waitress's face. It was instantly suppressed. Inspired with fresh courage by my treatment of her boss, she became more forthcoming. 'Man come here,' she explained, with flourishes of her hands. 'He give me money and message. Indonesian people.'

'Are you sure it was for me? *Kamu yakin ini untuk saya?*'

'*Yakin.*' She broke into rapid Indonesian which I didn't understand. I asked her to repeat herself. After another round of sign language, I reached the conclusion that this man had pointed me out.

'What was the man like? Was he young? Did he –?'

I broke off, for in the corner of my eye I could see the rat lurking, his wounded ego poised to exact revenge. I had to butter him up for the poor girl's sake – I didn't want her to lose her job.

So I turned and gave him my full attention, chatting about the restaurant as if he owned it. 'The food is wonderful here,' I gushed. '*Enak sekali di sini.*' The waitress, who wasn't slow on the uptake, took her chance to slip away and fetch my bill. As my flattery grew more preposterous, the rodent's chest puffed out further and further. Until eventually I was important enough to warrant a personal escort down the stairs.

At the bottom I was awarded the ingratiating smile once more. 'I trust we may welcome you here again, sir.'

In the dark street outside, I was hailed by a chorus of voices. On offer that evening, every imaginable service and pleasure. Did I need transport? Ganja? A woman for the night? I felt overwhelmed. Any one of this sea of faces could have delivered the message. As a *bule*, even in a tourist town like Ubud, I stood out. My every move could be monitored, while I could never return the gaze. The street seemed hot and noisy and breezeless. I set out for Ubud Palace, but my head was bleary with booze and I had a queasy feeling inside.

8

'How long does this thing last?' the boy behind me whined.

The mother consulted her programme. 'An hour and a half.'

'An hour and a half!' The wail of a torture victim.

An expectant hush fell over the courtyard, as if the Ubud Palace were holding its breath. A towering wall, built of honey-coloured stone, formed the backdrop for the action, tapering towards the sky in the shape of a triangle. In the base of the wall stood the performers' entrance, tiny from where I sat, like the door to a doll's house.

'You'll like it, Matthew. Won't he, John?' the mother urged the husband in a plea for support.

'It's not like English theatre,' the father explained, clearly intent that his son have a cultural experience. 'It's got music and dancing.'

'I'm starving!' the boy whinged, unmoved by the promise of a few dancing girls. 'When are we going to eat?'

'Just as soon as this has finished, Matthew.'

'But I'm hungry now!'

Harsh fluorescent light flooded the performance space, framed on left and right by the xylophones and gongs of a gamelan orchestra. At each end of the wall, as it sloped towards the heavens, a single candle burnt on every tier. Two stairways of flame stretching up into the black night sky.

'You had an ice-cream just five minutes ago!' the father snapped, his patience wearing thin.

The mother switched tactics to bribery. 'We can go to that restaurant you liked so much. Do you remember, where they had spare ribs?'

The musicians strolled on, in scarlet headbands, emerald jackets and patterned sarongs, and sat on the floor by their instruments. A man dressed in white quickly followed, in his hands a bowl of water. He sprinkled a few drops on each player and over the gamelan.

Matthew wasn't about to be bought off so cheaply. 'When are they going to start? This is really boring.'

As if taking their cue from his griping, the electric lights went out. Gentle illumination embraced the courtyard. Candles and the glow of the moon.

I turned in my seat and gave Matthew a glare, intending to shut him up. He was blond, sulky, maybe fourteen years old. He met my glare with a smirk. He might as well have just come out and said it. Stupid old git.

In my mind's eye, his moon-shaped head transformed into a gamelan gong and I held a nice big hammer in my hand.

'It really won't be that long, Matthew,' the mother cajoled, with an indulgent ruffle of his hair.

Matthew squirmed with embarrassment at this show of maternal solicitude. I gave him my sweetest smile. Aw there, mommy kiss it better. I turned my eyes to the stage and savoured my triumph.

The music sprang into life: the jangle of Balinese gamelan. As the gongs clashed and the hammers banged on the keys, the Barong appeared in the doorway, jagged teeth and bulging eyes.

The tourists shot up in unison and a hundred cameras flashed. Click click click click click.

It isn't easy to describe the Barong and do him justice. Dragon, lion, shaggy-dog. But as he stood motionless in the

86

doorway and stared out at the audience, he was quite spectacular. His feet began to jig and the mane around his head joined in the dance, as candlelight rustled the gold and made it shimmer.

Still the itchy fingers pressed their flash buttons, until the stage resembled a disco in the grip of a strobe. Click click click click click.

'Are you enjoying it, sir?' the man sitting next to me asked. He had a handsome face, typically Balinese, with even features and large brown eyes. I noted his presence suspiciously. Why had he spoken to me? Chosen the seat next to mine? He seemed the only Indonesian on the wooden seats at all. Why was he there, among all the *bules*?

'It's very good,' I said.

'This is the Barong, who protects the village from evil.'

'I know. I've seen it before.'

My less than subtle hint did nothing to deter him. 'Of course, this isn't a real *Calonarang*,' he explained. 'It's just a diversion for tourists. In the real *Calonarang*, the Barong does not appear first.'

I fixed my eyes straight ahead, to cut his presence out. Eventually the flashbulbs ceased and the Barong could hold the stage in all his glory. The mirrors along his back came to life like a swarm of fireflies, as each caught the light in turn and briefly spangled. He cracked out the beat of the gongs with his wooden jaws.

'Pah!' the man next to me spat, as an actor dressed as a monkey bounced on to the stage. 'This part has been added for the tourists, because they think it is funny!' He turned his face away from the stage with disgust.

I had to admit, in his black costume with big white spots, the monkey did look as if he'd stumbled in by accident from some Christmas panto. He sped through a slick routine: leaping around the stage, teasing the hapless Barong, peeling and gobbling down an enormous banana. Then he squatted next to a child on the front row and examined his hair for nits. It might have been fake, but the tourists were loving it. Click click click click click.

'It makes me ashamed,' the man fumed in my direction. 'The way we sell our souls to the tourists.'

'That's showbiz, I guess.'

'No, sir,' he hissed. 'You are talking about my culture.'

Oops. I figured I'd better cut down on the irony and keep my eyes on the stage.

The Barong and the monkey made their exits and moonlight bathed the bare ground. The gamelan subsided to a murmur, soft and brooding, like the sea before a storm. Then six young women in gorgeous sarongs fanned on to the stage and the gongs went wild again.

'This is black magic,' my neighbour whispered. 'A dance to bring evil to the village.'

I kept my eyes ahead and did my best to ignore him. I just wished he'd shut up. Why did he feel the need to explain everything to me? Why was he there at all, amongst all these tourists, on the chair next to mine?

'Watch their eyes and their hands. Can you see?' As the gongs clanged, the gaping eyes of the dancers shot from side to side, while their fingers weaved through the air, never still for a moment, edgy as butterflies flitting between flowers. 'Every position of their hands has a different meaning,' he went on. 'It is like a language to the Balinese people.'

I told myself to loosen up. This thumbprint stuff had really got me spooked. He was just the local bore, for Christ's sake. Or he was simply on the make and he'd ask me for money at the end.

'This is the holy man,' he explained, as an elderly figure limped on to the stage. 'He has been summoned to counter the evil of the women's dance.'

It had all gone quiet behind me, so I glanced around at Matthew. He was totally rapt in the story and seemed to have forgotten that his mission in life was to make his parents miserable.

To a burst of xylophones and gongs, the widow-witch appeared and challenged the holy man to a contest of magic. She lifted both hands and set a tree ablaze. The full moon glared down.

But the holy man's magic was stronger and, with a calm wave of a single hand, he restored the tree to full health.

'She has lost,' my neighbour murmured. The widow-witch skulked off, defeated. 'But she will transform herself and return. She will come back as Rangda.'

I looked in his direction to find him staring into my eyes.

'Supernatural evil.'

Rangda pounced through the gateway, her stiletto fingernails slicing the air. A tiny shake of her hand and the priest was sent sprawling. She was toying with him, this rag doll of blood and bones, a mere human being, who had dared to challenge her evil.

'It is up to the Barong now. Only he can protect the village.'

As his explanation echoed in my ears, the Barong returned. No jig of joy in the gateway this time, the Barong descended the steps to place himself opposite Rangda.

A group of young men rushed on, naked to the waist, with the sacred *kris* in their hands and only the magic of their black and white chequered sarongs to protect them. Rangda chuckled with relish at this human sacrifice. The gamelan crashed to a climax to announce the final battle between evil and good.

The pale moon glanced down, disinterested.

With the Barong at their side, the men fought without fear. They circled Rangda, dodging the slash of her fingernails, and the white cloth in her grip fell to the ground. The source of her power, without it she was helpless. Rangda raged in impotent fury.

It seemed evil had been defeated. But not destroyed. The white cloth exuded its malevolent force, even as it lay there on the ground. One by one, the dancers stepped over it and fell beneath its spell. One by one, each man turned his knife, his sacred *kris*, against his chest in an act of suicide.

'Do not worry. They are in a trance. The power of the gods will protect them.' He nodded to himself as he watched the stage. 'This is magic.'

I gave a little cough. Since my idea of magic was a guy in a cape sawing his lovely assistant in half, I always took this part of the performance with a pinch of salt.

'Can you see? The sword has entered his skin. But there is no blood.'

He stared at me until I acknowledged this fact. It was true. 'Yes, I can see,' I admitted. A tiny red dot marked where the sword had entered and yet not a single drop of blood flowed from the skin.

'Ah, but you do not believe in magic. I can see this.'

'No, I don't.'

He smiled indulgently at this sceptical westerner. It was only to be expected.

The man in white returned, sprinkling water on the dancers to remove them from their trance. The show was over. The audience clapped politely, but they'd lost their early enthusiasm. They had their snapshots for the folks back home and everyone felt greedy for fresh delights. Bodies stampeded out to Ubud's restaurants and bars. Soon Matthew's little fingers would be sticky with barbecue sauce.

Beneath a sky full of stars, the last surviving candles stuttered towards extinction. In the courtyard below, the xylophones lay abandoned. The Balinese man and I sat alone, amid the rows of empty chairs. I stood up to leave.

'Why are you always so angry?' he asked quietly.

'Angry?'

'Tourists come here to enjoy my culture. If I ask them, they say they admire my culture. And yet they never respect us, the people who make this culture.'

'I didn't mean to offend you. Forgive me.'

'This is my favourite moment of all.' He stared at the empty stage. 'When the *Calonarang* is over and the world is pure again. But the tourists never stay to feel this moment. They are too busy rushing off to their next experience.'

One more candle gasped its final breath and collapsed into the darkness. 'Don't you find this moment rather sad?' I asked.

'Yes, I suppose it is sad. It is frightening, too. But it is beautiful and mysterious.'

I sat back down and sniffed the cool night air. He turned to face me. 'I think you can feel it.'

'Yes, I can feel it.'

I might not have believed in the magic, but I could sense the mystery. A boundless sky, unimaginable stars, candles licking the darkness. The lost feeling that lingers on empty chairs.

'My name is Putu.' He held out his hand for me to shake.

'Graham.'

'Did you enjoy the Barong, Graham?'

'It's an amazing work of art.'

He allowed himself a wry smile. 'The *Calonarang* is much more than art. It houses the soul of my people.' He leant forward and placed his elbows on his knees. 'But we are selling our soul. Every day a little bit more to the tourists.'

'You have to eat.'

'Of course. We have to eat. But sometimes I think we are cannibals, eating each other alive. And one day there will be nothing to hand down to our children.'

'When I come here, I always feel Bali still has a strong culture. It's not like Jakarta, where everyone just wants to be western.'

'Do you live in Jakarta?'

I nodded.

'That must be why you are different from the other tourists. I could see it in your eyes when you were watching.'

'Different?'

'Less arrogant.'

'Are we really so arrogant?'

'Most of you. You think you respect us when you come here to share our culture. But the respect is never deep. We are always an exotic diversion to you.'

My mind flashed back to a visit to Kafe Batavia in downtown Jakarta, a famous relic from the colonial past. I was new to Indonesia and didn't know the ropes, so I took my driver inside and bought him a beer. The sneers on the other western faces, as if I'd brought my pet monkey along. And perhaps even worse, the sneers on the faces of the Indonesian staff, oozing envy and disgust at one of their own who had got above himself.

How guilty I felt for subjecting my driver to it all. The questions I asked myself later. Why had I done it? Just to parade my liberal conscience to the world?

The voice of my Balinese friend broke into my uncomfortable memories. 'I often speak to the westerners who come here. Forgive me, but I find you amusing.' The attendant began to gather up the wooden chairs. 'You watch a performance staged especially for tourists. Then you go back home and tell your friends about Balinese culture.'

I spotted a group of the gamelan players near the gateway, leaning against the palace walls. Laughing and smoking, still dressed in their emerald jackets and scarlet headbands. It felt almost sacrilegious.

'Last month I met a German man. He told me he liked the Barong because it was primitive. I said to him, "Don't you mean stupid?"' He laughed as he recalled the conversation, a surprisingly hearty laugh that shook his whole body. 'He reminded me of you, Graham.'

'Why did you choose me?' I asked. He gave me a puzzled look and opened a pack of clove cigarettes. 'There were a hundred *bules* here and yet you chose me. Have you been following me?'

'I didn't choose you, Graham.' He struck a match. 'May I speak frankly?' I nodded. 'I get the feeling you're troubled. Your soul isn't happy.'

'What are you – a priest now?'

I laughed, but I listened to the laughter as it struggled from my lips and the sound was hollow.

'You took your seat after I did, Graham.'

I struggled to remember if this was true. Blurred by all the gin, my mind had little recollection of my arrival.

'I didn't choose you. Perhaps you chose me.' His eyes were so steady that they frightened me. 'Or perhaps it was chosen for both of us. By Fate. But you don't believe in Fate, do you?'

'No, I don't.'

'You don't believe in Fate. You don't believe in magic.' He gave a strange little smile. 'Do you believe in anything, Graham?'

'Not really.'

'Perhaps that's why your soul is troubled.'

'Randomness. That's what I guess I believe in. Blind, stupid chance. Our brains make patterns all the time, because that's what we're programmed to do. Biologically. But there aren't any patterns. We just invent them.'

'So God plays dice with the universe?' A mischievous grin played on his lips. 'You're shocked when I quote Einstein?'

'Yes.' The whiff of his clove cigarette swirled around my head and made me giddy. 'Who are you?' I asked.

'A man from Bali who is able to quote Einstein.' He blew

a perfect ring of smoke through his rounded lips. 'And who can blow smoke rings.' He laughed out loud. 'That unsettles you, I think.'

'How come you can speak such perfect English?'

'There's nothing mysterious about that, Graham. I lived in Oxford for nine years.'

'Oxford?'

'Studying. Then lecturing. You see, there are patterns sometimes. The world can be logical.'

'You're a lecturer?'

'A professor of musicology, to be precise. But perhaps that confuses you even more. Indonesians should be lovable natives who make bracelets out of coconut shells.'

If his aim in saying this had been to embarrass me, he had succeeded. The lack of bitterness in his voice, the fact that he spoke it with sadness rather than anger only compounded my shame.

'You see? In a thousand little ways, you believe you are better than we are.'

'I'm sorry, I –'

'Don't apologize, Graham. Why shouldn't you believe it? In a thousand little ways, we still do.' The smoke from his cigarette spiralled up into the sticky night sky. 'They may have wiped the colours of the empires from the maps, but not from our minds.'

'What does a fingerprint in blood mean?' I suddenly spluttered.

A crash, as one of the wooden chairs went tumbling. I shot upright in my seat.

He sucked on his cigarette and studied me thoughtfully. 'In some cultures in Indonesia, it's a symbol of loyalty. It shows that we are ready to fight to the death for our cause. Why do you ask?'

'Nothing.' I caught the odour of burning clove. 'I'm sorry. I think I must still be a bit drunk.'

'The mysterious east. That's what you always say, isn't it?' He laughed. 'Perhaps you should say the mysterious west. You spend half your lives chasing logic and the other half getting drunk in order to escape it.'

All the chairs had been collected now, except for the pair we sat on. Putu pointed up to the stars. 'All those scientific straight lines, that marvellous logic, and yet it ends up in randomness.'

Another smoke ring faded into the cool night air. 'I hope you don't mind if I ask you something,' he said, as he tossed his cigarette to the ground. 'Are you Christian?'

'If I fill in a form, I say I'm Christian.'

'But it means nothing?'

'It's easier.'

'You only believe in what you can see, am I right? And you cannot see the invisible world.'

'Do you mean spirits and ghosts?'

'And many other things. You cannot see them, so they do not exist.'

'Oh, they exist, I guess. But only in our minds. Because we want them to exist.'

'This is very strange for us, the Balinese. For us, the invisible world is all around us. Every bit as real as this world we can touch and see.'

The last surviving candle suddenly flared up bright, as if it were scratching for heaven. I felt a cold wind at the back of my neck. One glorious leap and the candle flame died.

'This is the lesson of the *Calonarang*. Good and evil must always remain in balance. The west seeks to deny good and evil and replace them with logic. The concepts are out of date, they belong to the past.' He smiled. 'Like a Gregorian chant. But evil will not be banished so easily. It is inside us, every one of us. We must resist it, of course, but we can never destroy it.'

I thought again of my dream. Of how close I had felt to

evil. Not merely in its presence, but implicated in its existence. As if evil had plunged a hand in my heart and left something sweet behind.

'The *Calonarang* dance is more than just art to the Balinese people. It is a way of restoring the balance in the invisible world.' He gazed into my eyes. 'We must accept ourselves as we are. We must learn to embrace evil.'

'I think we ought to go,' I said. 'They want to collect our chairs.'

'Of course.' He stood up and held out his hand. 'Go back to your hotel, Graham. You are safe there.' He put his hand on my shoulder and guided me to the gateway. 'One day I will take you to a real *Calonarang*. In my village.'

I felt ashamed of ever considering he might ask me for money. 'I'd like that very much. Thank you.'

We stepped from the dim, hushed courtyard into a street full of colour and noise. How unreal it seemed, this world of tourists and traffic, of hawkers and restaurants and bars. It was a procession of masks, a carnival. Just pretend.

'Be careful, Graham. *Hati-hati*. We must be brave.'

Hati-hati. I felt far from brave. I felt pursued. I hurried along the frantic street, past the swell of strange faces, to the only spiritual sanctuary I knew. Not a church or a temple or mosque. And not some restful haven deep inside me. To Ketut's. Ketut's Bar, and oblivion.

9

Iran the gauntlet of dogs along Jalan Kajeng. Gateways to hotels and guest houses lined both sides of the lane, each guarded by a white beast baring its fangs. Their bark was worse than their bite – I hoped. This was my third stay in Jalan Kajeng and they hadn't bitten me yet.

It was past midnight, late by Ubud standards. With my usual persistence, I'd been the last person drinking in Ketut's Bar. In the end, the bravest waiter had come up to my table and told me they were closing.

'Is the waitress OK?'

'The waitress?'

'The girl who was serving here earlier.'

'She's gone home already.' The voice was curt. Perhaps he thought I wanted her for the night.

'Oh. OK.'

I don't know if the gin came from Holland, but it gave me loads of Dutch courage. 'Fuck them all,' I was thinking, as I stumbled along the lane. 'Fuck them all with their thumbprints and their invisible worlds.'

Jalan Kajeng was a kind of homespun Hollywood Boulevard. Visitors had inscribed messages in the paving stones over the years, some of them dating back as far as the seventies. I wondered what had become of these pioneers who had scratched their names in the concrete, if they'd ever returned to discover their mark had survived.

They'd be middle aged by now, these names, stuck in dull suburbia, the joy of their youth worn down by life's grind. And however happy their lives might have been since, I somehow doubted if they'd ever recaptured the carefree mood of these holiday messages.

Johan and Frieda, 1974. Such a long time ago. A lot of these names must also be etched on gravestones.

This sounds like a sombre thought, but I wasn't gloomy in the slightest. I was giggling at each hilarious name before staggering to the next. What a fine advert for Blighty! Here I was, in Ubud, centre of cross-cultural chic, and I belonged on the booze cruise to Calais.

The cheapest place in Jalan Kajeng, my guest house stood at the far end of the lane. That's the way of the world, I guess – the rich have less far to walk. By the end of the next millennium, perhaps, they'll have evolved vestigial legs. My own legs were pretty vestigial by now, after all that Dutch courage, so I rested against a wall beneath a spreading bougainvillea. The pack of dogs which tracked my wobbly progress began barking more loudly at this new threat to their territory. I was too drunk to care, and the night was too beautiful.

It had unsettled me, Putu's talk of good and evil, it gnawed at me inside. 'We must learn to embrace evil.' These words had lodged themselves in my brain, since they seemed so strange on Balinese lips. There was nothing mysterious about it, I tried to tell myself. He'd picked it up when he'd stayed in Oxford.

The moon bore down on me as I sprawled on the ground. A figure stepped out of the shadows of one of the gateways. A ghostly sheen picked out his cheekbones.

'Selamat malam.' I waved across, with a guilty little laugh.

He crossed his arms, strode his legs apart, and stared hard in my direction. It seemed wiser to get to my feet and carry on walking.

My hotel was designed in a style often found in Bali, with cottages laid out on terraces overlooking a central garden. Great spot to chill out, with one serious drawback – lots of treacherous steps on drunken nights. I edged my way down them with the exaggerated care of an inebriate who's proving he's sober.

Safely on my porch, I leant against the bamboo rail and stared up at the sky. Thick black velvet, clasped to the heavens by the brooch of a full moon. In the garden below, secrets seemed to be stirring. Frogs croaked, starlight rippled on the lotus pond and crickets scratched out their incessant whine. I felt tired, too tired to be drunk any more. I turned the key in the lock and switched on the light.

It was the third time I had seen a dead body.

The corpse had been laid out on the bed, face down. Neat, theatrical. Not a drop of blood.

At first I didn't even realize it was a corpse. I opened the door and turned on the light and someone was sleeping on my bed. I stared vaguely at the key in my hand to make sure I was in the right room, but the key was so old that the number had worn away.

I stood by the bed, breathing as softly as possible, frightened of waking him. If I woke him abruptly, he might panic and lash out. He might yell like crazy and wake the other guests.

Then I touched him. A shake of the shoulder to rouse him gently. He was cold and stiff. He must have been dead for some time.

I caught a movement in the corner of my eye. A cockroach froze to the spot and licked the air with its long antennae. It knew I was there.

I touched the body again, to make sure. I was expecting it this time, the shock of clammy skin, so it didn't send the same shudder down my spine. I laid my hand on his arm very lightly. I wanted to know the touch of a dead man. I wanted to know what it felt like, a body from which the human spirit had leaked. Nothing more than meat on a butcher's block.

I shuddered once again, but not because I was scared. It made my heart feel braver, taking hold of the corpse. I'd ceased to feel numb.

I turned the body over, face up, struggling as the inert flesh resisted. The bare bulb hanging from the ceiling cast a dim light, hardly enough to make out the face, crushed and twisted. Blue, purple, black: colours which lay unnaturally on a human skull. I guessed he'd been beaten to death; it seemed the only way he could have got so disfigured. Yet on top of the bed, on the fresh white sheet, not a single drop of blood.

Then I noticed the left hand. The thumb was missing.

A noise outside, and I froze. Some inexplicable sound from the jungle. A monkey perhaps, an insect, a bird. A moment later it had gone, swallowed by the cacophony of crickets.

I gazed around the hotel room. Naked, like every hotel room. A bed, a fan, a wardrobe, a chest of drawers. And they strip us naked, too, when we step inside them, these indifferent spaces. Until we have nothing left and nowhere to hide. They deprive us of the bric-à-brac with which we clutter our lives, stripping our meanings from us along with our names.

I stared again at the face on the bed. I had to struggle to breathe, as if the open mouth of the corpse were sucking all the fresh air from the room.

I suddenly gasped. It was Wawan, one of the two young men in the mall. For all the disfigurement, I felt sure it was him.

I edged a few steps away from the side of the bed. From there I stood and watched him, hoping he'd move, hoping he wasn't Wawan, hoping I'd wake up and find out it was all a dream. I wanted to turn him over and lie him back on his stomach, so that he looked as he had when I found him there, but I didn't dare touch him, not now I knew who he was and I could remember him alive.

I became aware of a strip of night where the curtains weren't quite shut and dashed over to close them tight. A long last look at the body, in the lunatic wish that I was wrong and he wasn't dead, then I walked over to the door and switched off the light. I edged the door open, just enough to squeeze my body through, and locked it fast behind me.

Outside the lifeless room, the world seemed shockingly alive. I sat on the porch and stared into the night.

This kind of thing only happens in movies. But in movies the hero is fearless and each new corpse makes him more determined than ever to root out the truth. I didn't give a damn about the truth. I was no hero – I just wanted this to end.

But I felt more alive than I'd felt in years. I'd thought I'd become deadened, that I was numbed to the point where irony was all I had left. As I stared into the jungle, my skin tingling, I found one emotion I was still able to summon. Fear. I could taste it at the back of my mouth. A bitter taste, with a metallic edge. Almonds maybe, or juniper.

I could leave. Disappear in the night. The maid would come to clean the room in the morning, find the dead body, and scream. But by then I'd be safely out of there, sipping wine on the plane to Jakarta.

These fantasies of escape comforted me for a few brief moments, but I knew in my heart that they were just pathetic dreams. The hotel had taken my passport number when I checked in; they had my signature, my name and address. It would prove my guilt for certain, if I slipped away into the night like that, and they'd come looking for me in Jakarta. They'd come looking for me in England.

I had to go to the police. It was my only option. I sat there, the questions they'd ask me flooding through my brain. What should I say when they asked if I knew him? I imagined the curl on the lips of the policemen as they listened to my answers. Their polite expressions. They wouldn't believe me whatever I said.

It's OK for heroes in movies and books: they can afford to be fearless. All they can bleed is words.

The greens of the jungle lay sprinkled in silver. The slim silhouettes of palm trees swayed against the midnight-blue sky. How precious they suddenly seemed – the cool night air, the trembling stars, the jungle and the moonlight. I wanted to stay on this porch for ever, wrapped like a baby in the cradle of this tropical night.

Hours passed. At least it felt like hours. I never reached a decision, I simply found myself walking up the steps to the hotel foyer: a battered desk beneath a sloping roof, open to the elements on three sides. It was deathly silent. I tapped on one of the doors where I knew the staff lived and called for assistance.

A dog barked in the distance. I tapped again.

A middle-aged man emerged from one of the doorways, hastily wrapping a sarong around his waist. He ran his hands through his hair and rubbed his eyes. Not even Balinese charm could disguise his irritation.

'What do you want?'

'There's a dead man in my room.' I sounded preposterous. I felt like the straight half of a comedy duo, waiting for the punchline: 'Don't talk too loud – they'll all want one.'

'*Ada orang yang meninggal di dalam kamar saya,*' I repeated. It didn't sound remotely as ridiculous in Indonesian. Not to me, in any case. And not to him, apparently. He blinked at me, showing no great surprise, nor even much interest. He shrugged his shoulders and held out his hands, baring his palms. What could he do about it?

102

I shook my head. Perhaps he hadn't understood my Indonesian. Perhaps it would be better just to show him.

'Come with me. Please.' I beckoned for him to follow. 'Please.' He gave me the kind of stare that suggested he was about to slam the door in my face, but thought better of it, grudgingly wiped his eyes and slipped on some sandals.

It should have been quite a *coup de théâtre*. The descent down the steps in the floodlight of a full moon, past the sleepy bamboo cottages, to the sounds of a tropical night. The twist of the key in the lock, the creak of the door, then the moment of high drama when I switched on the light and revealed the dead body.

He fluffed his lines. No shock, no horror. Not much reaction at all. He gazed absently at the corpse, as if I were showing him a light bulb that wasn't working or a toilet that didn't flush. After a cursory inspection to convince himself that the man was dead, he looked across at me.

'Does this man stay with you?'

'I've never seen him before.'

'This man is your friend for the night, yes?'

'I've just told you, I've never seen him before.'

'Bali people?'

'Javanese.' Then, realizing this hardly fitted with my claim that I didn't know him, I quickly added, 'I mean, he looks Javanese. *Dia kelihatan orang Jawa.*'

'Wait here,' he ordered. 'I will phone the police.' He sighed and glared in my direction. He'd get no more sleep that night and I was to blame.

I sat alone on my porch, sipping the cool night air. The taste of fear had left my mouth and something close to calm fell on my heart. This was like a dream. This was so much like some helter-skelter dream that it was hopeless to fight it. I had to follow the twists and turns of its surreal logic.

I pondered the manager's reaction to the dead body. How different it had been from a westerner's in the same situation. In our rational universe, corpses don't turn up in hotel rooms and if strange things happen we scratch around for reasons, for a box we can place them in. But this skin of western logic soon peels off. Indonesians seem ready to live in a world with fewer boxes and certainties, where the border between reality and dream becomes more hazy. The invisible whispers in their ears.

I was jolted from these ramblings by the sound of voices. I stood up and straightened my clothes. The manager reappeared, torch in hand, anxiously lighting a path down the twisting steps. Behind him, at a polite distance, two young Balinese police officers. Behind them, the shadow of a figure I was getting to know rather well.

'Good evening, Mr Young.'

It was the voice of Detective Suprianto.

10

Suprianto and I had reached an understanding. In theory, at least, though I'd yet to see the colour of his money. We zipped along the toll road from Soekarno-Hatta, beneath a sky that was threatening rain. I had no idea where he was taking me.

'It is my secret,' he whispered, with boyish glee.

The suggestion of a deal came from Suprianto. The Bali police didn't know me, he'd said, and they would assume I was guilty. I'd be handled like a criminal. It would be much easier for everyone concerned if I accompanied him back to Jakarta. In his custody, officially, but that would be just protocol. He could head the investigation from there himself. Go through the motions of interrogating me, while focusing all his attention on catching the real villain.

I didn't see how this was possible, I'd objected. Wherever they are, cops don't like outsiders muscling in on their patch. In any case, how could he head a murder enquiry hundreds of miles from the scene of the crime?

He listened to my objections, with that air of quiet indulgence he often showed me, before spreading his hands behind his head and easing into a smile. 'This is my country, Mr Young. Please trust me.'

We sat on the porch of my hotel room and negotiated.

The Bali police would be glad of the chance to wash their hands of the crime, he told me – the last thing anyone wanted on Paradise Island was a *bule* embroiled in a murder enquiry. This was Indonesia. Things could be arranged.

And sure enough, things were arranged. Half an hour in a sweaty hut on the outskirts of Ubud, and I was whisked off to Denpasar, the regional capital, to be presented before a pompous official. He sat at his shiny desk in his khaki uniform and posed a long list of questions with agonizing seriousness. I needed to realize I was in the presence of an important man.

Suprianto answered with exquisite politeness on my behalf, but it was obvious that he was even more important. All the same, the status of the official had to be acknowledged, so there was a procedure to respect. It seemed that tedium was the proper way to achieve this, by dragging out the interview for as long as possible and asking all kinds of irrelevant questions about long-lost relatives and how often I went to church.

At least sitting still in the dim little room helped to calm me down. And gave me time to sober up. By the time the Balinese dawn crept through the dust-caked window, I wasn't scared any more. I wasn't even nervous. I was bored.

My passport was demanded. I glanced up at the clock on the wall. 7:34. The official turned the pages one by one, tongue resting dubiously on the edge of his teeth, as he inspected each stamp with bureaucratic fussiness. I felt sure he had no idea what he was supposed to be looking for. He got to the back page at last and checked the personal details listed there. A squint at the photograph, a perusal of my face, then he handed the passport to Suprianto. It was slipped inside the detective's jacket pocket.

Collecting the documents on his desk into an orderly pile, the official finally declared himself ready to put us all out of our misery. I was taken away to be fingerprinted. Less than one hour later, Suprianto and I were stepping aboard a plane at Ngurah Rai airport.

Jakarta and the toll road seemed even uglier after the rice fields of Ubud. I sat in Suprianto's car and waited for him to deliver his part of the deal. In short, he would tell me everything he knew once we got to the capital. I'd never believed this, probably, even in Bali. But there hadn't seemed much choice other than to trust him and at least I felt pretty sure I wouldn't wake up in a cell with bruises tomorrow. He was much too wily for that.

He lit the latest in a long line of Marlboros. Why did he have to do everything so painfully slowly? Except drive. A typical Indonesian, he seemed to believe he became invulnerable when he took to the wheel. Trucks the size of oil tankers roared either side of us and still his foot stayed jammed on the gas. I tried closing my eyes. It didn't help. I preferred to see what we hit.

A little-boy grin spread over his face as he teased me about our mystery destination. I was stupid enough to play the game at first, asking him where we were going, to be greeted with a wall of silence. I fell for it twice. Then I learnt my lesson and shut up. Asking him a third time would only serve to underline my powerlessness.

We drove past Taman Mini and exited the toll road at Ragunan. A few minutes later, the black BMW floated into the car park at Jakarta Zoo.

The detective beamed with pride, like a magician who'd pulled a rabbit from his hat. 'You have never been to Ragunan Zoo before?' Mock surprise.

'Never.'

'Then *Pak* Suprianto must be a tourist guide today.'

I unfastened my seatbelt. Suprianto hadn't worn his. A horde of grubby children surrounded the car, jostling for pole position. I opened the door and they thrust their wares in my face.

'Peanuts, mister?'

'Coca-Cola?'

'Banana, mister? Banana for monkey?'

Achingly skinny, most of them, but nothing much wrong with their vocal cords. They circled me and pushed up close, each fresh face bawling louder than the last. An astonishing range of goods was on offer in their tight little fists, from traditional wooden carvings to US baseball caps.

Very English of me, I know, but I always felt uncomfortable in this situation, even after living in the country for a year. Suprianto surveyed my predicament with quiet amusement. He stood back for a while and indulged the budding entrepreneurs, before barking out a command and shooing them away. The gang dispersed at once, without a murmur of protest.

'I wish kids in this country would go to school occasionally,' I griped to myself.

'If you give them money, Mr Young, I am sure they will.' I looked away, but could still feel his stare and its accusation.

A weekday afternoon, and the car park was virtually empty. The hawkers on the stalls outnumbered the visitors. I fixed my gaze on the ground as we made for the ticket office. Suprianto looked up at the sky. 'It will rain soon.' He held an imaginary umbrella high in the air.

Moments later, a bewildering array of real umbrellas burst open in the hands of the same gang of children. As far as I could see, it was a simple matter of which colour to choose. But apparently not – there was a science to buying an umbrella. The detective subjected each one to a thorough test until he found a plain black model that met his standards. He slipped it under his arm and strode ahead.

Long years of tropical rain had all but rotted away the wooden counter where Suprianto paid our entrance fee. The attendant grinned as he handed over the tickets, exposing large gaps which once held teeth. The tickets were nothing fancy – the kind you might get on a bus.

A rusty turnstile creaked, and Suprianto and I entered a world where all the clocks had stopped.

'Why have you brought me here?' I asked.

He chose not to answer and stared up at the sky. 'Heavy rain, I think. Perhaps a storm.'

'Look, we had an agreement,' I reminded him, as sharply as I felt able to. 'I'd like you to tell me what's going on.'

'This is not the west,' he stated, in a matter-of-fact way, as he spread open the umbrella. 'You must learn to be patient.' Having forced home its point, the voice defrosted. 'I want us to understand each other, Mr Young. The work of a detective is not only about facts.'

The first drops of rain fell and he shielded me with the umbrella as we tramped along. The air was hushed, the wind smelt clean and we were completely alone – two shadow puppets outlined against the screen of a darkening sky. It was hard to believe that Jakarta still bustled, brash and chaotic, a short walk away.

His face wrinkled into a frown. 'How do you say it in English? *Aduh!* Already I am like an old man who forgets it all.' Then a smile lit up his face with the unrestrained joy that a child might show on Christmas morning. 'All in good time. That's right, yes?'

'That's right, yes,' I echoed, in a flat voice. No wonder he'd remembered it – the sentiment was so Indonesian.

He gave a little nod, ridiculously proud of himself. 'Patience, Mr Young. All in good time.'

A heavy mood weighed down the earth and the damp air clung to my skin. The soil lay leaden beneath the thickening clouds. Dead as mud, just waiting. A wide road spread before us, a long line of trees on either side, with bare stretches of grass to the left and right. The trees strained upwards, like the hands of beggars, branches cupped tight to catch each drop of rain.

Suprianto seemed to soak in the doleful mood and

become reflective. 'I am not happy to live in Jakarta, Mr Young. It is my home for twenty years, but I do not enjoy it. It is never *tenang*.' He muttered to himself, '*Apa tenang?*'

'Calm,' I translated.

'Ach, my English is so bad today!' He shook his head. 'I come to the zoo because here I can think. When I have problem in my work and my mind is confused.' The umbrella brushed the top of my head. 'There are children from school sometimes. But I do not mind them. They come here to learn and do not disturb me.'

I stared ahead, through unremitting grey rain. The first animal enclosures had appeared on either side, desolate spaces behind high walls of wire mesh. Any creatures they housed were hidden from sight, sheltering from the storm.

'I had nothing when I was a child,' Suprianto murmured to himself. 'But I had hope.'

At last, in a field of bleached grass behind a mesh fence, I spotted an animal. A deer that looked so fragile it might have been made of glass. The rain streamed down and melted the trees. In the wild, this helpless creature would be food for everything else that lurked in the jungle.

'But I am lucky. I have my work. I have my family.' He reached into his inside pocket, took out his wallet and showed me a photograph. 'One boy, one girl.'

I took the picture from his hand. A proud young girl with long straight hair, head poised high, very much Suprianto's daughter. She wrapped a protective arm around a younger brother in a Del Piero T-shirt. Despite the boy's dutiful smile, the camera had captured something dark, an inexplicable sorrow, at the back of his brown eyes.

I thought briefly of my own children. A fat drop of rain plunged from one of the umbrella tips and landed on the snapshot with a plop. Suprianto took the picture from my hand and wiped it dry. 'I must stay here in Jakarta. It is God's will.'

The deer became aware of our presence and ceased nibbling grass. It looked up, startled. The nostrils took an anxious sniff of the air. Aesop's fable sprang to my mind: the tale about the one-eyed deer who kept his good eye on the land, only to meet his death at the hands of hunters who had sneaked up by boat.

'Life is dangerous in Indoncsia at the moment, Mr Young. My people want change so much. *Reformasi*.'

We stared into the enclosure. The myriad shades of green ran into each other, dissolved by the rain, soft as a watercolour.

'I watch you when you walk, Mr Young. You walk like a free man.'

I wiped the rain from the side of my face. 'Then how come I'm in police custody?'

'My people all want to be western, just like you. They think it is so easy. When I watch you, yes, I think this, too. It must be easy. I can see the freedom in your footsteps. I can hear your freedom in your voice.'

'I'm not sure what freedom is,' I said, with a stiff laugh. There was something snide about it that I didn't like.

He cast me a puzzled look and took a Marlboro from its pack. 'You do not think you are free?'

'Oh, I'm free enough, I guess. Freer than people here, anyway. I mean, no one's going to lock me up just for speaking my mind.' He struck a match and hunched over the flame, to protect it from the storm. 'But if you ask me, are we really free in the west? Then I'm not so sure. Sometimes I think it's all a conjuring trick.'

'I do not understand you, Mr Young.'

'Like a magician with a pack of cards,' I explained. 'It looks real, but it's just pretend. It's just a show.'

'You have so much in the west!' he sighed, dragging on his cigarette, staring sadly ahead.

'Perhaps there's no such thing as freedom,' I went on.

'Perhaps it's just an illusion that our minds create.' I regarded him closely. 'You're Javanese, Detective Suprianto. So I guess you believe in destiny?'

He glanced at me suspiciously, as if my question were some kind of trap.

'And that everything that happens is the will of God?'

'Of course I believe this.'

'How can you hope to be free, if that's how you think? That some God in the sky sets everything in motion, then sits back and watches as we struggle like flies in a web?' He gave me a hard stare. 'A God who creates us just to destroy us? I wouldn't want to believe in a God like that.'

'Perhaps you have too much in the west,' he said, in a bitter voice. 'Too much freedom, too much everything. So you think you do not need God, because you have so much.'

I peered through the teeming rain into the bleak enclosure. The colours seemed even more liquid, a blend of mournful greys and greens.

'You have so much,' he repeated. 'In the west. Rich people.'

'This isn't about money. I wasn't born rich. My parents were poor.'

'Poor, same with Indonesia?' he asked, resentfully.

I looked down at the ground. 'No.'

'My father and mother were farmers from the *kampung*, Mr Young. All their life they work so hard and all their life they are poor. My baby brother died because they could not buy medicine.' On the other side of the fence, the shape of the deer became blurred, a blob of brown, as if the rain were rubbing it out. 'I do not believe you can ever understand this.'

'No, I don't think I can,' I said. 'I don't know how some of the people I see here go on living.'

'When people are young, they have hope. It is God's gift

to them.' One by one, the raindrops on the umbrella grew fatter and more bulbous, until they could hang on the tips no longer and plunged to the ground. 'When I was a young man, I had dreams, Mr Young. Like every young man, I suppose. I dreamed of being a rich man. For me, only a rich man was free because his stomach was full.' A raindrop landed on his cheekbone and trickled down his face. 'But I was lucky. I won a scholarship to Gajah Mada University. Now I have a house and a car and my children are never hungry.'

He slipped his fingers between the gaps in the wire netting. 'But I am not free.'

A peal of thunder sent a shiver along the skyline. 'He is not free,' he said, gesturing towards the deer in the enclosure. 'But he is safe. He has food and someone take care of him. Tomorrow, we will put him in the jungle and he is free, but he is not safe any more. Perhaps a tiger will come and eat him.'

The mood grew strangely intimate beneath the shelter of our umbrella, as we huddled close to each other in our cage of rain.

'I will be an old man soon,' he said. 'I must look into the eyes of my God and not feel ashamed.'

'You couldn't do that?'

'No, Mr Young. I couldn't.'

Another peal of thunder rumbled, a softer sound, stroking the earth. It seemed to shake the detective out of his melancholy.

'What do you think about my country, Mr Young?' he asked. 'My people. Are they ready for freedom?'

'Does it matter what I think?'

'To me it matters, Mr Young. I don't know why. Because you are a clever man.'

A drop of icy water trickled down the back of my neck. 'So you keep telling me.'

'My people think *reformasi* is easy. They see the west on television and dream they are free, same with you.'

The next peal of thunder was even more distant. The storm would pass us by.

'You talk as if that's a bad thing.'

He shook his head. 'They are like children, my people. They do not understand. *Reformasi.* They write this on the flags. But it is never easy, *reformasi.* It is never easy to change. For a person, or a country.' He tugged at my arm. 'Please, Mr Young. I want to show you something.'

'Where are we going?'

He hurried me along the deserted road, oblivious to the rain. I scurried behind, struggling to keep dry beneath the umbrella. We reached a crossroads where a banyan tree spread its huge green branches above a circle of white stone seats. Moments later, we stood face to face with a row of big cats.

The zoo had been shabby until now, but humane enough, as far as zoos go. There was a neglected look about the creatures in their tatty enclosures, but at least they had plenty of space to roam freely. The cages that confined the big cats, though, would not have looked out of place in an old-fashioned circus. The glorious creatures paced back and forth. Madness was stalking them.

A tiger paced and snarled in the cage before us. 'Often I come here and watch him. I look into his eyes and we understand each other. *Kasihan.*'

I echoed his expression of pity for the beast. '*Kasihan.*'

'When I stand here, Mr Young, sometimes I think I go a little crazy. I get strange pictures in my head. In my hand I have a key and I set the animals free. But then I am frightened. The animals will go crazy, so long they are locked in their cage.'

I ran my eyes along the line of big cats. Leopards, panthers, a single king of the jungle. Each of them stalked by the same unrelenting madness, each of them doomed to their prisons of obsession. The horizon swallowed a peal of thunder until it was barely more than a sigh.

'You think you can turn your face from God, Mr Young. Western people. You think you can escape Him, there is somewhere to run. But perhaps He will not let you.' He let out a peal of laughter, cracked, like off-key bells. 'We are all in a cage. Yes, even you. Often it is beautiful. But we grow lazy and selfish there. We forget our God because we want to stay there so much. We feel safe in our cage, as if nothing will ever change. But I must look my God in the eye soon, and I cannot.'

I struggled for something to say. But before I could speak, he had blinked and shaken his head, as if rousing himself from a dream. He struck a match and lit another cigarette.

The rain had softened to a mist, wrapping itself around us like a silken shawl.

'Forgive me, I talk too much. Let's leave here now.' He turned and bowed his head towards the tiger, as if he were visiting an old human friend and it was time to say his goodbyes.

He put his hand on my shoulder and guided me away. I glanced up at the sky – a hot white sun already sliced through the layers of cloud. We turned a corner to face the banyan tree. A figure stood motionless in the shadows beneath its branches: a young man, short and squat, with heavy features. I was looking at Wawan.

11

The sky was a blank sheet of paper, and if I raised my hand I could tear the whole thing down. I had exited my body and stared at a landscape scratched in black lines on canvas, a world from which the life and the colour had been sucked.

'Mr Young? Are you all right?'

An answer left my mouth, but I listened to the words, the voice of a stranger. I was outside my flesh, watching this person speak.

'I will take you to the café. You are cold and wet.'

My legs and feet followed, on strings. I couldn't feel the ground.

He placed a hand of encouragement on my shoulder. 'The café is not far.'

I stared into the darkness beneath the banyan tree. I was back in my dream. Back in the presence of something evil which was hunting me. It spread open like a poisoned rose until its perfume tainted everything. It stank in the sky, in the sunlight, the clouds, the leaves on the trees. The breath of God.

'Forgive me, I talk so much. It is never easy, the life of a detective. He must keep many problems in his heart.'

A little better now, just a little. I could feel myself slipping back inside my skin. Whatever it is, this thing that I call myself. I looked behind me. The banyan towered alone, supreme. No one stood in the tangled knot of its shadows.

Suprianto marched back from the counter, two cups of hot coffee steaming in his hands.

'Please, Mr Young, you must drink. I think you are sick.' He took hold of my hand and wrapped my fingers around the plastic cup. I felt nothing at all. 'Your face is white.' He touched my hand once more. 'You are cold, like ice.'

'The man in my hotel room. Was he dead?'

He piled sugar into his cup and showed no reaction. 'Of course he was dead. You saw him, Mr Young. His face was ugly.'

'Yes.' I swallowed a mouthful of coffee, so hot that it singed both my lips. I was relieved to feel the pain, it had a strange tenderness. I was back inside my body.

'Who was he?'

His eyes glazed over. 'I don't know, Mr Young.' He lit a cigarette and sighed.

Another sachet of sugar was shovelled into his cup. 'You don't want sugar, Mr Young?' I shook my head. 'You're right, it isn't healthy. But I have – how do you say? – a sweet tooth, yes?' He glowed with satisfaction at recalling the idiom.

I rose from the plastic chair and perched on a wall overlooking the lake. The storm had blown over quickly and sunshine sliced open the grey sheets of cloud. I wrapped my hands, drained of blood, around the hot plastic cup, enjoying the burn on my skin. A few deep breaths, and I tried to make some sense of what had just happened to me. An anxiety attack, I told myself. I'd read about them somewhere. It was a label, anyway, and labels are comforting.

Suprianto came and sat beside me on the concrete ledge. He tore up some bread and threw it to the geese below.

'There is a problem, Mr Young. I can see this.'

'Is the young man dead?'

'Why do you ask me this again?'

'I don't know. No reason.'

The geese honked viciously as they squabbled over the scraps. He leant his hands on the ledge and edged closer towards me. 'Mr Young, I do not like your eyes. They look very frightened.'

I sucked in a mouthful of air. 'I saw him.'

'Whom did you see?'

'The dead boy. I saw him standing under the big tree.'

'You saw a ghost, Mr Young.' I had feared ridicule, but I received a kind of sympathy instead.

'I don't believe in ghosts.'

He gazed out at the water. He reminded me of a sailor as he sat there, the lake reflected in his eyes. 'There are ghosts everywhere.'

'I don't believe in ghosts,' I repeated.

'Oh, they are out there, Mr Young. You can't feel them in the branches? In my country, there are many ghosts.'

'You asked me once if I believed in evil.'

He looked at me with interest. 'I remember this conversation, yes.'

'And you, Detective Suprianto? Do you believe in it?'

'Of course.'

'Do you believe it can enter our soul?'

'If we are not careful. If we forget our God.'

'And if we don't believe in God, what then? If we don't believe in an invisible world?'

He looked at me with pity. 'Then we are lost.'

A feeling close to hatred swept over me. For Suprianto, his culture, his country. For the barren hole in which we sat, this cavern of plastic and concrete. We both fell silent. I struggled with the notion that I was having some kind of breakdown. Another label, another box.

He finally spoke. 'Yes, then we are lost.'

It should have been an enchanted setting, like a sketch

from a book of fairy tales, this beautiful spot by the lake. Silver water, cascading trees. Why had no one tried to make the café more attractive, not even a simple gesture like some flowers on each table?

I felt a need to talk. I longed to put the panic attack behind me. 'Have you always been a policeman?' I found myself asking.

'I was a soldier first. There is no respect in Indonesia for work of the police.' He tore up more bread and tossed it to the snapping beaks. 'But it was always my dream to be a policeman. A cop. Because of the novels I used to read, with the clever detective who solves the crime.'

'You must see a lot of evil in your work.'

'I meet with many bad people, this is true.'

'And does it enter your soul in the end? The evil? Does it seep in like poison?'

'I have my God, Mr Young.' Something strong and stiff came into his voice, an impenetrable shield.

My eyes fell shut, I was exhausted. For the first time since I'd arrived, I felt tired with Indonesia. I wanted to leave.

'But not many people are evil,' he went on. 'Inside their soul. Generally, there are reasons why people are not good.'

My body felt brittle, stretched out like dried leaves in the sun. A panic attack, I told myself again. Quite normal, quite explicable, given all the things that had happened to me. I wished I could find the courage to talk about it, so I could hear my voice describe it. Get it outside my body, into reality.

But I felt too ashamed to talk about it. These moments of madness were always locked away. They were things you never admitted.

'To be evil, you must be strong,' Suprianto continued. 'Not many people can be so strong.' He moved closer and whispered in my ear. 'But sometimes, Mr Young, I see something different. I see a darkness I cannot understand.'

119

'When is this going to end?' I cried out. He squeezed my shoulder gently. 'Why did you follow me to Bali? Why did Wawan follow me?' The beaks of the geese cracked like dry wood as they gobbled up the bread. 'Am I still in danger?'

'The man who attacked you is with my men now.'

'Who is he?'

He stirred his spoon around his cup in his laboured manner. In the same painstaking fashion, he slid another Marlboro from the pack.

'Why did he attack me?'

'He is girl's father.' I stared at him vaguely. 'There was a girl, Mr Young. Fourteen years old. Doctor White –' His voice broke off as he struggled to contain his emotion.

'So why did he attack me?' I glanced around the café. Now that the storm had blown over, figures were emerging from the shadows, like stick insects. I was the only *bule*. 'Does he think I'm Doctor White?'

'It is possible.'

'Then tell him I'm not.'

'That will not be easy, Mr Young. Indonesian people do not believe the police.' He placed his hand on my shoulder. 'But please, do not worry. He is with us' – he struggled for the phrase – 'in our custody.'

Steam hissed from the leaves as the sun scorched them dry. I put my head in my hands. I was scared. It wasn't the dead bodies that scared me. It wasn't the blood. I could cope with those. It was the thoughts inside me that were spinning out of control. It was a terror that I could never bring up to the light.

'Hello.' The young voice of an Asian woman rang out in singsong chimes. I lifted my eyes to face a female in a tight red top and a flimsy black skirt. The powder caking her skin made me think of a death mask.

'German, mister?'

'English.'

120

'Oh, English! London!'

'No.'

This stopped her in her tracks, since London seemed to be the only place she knew in England. Her face froze in a jarring smile, a primitive clash of colours – mascara, powder, lipstick. Her sickly perfume seeped into my skull.

She brushed the top of the wall with her hand and sat down beside me. 'On holiday, yes?'

I edged closer to the detective. 'Working.'

'Oh, working here. Working in Jakarta.'

'That's right.'

'Why you not working today?'

'Holiday.'

'Ah, free today, yes? Want some fun, perhaps.'

I looked at her more closely, to see a face that was surprisingly beautiful. Or would have been beautiful, had a natural beauty not been smothered beneath so many fake layers of paint.

'Relaxing by the lake,' she babbled.

'Yes. By the lake. With my friend here.'

She glanced at Suprianto and flashed a brief smile of acknowledgement, but her annoyance at his presence was obvious. The policeman responded with the grimmest of nods.

'Very beautiful here, yes?' She ran her hands down her body, stretching her shiny top tighter to push out the curves.

'Yes, isn't it?' I was pretty sure she could sense my hostility towards her. What I didn't know was whether she sensed my fear. The thought of making love to her made me shudder. It would be like kissing a corpse on the lips.

I avoided her eyes. For a moment, she sat there, motionless, a defeated slump to her body, and I thought maybe she'd leave. It suddenly seemed such a burden, this mask she clamped on herself. The veneer cracked and a very different woman, an ordinary woman, poor and tired and desperate, gleamed like a skeleton through the manufactured sexiness.

The mask was yanked back into place and she buoyed herself up for another assault. 'You have ring,' she cooed, pointing to my wedding finger and taking my hand in hers. '*Perak*, yes? Silver?'

'Yes.'

'You buy in England?'

'Thailand.'

'Oh, Thailand! Very expensive, I think. How much?'

'What's it to you?' I snapped.

For God's sake, what was wrong with me? Propositions like this went with the territory for middle-aged *bules* in Jakarta, especially in the sort of bars where I hung out. I could handle this kind of situation in my sleep. I knew how to decline gracefully, with a joke and a smile, so that no one need ever lose face.

'I think maybe your wife buy you this.'

'No.'

'But you have wife in England, yes?'

'No, she's here. She's with me, in Jakarta.'

I flashed a silent appeal for help in Suprianto's direction and got just a grin in return. She spotted the grin and guessed it meant I was lying. She may not have been subtle, but she wasn't stupid.

'I don't believe you,' she said, tightening her grip on my fingers and staring into my eyes. 'I think your wife in England. I think you very lonely here.' I looked at her and pondered the contrast. Such delicate features, such a gross mask.

But why shouldn't she wear a mask to protect herself? Everybody else did in Jakarta. The rich encased themselves in a porcelain calm, like those masks at the Venice carnival, smooth and elegant. Beneath such a blank exterior, they could bury their anxieties and fears. The poor disguised their hatred behind a permanent smile. Frankness seemed impossible in this city, faintly ridiculous. I snatched my hand away.

'Where you work in Jakarta?' My silence was met by a toss of the head and a knowing laugh. 'Ah, but it is secret.' She giggled. 'I know this.'

'Look, I'm not interested in you, OK?'

Her pride was stung, perhaps, or she simply grew more desperate. 'I will give you my number, *tuan*,' she said, glancing over at Suprianto. 'You are with your friend now. I understand.' She clicked open the shiny black bag that dangled from her shoulder and searched for pen and paper. 'You can call me later, perhaps.'

A bridge too far for Suprianto, who seemed to have extracted all the amusement he could from the moment and finally decided to call a halt to the game. He rose to his feet in a formal manner, straightened up his body and addressed her with a few clipped words. She tossed him the kind of careless glance you might give a fly as you brushed it aside, before tearing a page from her notebook and beginning to write.

Bad career move. For all his politeness and his Javanese humility, Suprianto was much too proud to allow such an insult to stand. The police ID shot from his pocket and was flashed in her face. He proceeded to chide her, with patience and reason, as if she were a wayward child in need of correction. It was a savage humiliation, all the more cutting for a gentle delivery which bore the self-righteousness of a priest.

She fixed her eyes on the ground and placed her palms together in a gesture of supplication. '*Ma'afkan saya, Pak. Ma'afkan saya.*' All the brash confidence had evaporated. Even her pert little breasts seemed to droop.

Suprianto surveyed her show of contrition. It was utterly

insincere, of course, this fulsome remorse, and all three of us knew it. What she longed to do, in her heart of hearts, was spit in his interfering face.

'Only joking, *tuan*,' she said to me, with a nervous smile, as she edged away, her head bowed low. She held up both palms. 'Sorry, yes?'

And suddenly all my bad feelings towards her were gone. She had ceased to be a death mask, some omen from an invisible world, and had become just a desperate woman with a family to feed. I scanned the smudges of her make-up, clumsy and sad. If they brought anything to my mind now, it was the markings of a clown.

She continued to retreat, step by step, keeping her face towards us. Then she stopped and pulled her body up straight. In an instant the contrition had vanished. She felt safe now, so she swept her fingers through her long black hair, thrust out her breasts and swaggered into the distance with lascivious swings of the hips. Exit stage left, flamboyantly. This poor woman had her pride, too. She needed to salvage a scrap of self-respect from an encounter that had humiliated her, even if her revenge could only be a tiny one.

Suprianto laughed. 'She likes you, Mr Young.' I think he sensed my disapproval of his laughter, for he rapidly changed tune. 'So many same with her now, after *krismon*,' he sighed. 'You know *krismon*? When the markets crash in Asia?'

'Last year. Just after I arrived.'

'It was different in my country before then, Mr Young. Now even rice is expensive and my people need money so much.' He shook his head. 'But here, in zoo! She should not. It is not right. Many children come here. And perhaps she is a mother herself. What do her children learn?'

'She has to eat.'

'Yes. It is not always so easy to be good.'

Dragonflies skated on the silver surface of the lake. 'I often wonder why you don't hate us more,' I said. 'For the things we've done in the past. What we're still doing now.'

'Hate you, Mr Young?'

'We caused the crash in Asia, didn't we? The west. Our speculators.' The geese screeched out for more scraps of food. 'What kind of life do people like her have, selling herself to *bules* like me?'

He lit a cigarette and gave a triumphant smile. 'You are a romantic, Mr Young!' He patted me on the back.

I spotted him off his guard. 'When did the little girl die?'

'One month ago. Six weeks, maybe.'

I tried to match her with one of the newspaper cuttings on my desk. 'Did she suffer a lot?'

He flinched. 'I have a daughter, Mr Young. Sometimes I think, how if this happen to my daughter? To my little Dewi?'

As I looked at him, for the first time I felt some emotion about these killings. A report appears of a brutal murder and because it's nothing but words, markings of ink on an empty page, the story stays disembodied. As if real flesh never shed real blood and no one ever felt pain. But when I heard the quiver in the policeman's voice and saw the tears well up in his eyes I suddenly pictured an ordinary little girl lying bloodied and dead, with a mother and father who had loved her, who now grieved for her.

Suprianto puffed nervously on his cigarette before tossing the half-smoked stub into the lake. 'Do you have a family in England, Mr Young?'

'Yes, but I never see them.' I was ready for his look of surprise and embarrassment. 'I'm divorced and my wife has custody.'

'Oh.' He stared at the ground. 'Forgive me.'

'It's normal in the west. Maybe some of us weren't meant for family life.'

'I love my family, Mr Young. Without my family, I do not know what will happen to me. I know he is wrong, but I pity the man who try to kill you.'

'Yes. So do I.'

The sun seared the water, steam hissed from the leaves, and the air around us grew sticky. I took a paper serviette and mopped my brow. 'Why did you follow me to Bali?'

He said nothing. I turned my gaze from the lake and stared inwards, at a concrete tunnel of plastic tables and chairs. When George had asked me what I missed about the west, I hadn't been able to come up with anything. Maybe I could at last. I missed western-style restaurants.

'There's a place I used to go to,' I whispered. 'Near Boulogne, in France. My wife and I used to catch the ferry.' I shook my head. 'Just a restaurant. Nowhere special.'

'You miss the west, I think, Mr Young.'

'What is there to miss?'

'It is your home. Your culture. It is natural you miss it.'

'Who killed the man in my hotel room, Detective Suprianto? Do you know?'

His eyes met mine in quiet exasperation. 'Please, Mr Young, you ask too many questions.'

'You gave me a speech about freedom before. One of the basic freedoms is the right to know.'

'And you think I know? You think I know everything? It is better sometimes if we do not know.'

'Better, or more convenient?'

'It is safer. You do not need to know about this young man. He is dead now.'

'Oh yes, he's dead. Dead as a doornail, and they're tossing his body into the sea right now. You're not heading any investigation into his murder. He's forgotten. Just another statistic.'

'The military were interested in him,' Suprianto suddenly snapped. 'Important people. Maybe he is a communist.'

126

'Oh, come on, Detective Suprianto! I'll just about accept you believe in ghosts. But communists?'

He stared at me defiantly. 'They make revolution here, in days of *Pak* Sukarno.'

'That was thirty years ago. There aren't any communists any more. They're extinct, like the Java tiger.'

He blew out a mouthful of smoke with sulky resolve. The ridicule in my voice had stung him. 'Sometimes you think you are so clever, from the west. But this is my country and I know!' He drained his cup and rose to his feet. 'It is time we leave now.'

I had no chance to argue before the waitress had been summoned and the bill paid. He tore up a last scrap of bread and tossed it to the geese.

The pique had been conquered and the politeness returned. 'Forgive me, Mr Young, if I become emotional. It is difficult for me, this investigation. May I drive you home?'

'Am I free to go?'

'Of course. I promised this in Bali.' He reached inside his jacket pocket and took out my passport. 'This is yours, I think.'

'Don't you have to keep it?'

'It is yours.'

'But you told the police in Bali that you'd keep it. It was part of the deal.'

'That was just sweet words.'

'Suppose I disappear? Suppose I leave the country?'

'We must trust each other.' The passport was placed in my hand with excessive care. 'You are free now. Perhaps you take a plane to England and I will get in bad trouble for this. But it is my duty.' He took hold of my fingers and wrapped them around the passport. 'We must trust each other.'

I looked at the little book in the palm of my hand, before

slipping it inside my pocket. I got the feeling he was washing his hands of me. I was no longer his responsibility.

'Would you like me to drive you home?'

'No. Please.' I was much too sober to face those stark white walls. 'Could you take me to Blok M, perhaps? Pasaraya?'

The zoo seemed a different world now that the sun was shining. Friends strolled together in the shade of the trees, laughing and joking, and the road which had felt so gloomy was bathed in light, cool and refreshing and green. I saw the figure of a dark-skinned man crouched beneath one of the trees and it might have been any of a thousand young Indonesians.

I went a little crazy for a moment, I told myself. That was all it was. Just a panic attack, a normal reaction to stress. I hadn't seen Wawan. I hadn't seen a ghost. I wasn't losing my mind.

I sat in the soft leather seat of Suprianto's BMW and fingered the edge of my passport. I was free to go. I should have been overjoyed, perhaps, but instead I felt uneasy. It made me nervous, having my passport in my pocket again. It made me feel unprotected. The streets of Jakarta, teeming and grubby, slipped past the car window. Tomorrow, maybe, I would say goodbye for ever to these unlovable streets.

12

I held my passport in my hand. Not the stiff, black bible of the British Empire, but the European paperback version: a flimsy red booklet that had got battered and creased in the careless hands of immigration officials. I flicked through the pages. Just twelve months in Jakarta and already page after page of black stamps, granting me permission to enter, permission to leave, permission to stay, permission to work. Here we were in a global village, the world's leaders loved to boast, yet still I needed to scale this mountain of bureaucracy, to trek through this jungle of black stamps, just so I could live and work in another country.

I stared long and hard at the photograph. Only three years ago, yet how much younger I looked. No streaks of grey in the hair, while the shine of the studio lights had wiped out the wrinkles. Inside the back cover, the bare data of my existence: name, citizenship, date of birth, place of birth, who to contact in the event of an emergency. A number. At the bottom, the scrawl of my signature. If I were killed in a car crash and a stranger's hand reached into my pocket to find this red document, it would represent the sum total of my life, this list of facts in functional characters on an insignificant page. My life's blood reduced to statistics.

I sat in the swish café on the fourth floor of Pasaraya shopping mall in Blok M. Gamelan played softly in the background – Javanese gamelan, stately and solemn. The floor was stuffed with fabrics and handicrafts from every far-flung corner of the nation, a treasure chest for Jakarta's ex-pats seeking ethnic *objets d'art* to sprinkle around their luxury residences. It was all terribly authentic and third world, except for the first-world prices, so the only Indonesians you ever saw here were the sales staff looking awkward in their traditional costumes. How different from the other floors of the building, which were crammed with consumer goods and the latest western fashions, and so became a magnet for Jakarta's nouveau riche, with their handphones and Calvin Klein T-shirts. East met west, greedy for each other, and neither seemed aware of the irony.

I flicked again through the pages of my passport. Why had Suprianto given it back to me? Was he warning me to get out quick? Giving me a chance to slip away? Or was he setting me up? Was it all a ruse so I could be apprehended at the airport when I tried to leave? A corpse and a one-way ticket to England – Perry Mason would be hard pressed to squeeze victory from that one.

The coffee was as overpriced as the primitive art from Irian Jaya, but at least it was good. It came in a cafetière with a dainty plate of nibbles, which must be the ultimate in western chic if you're an ambitious Jakartan with the money to match your pretensions. They had little interest in the ethnic bric-à-brac, these wealthy Indonesians, but it was the height of fashion to be seen partaking of the coffee here and the élite who dangled their china in the air radiated opulence and privilege. A party of these urbanites sat and posed at every table, except for a lone group of *bules*, surveying the territory before them with the serene detachment of colonials in old photographs. I imagined them in safari hats and knee-length khaki shorts, griping about the natives and sipping Pimm's. God help me, but to the waitresses and the kitchen staff, I must have looked the same.

In the end, it all came down to a simple question – could I trust Suprianto? I felt probably yes, but how the hell could I know?

'Graham Young!' a high-pitched voice squealed across the café. It belonged to Lucy Palmerston, an ex-pat wife I often came across at functions and on committees, secretary of this charity, chairperson of that. She trotted over in a flurry of excitement.

'You have saved my life, Graham!' she gushed, as she flounced down at my table, 'This city is like Dante's Inferno!' She filled the empty chairs on either side of her with parcels and bags. Lucy had been doing what Lucy did best – shopping.

I had no time to reply before the whirlwind gusted again. 'You have no idea how thirsty I am!' she announced, with an impatient wave in the direction of the waitress. 'What a morning I've had! Frantic isn't the word. There aren't enough hours in the day.'

I gazed longingly at my passport before slipping it back in my pocket. Lucy Palmerston was the kind of person you'd emigrate to avoid.

She ordered coffee and biscuits with the glacial charm of the lady of the manor. Marcus and Lucy Palmerston were luminaries of the local ex-pat circle, big fish in Jakarta's murky pond. He was some kind of financial whizz-kid whose work was connected with the IMF. In his spare time, he acted as treasurer of my NGO. I found him pleasant enough, I suppose, but rather reserved, with that difficulty in forming relationships that often seems to come with a public-school background.

Lucy more than made up for her husband's reticence. She may have looked like the perfectly coiffured ex-pat wife, but she had drive and intelligence, serious drawbacks in a life that was meant to consist of leisurely trips to the hair salon and visits to your aromatherapist. I got the feeling that her life there was a constant fight against boredom and so she spent her days looking for dragons to slay. In between her busy schedule of shopping and hosting bashes, she seemed to find time to sit on every well-meaning committee in the city.

I could see that the waitress had taken an instant dislike to this haughty *bule*. She wrote down the order as sourly as she could, before loping away from our table with exaggerated lethargy.

Lucy dipped her fingers into a shiny black Pasaraya shopping bag and produced a wooden statuette of a water buffalo.

'Isn't it just divine?'

'Divine.'

'I have a chum in England who's going through an acrimonious divorce. The husband's behaving like an absolute pig.' She clicked her tongue. 'The usual story. A secretary whose breast measurement outnumbers her IQ.' She stood the statuette in the centre of the table and studied it from various angles. 'I thought this might cheer her up.'

'Indeed, it might.' Well, it cheered me up. I laughed aloud. She frowned and gave me a hard stare.

'Are you having it shipped all the way back to England?' I asked.

'Oh. You didn't know? I'm flying out there next Tuesday. I have one or two matters that need attending to.' She caught me looking across and explained in further detail, as if I'd expressed an interest. 'Investments and the like. Terribly boring, I'm afraid. But one simply can't trust these things to accountants. You know how it is.'

I felt pretty sure I didn't. The Palmerstons were out of my league financially.

I suddenly found myself promoted to the post of confidant. 'Between you and me,' she whispered, placing a hand on my arm, 'I need a break from this dreadful place.'

'Is it really so bad?'

'Oh, Graham, you're an absolute delight sometimes. But that's your job, I suppose. You insist on seeing the positive side to everything.'

I gave a weak smile. Nothing was farther from the truth. I was an old jade whose last glimpse of the positive side came when England won the World Cup.

The buffalo was carefully dispatched back into its bag. 'Does your maid live in?' she asked me, abruptly.

'No, she comes in every day and goes home.'

'Very wise decision,' she sighed, with a nod of the head. 'I only wish I could do the same. But I simply have too much on my plate, what with hosting clients for Marcus and the like.'

'I thought you were happy with this one,' I said, guessing she'd sacked yet another *pembantu*. Lucy went through maids like lesser mortals go through disposable napkins.

'Oh I was, at first. She seemed quite delightful. You can just never trust them, Graham.' She became aware that her coffee had yet to arrive and glared in the direction of the kitchen. 'I had to dismiss her, of course.'

'Of course.'

'I came home one evening and found her going through my bedside cabinet. And would you believe she had the gall to deny it? I'd watched her with my own eyes, Graham, as near as I'm sitting to you. The barefaced cheek! She looked me in the eye and she denied everything.'

The waitress sauntered across with a cafetière and a plate of wafer-thin biscuits. Lucy thanked her with charm and even greater condescension. 'You simply cannot trust them, Graham. I'm sorry, I know it's not acceptable to say such things these days, but it happens to be true.'

Struggling to suppress her intense dislike of this white mistress from the plantation, the waitress placed the sugar bowl down before her with a carefulness that bordered on irony.

'Thank you, my dear,' Lucy's voice clinked.

The eyes of the waitress glinted like two wet stones. 'You're welcome.'

'There's no need to tar them all with the same brush,' I argued.

'Oh, I quite agree,' Lucy said, with passion, as she plunged the handle on her cafetière. 'The Baileys – do you know them?' I shook my head. 'Delightful couple. He's from somewhere in Yorkshire. Harrogate, I believe. She's Singaporean. Anyway, their maid is simply wonderful. Salt of the earth. They've had her for years, apparently.' She sniffed the aroma from the cafetière. 'Mmm, this is the only place in the city which serves decent coffee!'

'At a decent price.'

She ignored my detour into the cost of high-grade Kenyan and returned to the vexed subject of domestic staff. 'If you happen to find a good one, of course, they're worth their weight in gold. I'm not denying that. I just seem to be cursed with the most dreadful bad luck.' She shook her head in genuine bafflement. 'I always have the most horrendous problems.'

I poured the last of my coffee and maintained a tactful silence.

'Brown sugar!' she purred, as she measured out half a teaspoon and stirred it into her cup. 'They know how to do things properly here. I do believe I'd go quite mad without this place.'

I watched her pecking at her biscuit like a bird. Before I came to Jakarta, I wouldn't have believed that ex-pats like Marcus and Lucy still existed, less than eighteen months short of the third millennium. But exist they certainly did, these elegant remnants. Living proof sat before me now, fragrant in the tropical heat.

She turned her attention to straightening the paper serviettes in their dispenser. 'I hear you won't be leaving after all.'

'Did you think I might be?'

'Well, one hears such a tremendous amount of gossip. But I'm so glad you've decided to stay,' she cooed, with the mellifluous insincerity of a company wife performing her duty. 'Your organization does such sterling work, Graham. At least some of the aid gets to where it's meant to go. And it's so important for the rest of us to have friends here right now. This city has become so frightening.'

I raised my eyebrows. It was hard to imagine Lucy P being frightened by a Java rhinoceros charging headlong towards her. 'I think the worst is probably over,' I suggested, in a consoling voice.

'Do you think so? The embassy issued another travel warning this week.'

'Oh, they're just covering their backs because they were such a waste of space during the May riots.'

'You may be right,' she conceded, in a distinctly cool tone of voice. I got the feeling she didn't appreciate my bad-mouthing the great and the good at the British Embassy. Many of them were probably her chums.

'Dear me, these biscuits are terribly moreish,' she tutted, as she nibbled guiltily on her third. 'I shall pay for this later on the scales.' She leant towards me and gently held my wrist with an intimacy that I found rather embarrassing. 'Strictly *entre nous*, I'd leave here myself given the chance.'

I drank my coffee and tried to look interested.

'Oh, if only Marcus would be transferred to somewhere civilized! Did I ever tell you, we turned down Vienna for this? Do you believe that?' She leant even closer and whispered in my ear. 'Now this is off the record, naturally, but I'm sure Marcus would pull some strings if you wanted a change of direction. I know how highly he regards you.'

135

I remembered the little red book nestling in my inside pocket and ran my fingertip along the edge, to check it was still there. 'You mean, give up my kind of work?'

'Well, it can't be terribly lucrative. Surely you've done your stint, Graham. You're hardly young any more. You have to consider your future.'

'I've made a rule of never considering my future,' I joked. 'That way I can still pretend I'm twenty-five.'

'Well, we all know what happened to Peter Pan,' she said as she peered into each shopping bag in turn. She located the one she wanted and a piece of dark blue silk was brought forth, with a golden motif in the shape of a lotus flower. 'I thought it would make a dress for my sister. She wears blue terribly well.'

I gave a tiny nod, anxious not to express too much enthusiasm for fear of the treat of being shown every purchase.

She unfolded the silk to inspect it more carefully. 'And now there are all these dreadful killings,' she fretted.

I assumed she was referring to Banyuwangi, a small town on the edge of East Java which had recently been the site of a spate of murders by mysterious groups of 'ninjas', masked men dressed in black.

'I heard there were some in Jakarta last week and it all got hushed up. But it may not be true, of course. Everyone is so jittery nowadays that the rumours simply fly.'

'The police say it's the work of communists.'

She gave a click of her tongue and flashed a look of disbelief in my direction. 'I read a piece in the *Jakarta Post*,' she said. 'They seem to think it's a power struggle within the military.'

'Could be, I guess. But if there's a rogue faction of ABRI who remain loyal to Soeharto, what do they hope to gain by killing Muslim leaders in Banyuwangi? It's a godforsaken hole in the middle of nowhere.'

'Oh, don't ask me,' she snapped. 'I've long since given up trying to understand them.'

'Banyuwangi has a reputation for black magic,' I ventured. 'Lots of the victims have been shamans. Maybe it's something to do with that.'

'You don't believe in that nonsense, do you?' There was an undeniable edginess to the fingers as they folded the navy blue silk back into a square.

'Maybe not. But most of the people here believe in it and that's the important thing.'

'Marcus is convinced they're contract killings,' she stated firmly, as she continued to fuss over her bags. 'He says he could arrange to have someone killed for half a million *rupiah*. That's less than fifty pounds – the life of a fellow human being! What kind of dreadful country is this?'

I smiled. 'It's a pretty weird place, that's for sure.'

The intimacy returned as she looked into my eyes. 'I don't feel safe any longer in this city, Graham.'

I couldn't help but feel a little sorry for her. A lifetime of being in control, and here she was, trapped in a country spiralling headlong out of control. In the twelve months that I'd known her, this was the very first hint of human frailty I'd seen in Lucy P. I felt a disconcerting urge to reach over and take her hand.

It lasted five seconds at most. 'The whole place is a shambles,' she rasped. 'The economy's in ruins, they're on the verge of a civil war and no one seems to have the slightest idea what to do about it.' Her face set in a grimace and any fleeting vulnerability had long since departed. 'Why can't these people organize their lives, for goodness sake?'

'Indonesia was colonized by the Dutch for hundreds of years. They don't have the political experience.'

'Oh really, Graham! That's the sort of woolly nonsense I'd expect from an undergraduate! It's fifty years since we gave them independence. They can't keep blaming the Dutch for their problems. They have to start taking responsibility for themselves.'

She summoned the waitress with an imperious sweep of her hand, as if she could direct all her frustration with this indisciplined country at this one hapless girl. The waitress leant against the counter and stared defiantly back. She wasn't about to be summoned, and ambled over in her own good time.

'I want to pay, my dear,' Lucy said, in her crispest voice. 'Two black coffees, with biscuits.' She brushed aside my protests with a flick of the hand. 'No, Graham, I insist. You've rescued my day. It's the least I can do.'

The waitress meandered back to the counter and leant gossiping to the cashier as he totted up the bill. Lucy could only wait, purse in talons, as the minutes ticked by. Her foot tapped the floor as her agitation grew. The waitress, enjoying her power and quite unperturbed, adroitly avoided Lucy's evil eye.

The bill arrived and Lucy snatched it from her grasp. The eyes of a hawk peered at the sheet of paper, scrutinizing every detail in the hope of finding an error. But everything was in order and Lucy could do nothing except dip her hand in her purse as graciously as she could bear.

'This is for you, my dear,' she said, with a frosty smile, placing a folded note in the young girl's palm with ostentatious largesse. But the waitress refused to be put in her place, even by generosity, and met Lucy's kindness with a winning smile.

One for the home team.

Lucy gathered her purchases. With these tools of her trade in her grip, she transformed in a trice to the perfect company wife. Any glimpses of frailty I'd been privileged to behold were safely secreted once more behind the cut-glass façade.

I was awarded a peck on the cheek. 'Graham, how can I ever thank you?' she gushed. 'You've given me the will to go on.' Two little fingers wiggled farewell through her panoply of shopping bags. 'Sorry, simply must dash!'

I had been dismissed and was left feeling both honoured and belittled, like some humble official granted a brief audience with the Queen.

I smoothed the bare white tablecloth. There was a feeling of emptiness at the table now, with its vase of tired orchids and its ashtray that no one had used. Like all those people who need to dominate every conversation, Lucy left a void in her wake. A pleasant void, to be sure, like the end of a nagging headache, but a void all the same. I felt at a loss about what to do next, as if I couldn't possibly make a decision for myself.

So I ordered another coffee. The waitress eyed me suspiciously, as if I had an ulterior motive, before trudging over to the counter to sort out my order.

I allowed myself a wry smile. Lucy P would never find herself in the mess I was in. No one would dare leave a corpse in *her* hotel room. Nor would she sit lamely around like me, chewing over each course of action and rejecting every one. She'd be out there, guns blazing, and heaven help any poor sod who got in her way.

But I wasn't Lucy P and I had no idea what to do. The passport lodged in my pocket felt like a stone. My ticket to freedom, but did I dare use it? I shredded one of the serviettes and let out an empty sigh. What was the point of going through the motions of deliberating, pretending to myself that I might reach a decision? I knew only too well what I'd do next. What I always did when the going got rough. Buy myself a bottle of gin, take it home and wake up beside it in the morning, bleary-eyed.

13

I couldn't bear the house any longer. Enti fussing over me, a flurry of fingers and smiles, determined to prove she was the perfect *pembantu*. I couldn't stand my gardener and his pathetic macho posturing, as he hung his hand from his trouser belt and performed his cock-of-the-walk strut for passing maids.

Most of all, I think, I couldn't bear the cavernous echoes and anonymous white walls. As if I were entombed.

Beyond the front gate, the complex seemed devoid of life. No birdsong, no stray dogs growling, no haughty cats stretched out in the sun. Squares of lawn lined either side of the street, as if someone had mapped out slabs of concrete and daubed them green.

I beat a path to the swimming pool, the only place in the complex where I found some relief. My head was thick from last night's gin; my stomach felt delicate. I hadn't been able to cope with breakfast.

I felt my passport in my trouser pocket as it pressed against my thigh with every step. I'd heard nothing from Suprianto since the previous day. I wasn't exactly anticipating a billet-doux. The more I thought about our chat amid the animal cages, the more certain I became that he'd washed his hands of me.

Wooden loungers lay unattended beneath the noonday sun. There hadn't been a sky this blue for weeks. The water mirrored its colour, no longer pale and rippled like frosted glass, but dyed a deeper shade. I pulled a lounger close to the edge of the pool and sat down. This stillness and this unearthly blue had me mesmerized. Psychics say we all have an aura of colour surrounding our body. Mine must be tinted this transient shade of blue.

'Hello, Graham.'

I looked up. The lean black silhouette of a human form was pinned against the sky.

'What are you doing here?' I asked.

'I came to visit you. Is it OK?'

'Do I have a choice in the matter?'

'I've brought some beers.' He took half a dozen small cans of Bintang from his backpack. 'They're still cold.'

'Isn't it a bit early in the day?'

'No problem. I've lived in Australia, Graham. If you want to drink at this hour, it doesn't shock me.'

Odd, but I wasn't in the least surprised to see Santo. He placed the cans on the nearest table, jerked up the red and white umbrella, and dragged the whole thing closer towards me until my body lay under its shade.

'You might get burnt.'

'Does security know you're here?'

'I slipped through the gate. There was no one around.'

'I could have you thrown out.'

He crouched down beside me and looked deep into my eyes. 'Why would you need to do that?' This was such a different Santo from the young man I'd met just a few days before. The swagger and the nonchalance had vanished. 'Well, Graham? Are you going to have me thrown out?'

I opened one of the beers. 'Why have you come here, Santo?'

'I need to talk to you.'

'Sounds like a line from a *sinetron*.'

'Then I will try not to be so melodramatic.' He took out a

pack of Lucky Strikes and offered me one. 'I'm sorry, I forgot. You don't, do you?'

'So what do you want to talk about?'

He struck a match. 'I want to ask you a favour.'

'And what might that be?' I noticed he inhaled very little of the smoke, but blew it moodily through pursed lips instead. It was hard to believe this was the jaunty young man who had streaked before my eyes a few days ago.

'It must be easy to relax here,' he remarked.

'I guess so.'

'Do you often swim in the pool?'

'No. I just sit here.'

'It's weird, isn't it? That pebble on the bottom there. There's just a few feet of water between us and the pebble. But it still looks distorted.'

'Are you making some kind of point?'

'The point I'm making, Graham, is that even when we think we can see something straight, that doesn't always mean we know the truth. Things aren't always what they seem.'

'I'm sorry about your friend, Santo.' I suppose I said this because I assumed Wawan's death lay behind his sombre mood. He hardly reacted. 'You know about your friend, don't you?'

'I know.' He dragged impassively on his cigarette. Santo appeared a young man of high principle, yet a coldness remained, something that kept him aloof from the rest of the world. For all his idealism, he seemed to find it easier to embrace the whole of humanity than to love one other person.

'How did you hear about it?' I asked.

'Bad news travels fast. That's what you say in the west, isn't it?' He walked over and threw his cigarette into the strip of bushes that lined the pool area, as if he were tossing away the memories at the same time.

'Oh, I didn't tell you yet,' he said. 'My tape – it was excellent.' He raised his right thumb in approval. '*Fat of the Land*. Do you remember?'

'I remember.' I had drained the first can of beer and picked up a second. 'Aren't you going to join me?'

'I'm Muslim, Graham. I'm not allowed alcohol.'

'That doesn't stop most of the Muslims I know.'

'That's their business. It stops me.'

The can spat open with a pop, like a toy gun. 'So, what is this favour you want?'

He avoided my eyes as he answered. 'I'd like you to come and meet the man who tried to kill you.'

'Oh sure.'

'So that you understand.'

'Do you think I'm crazy?'

'You don't need to speak to him, Graham. I want you to see him. That's all.'

'Why? So he can do a better job second time around?'

He was already lighting another cigarette. 'I know the whole idea sounds off the wall.'

'Too damn right it does.'

'But just hear me out.'

'Forget it, Santo.'

He tossed the dead match into the clump of bushes. 'Suprianto's done a fine job on you, hasn't he?'

'What's that supposed to mean?'

'It means, Graham, that things aren't always what they seem.'

I let out a sardonic burst of laughter and polished off the second can. 'You can say that again. This is one hell of a dream.'

'I know it must be difficult for you.' This was expressed with curiosity rather than concern, as if I were some zoological species he was studying in the field. 'A western guy, I mean.'

'Is Wawan really dead, Santo?'

The bemusement that flashed across his face seemed genuine enough. 'Of course he's dead. You saw him, didn't you?'

'This would be a great place for a ghost, don't you think? By the pool. It could haunt the trees over there and no one would ever disturb it.' I leant down and dragged my fingers through the water. 'Perhaps people would see it from time to time when they stared into the pool. Catch a glimpse of its face behind them, grinning.'

He squatted on the ground beside me. 'What are you afraid of, Graham? Do you think I'm part of some plot? To ambush you and kill you, perhaps?'

'The thought had crossed my mind.'

'Now who's being melodramatic?' He took out a third cigarette and lit it from the stub of his second. 'You're a rational guy. So ask yourself – why would I bother going to all that trouble?'

'I don't know.'

'If I really wanted you dead, there are a thousand easier ways.'

I glanced across at him and picked up another beer. Beads of condensation sparkled on the ice-cold can.

'You're an outsider. There are so many ways you could be disposed of.' This was stated in such a matter-of-fact voice that it didn't feel remotely like a threat. The opposite, in fact – it felt strangely reassuring.

'I don't owe you anything, Santo. Why should I help you?'

'Friendship, perhaps.'

'I wasn't aware we were friends.'

'I'm sorry you feel like that.'

'And if I did agree to meet this guy?' I noticed how his body stiffened when I said this. 'What do I get from it?'

'What do you want?'

'The truth. I want you to tell me the truth.'

'Of course.'

'So who is he? This man?' He sat rigid and made no reply. 'Is it true his little girl was murdered by Doctor White?'

'Did *Pak* Suprianto tell you that?' He dragged on his cigarette. 'What else did he tell you?' When I said nothing, he whispered, 'It's true.'

'So why did he attack me?'

'Why do you think?'

'I imagine he believed I was Doctor White.'

'It didn't take a lot of figuring, did it?'

'And why would he think that?'

'Because that's what *Pak* Suprianto told him.'

'I don't believe you, Santo.'

'It's up to you what you believe.' His self-control slipped for a second and a spark of impatience flared up at the back of his eyes. 'Fair enough. So I can't tell you for certain that *Pak* Suprianto lied. He's a smart guy. Perhaps he merely led Wawan to believe what he did. And Wawan was too stupid to realize he was being worked from below like a *wayang* puppet.'

'And how about you? Did you ever believe I was Doctor White?'

For the first time so far, he allowed himself a smile. A tiny curl of the lips, arrogant and friendly in equal measure. 'Of course not.'

'So why didn't you say anything to the man who attacked me? Or to Wawan?'

'You didn't know Wawan. He had the mind of a child, Graham. He was innocent.'

'He didn't look so innocent to me.'

'That just goes to show you didn't know him.' He flicked ash into the pool. 'Once something got fixed in Wawan's mind, he became pretty stubborn. It was impossible to change it.'

145

'You could have persuaded him. I saw how much he respected you.'

'Wawan was a nice guy, Graham. But he wasn't too smart.'

'I suspect you're smart enough for both of you.'

He stared at me without blinking. 'Yes, Graham. I suspect I am.'

This felt like a challenge and I picked up the glove. 'That's an interesting fairy tale, Santo. There's just one major flaw in it. The guy attacked me afterwards. Doctor White was dead by then.'

He blew out a puff of smoke and dangled the cigarette high in the air, between his fingers. Then the hand swooped down and stubbed it out on the ground. A moment of theatre, almost certainly for dramatic effect.

'Doctor White isn't dead.'

'I saw him, Santo. That's one corpse who's never going to walk.'

'You saw a dead body. A piece of meat that *Pak* Suprianto told you was Doctor White.' He launched the crumpled stub into the pool with a flick of his thumb. 'The body you saw in the morgue belonged to some sick creep who used to arrange the victims for the doctor. His pay-off was he got to have sex with them first.'

'I don't believe you, Santo,' I said for a second time. The words were the same, but the tone of my voice had grown shakier.

'Why not? Because *Pak* Suprianto is a policeman and policemen never tell lies? Get real, Graham. You're not in England any more. Suprianto isn't one of your bobbies on the beat.'

'And why should I believe you rather than him?'

'Fair enough. Why should you?'

I crunched an empty beer can in my fist. I got the uneasy feeling I was losing this conversation.

'Make your own decisions, Graham. But get the facts right first. Come and see this guy. What are you scared of?'

I stepped from under the shade of the parasol and knelt by the side of the pool. 'Why does this matter to you?'

'I want you on my side. People in your line of work support *reformasi*.'

'It's your country.' I shrugged, running my hand through the water. 'It's nothing to do with me.'

I heard the scrape of a match along the side of the box. 'I'm disappointed in you, Graham. I thought you'd be intrigued. Wouldn't you like to hold that stone in your hand and see what it looks like?'

'And did it ever occur to you I might just be scared?'

I fixed my gaze on the pool, but I sensed him move until he came and stood close behind me. I could feel his shadow hanging over me.

'You think you can always run away,' he said. 'Rich people. Just buy a ticket and go some place else. Like you did in May.' I lay in his shade and grew suddenly cold. 'But most people can't afford to run. They have to stay no matter how bad things get. And perhaps the day has come, Graham, when you can't run any more. Perhaps they'll follow you no matter how fast you run.'

'I'm no hero, Santo. I'm just some sad old fuck who's drinking himself to death.'

He cracked open another beer and handed it to me over my shoulder. 'I'm not asking you to be a hero. Wawan liked to play the hero. And look at him now.'

I smelt the nicotine that lingered around his body and coughed out loud. 'Why can't you leave me alone?'

'We can play it any way you like, Graham. We can use your car if you want.' I stared into the water. 'Or we'll walk to the main road and hail a taxi, if that feels safer. A Blue Bird.' This was the top company in the city, recommended by the embassy for safety reasons.

I turned my head and looked up into his eyes. 'Just answer me one question, Santo. Why the hell should I get involved?'

He strolled over to the bushes and plucked a bright red flower. 'I think you need to understand something, Graham. You're involved already.' A quiet sense of triumph glowed in his eyes. '*Pak* Suprianto's seen to that. You think you can stay neutral, but you can't. You're implicated.'

'In what?'

'Wawan's murder, for a start.'

'I had nothing to do with that and you know it.'

'That might not stop them pinning it on you.' He tore off the petals one by one and let them float like scarlet parachutes down to the water. 'Aren't you scared the same thing might happen to you that happened to Wawan? If they decide you've become too troublesome?'

'Who are they, these people you keep talking about? Why should they be interested in me?'

'I don't know, Graham. Your NGO made quite a splash in the papers a while ago. You uncovered a lot of dirt.'

'So?'

'This isn't the best of places to play Robin Hood. Perhaps you've made enemies.' He knelt at my feet and gazed up with an ironic smile. 'Yes, everyone seems fascinated by Graham Young.'

'Who are you talking about? The military?'

The sun burnt a hole through the sky like a cigarette through paper. 'So I'm fascinated, too. I ask myself why.'

One of the petals had drifted loose from the others and now rested at the side of the pool. I stretched down and cupped it in my hand. It lay like a tiny drop of blood in my palm.

'They've bled Indonesia dry for thirty years. Do you think they'll let go of their power without a struggle?' His voice grew in confidence as I felt my body shrivel, as if he were feeding on me. 'If you stand in their way, they won't give

148

you a second thought. They won't care you're a *bule*. So what are you going to do? Stay hidden here, scared to step outside your front door? Wondering when you're next?'

He offered me the final can. 'Perhaps you need friends right now. Perhaps we need each other.'

'How far is this place you want me to go?'

It's one of life's great mysteries, up there with Jack the Ripper. Drive along any Jakarta street, even some potholed back alley, and you're sure to spot two or three signs advertising *knalpot* – car exhausts. Yet there doesn't seem to be a single vehicle in the entire metropolis which doesn't have noxious black shit belching out of its rear.

Our taxi lay downwind of one of these environmental disasters, a bright orange minibus we could never squeeze past because the road was too narrow. The AC in the taxi was *rusak*, naturally. So I didn't have the best of options – I either melted in a malodorous pool on my seat, or opened the window and ravaged what was left of my lungs. I wound down the window and spluttered.

All the same, I was feeling strangely merry. My early morning nausea had disappeared and Santo's beers had topped up last night's gin quite nicely. I sighed to myself. The world was regaining that soft-focus edge I loved so much. We turned off the clutter of Ciputat Raya and emerged in a parallel universe, as we threaded our way through a maze of bumpy lanes, dodging suicidal cyclists and manic chickens.

'Where are we?'

'Welcome to the real Jakarta, Graham.'

'How much farther is this place we're going?'

'It's not long now.'

The *kampung* that we drove through was worlds apart from the glossy malls and gleaming skyscrapers of the Golden Triangle. At times it became semi-rural, this sprawling mass of dilapidated buildings, with its stray dogs and chickens and its wooden stalls where bananas hung for sale. But I'd seen far grimmer places in this city. The corrugated hovels opposite Pondok Indah Mal for a start, and the flooded shacks of tin which teetered above the swamplands on the way to the airport. These simple streets at least had greater dignity. The poverty felt less crushing here; it didn't seem to have seeped inside people's souls.

'OK, Santo. You've got me where you want me. What are you really after?'

'There's no need to be suspicious, Graham. I haven't lied to you. I want you to meet the man who attacked you.'

'What for?'

'It might help everyone.'

Fewer and fewer buildings slipped past the taxi window. Haphazardly spread out, separated from each other by strips of wasteland where bananas grew wild next to palm trees and papayas. I'd been to places like this, but in the backwaters of the nation, on the edge of the jungle – not a stone's throw from the skyline of the business district.

I was attracting attention as a white face in this part of the city where white faces never strayed. 'Where do you come from, *mas*?' I asked the taxi driver, an excuse to break the silence and to hear some English.

'Semarang, *tuan*. Jawa Tengah.'

Santo had fallen silent and stared with pensive eyes through the taxi window. The narrow road snaked past a school and a mosque, simple buildings which seemed almost grand in contrast with their modest surroundings. The driver took a left, down a lane that wasn't asphalted. A bumpy ride later, the taxi drove through a gateway and pulled to a halt on a flat stretch of grass. Through the open window, I heard the sound of a human voice. A creature howling.

'Where are we? What is this place?'

'A hospital.'

Birdsong assailed me as I opened the taxi door. Rarely heard in Jakarta, it seemed out of tune, slightly cracked. The human voice continued to howl. I double-checked that the driver would wait for me.

A woman emerged from the doorway to greet us. She wore the *jilbab*, the Muslim scarf that shrouds the hair and wraps a soft white circle of cloth around the face. Its simplicity brought out the fierce sense of purpose in her eyes.

We were introduced briefly, but she declined to shake my hand. I followed them both round the side of the building, into a kind of inner courtyard. As we clambered over the stones, pictures of newsreel from war zones shot through my mind. Some forlorn place like Beirut, where I'd seen plaster crumbling off the walls like this, in the same flaky way. The howling was fainter here, but still I could hear it.

We entered a building. From the outside, it looked abandoned. I followed them along a corridor, lined on both sides by a row of closed doors. At last the howling had stopped, or maybe the walls had blocked out the sound. The woman tapped very gently on one of the murky brown doors. She waited, but seemed to know that no one would open it.

Santo placed his hand on my shoulder. 'Don't worry. It's safe.' He turned the handle of the door and let it swing open.

The man who had attacked me sat, nearly naked, on the edge of a wooden bed, gaping into space.

'Go in, Graham. Please.'

I remained on the threshold, staring in. Santo walked over to the figure on the bed and moved his hand up and down in front of the face. Nothing stirred in the motionless eyes.

'Is he always like this?' I asked, as I edged two steps closer. 'Doesn't he move?'

'Sometimes. Sometimes he cries.'

It was dark and hot in this cramped little room and it

smelt as if nobody lived there. A dusty window which let in hardly any light, a wooden bed, a wardrobe, a concrete grey floor. Like some run-down hotel room long relinquished to cockroaches.

The woman in the *jilbab* stepped to one side, away from the bed, to make more space for me. Our eyes met and she glanced demurely to the ground.

'Do you think he can hear us?' I asked Santo.

'I don't know.'

'How long has he been like this?'

'Since he attacked you.'

I edged another step closer and waved my hand in front of his eyes. 'Is he under sedation?'

'Allah is merciful, Graham. When the pain of life is too great, He takes it away.'

But I didn't get the feeling that the pain had been taken away. It had been frozen, that was all, deep inside this man.

'Take hold of his hand, Graham. Please.'

I let out a tiny laugh and shook my head.

'Perhaps it will help. If he thinks you forgive him.'

Through the little window which let the only natural light into this room, I heard the sound of a mosque calling the faithful to prayer.

'What is this place?' I asked. 'What kind of hospital?'

'Somewhere people can hide when life is too much for them. When there's nowhere else they can run.'

'It's nothing to do with the police?'

He seemed genuinely puzzled by my question. 'Graham, it's an Islamic hospital. Staffed by people like this woman.'

'But Suprianto told me this man was in custody.'

'Perhaps the policeman lied.'

The call of the mosque grew more insistent. A procession of believers filed past the window, prayer mats in hand.

'Get closer to him, Graham.'

'I can't.'

'He won't hurt you.'

I wiped the sweat from the back of my neck. It was unbearably hot in this tiny, airless room.

'He can't see you or hear you. He's lost forever to this world. He's killed himself, Graham. In my religion, suicide is a terrible sin. To take the life which Allah has given you. So he's killed himself in the only way he can. By renouncing this world. The women here take care of his body. Allah must guard his soul.'

The call of the mosque suddenly stopped. Silence swallowed us up.

The man rose to his feet, walked over to the wardrobe and opened the door. From a little drawer on the right-hand side, he took out a chequered sarong and wrapped it around his waist. Then a prayer mat in green, with an abstract design that suggested Arabic lettering, was laid carefully out on the floor.

I went to speak, but Santo placed a finger to his lips to command my silence. In this bleak room, which God seemed to have forgotten, the three of us watched as this ghost of a man set out his humble prayer. He lifted both hands until they lay either side of his face, before lowering his arms and crossing them over his chest. He murmured a few words of Arabic, too faint to understand, even if I'd spoken the language.

The room seemed to grow darker around us, as if the sun had gone in.

'Why are you showing me this?' I whispered.

'I want you to understand.'

The man leant forward at the waist and laid a hand on each knee. The stranded eyes bore no glimmer of life as he knelt on the floor. I longed to get out of the room, away from the stifling heat and the crushing silence. But I was fascinated, also, by the eloquence of this curious mime. His forehead kissed the ground in submission to Allah.

'You see. Allah speaks to him. Even if we cannot.'

'What do you want me to understand?'

Once more he bid my silence.

His prayer concluded, the man folded his sarong and prayer mat back into two neat squares and returned them to the drawer. He closed the wardrobe door with great delicacy, careful not to offend the sacred objects within.

Then he looked at me. Into my eyes at first, until his gaze came to rest on the bandage around my arm. For a fleeting moment, I saw a memory flicker to life at the back of his eyes. Some fragment buried deep in his darkened mind. I glanced at Santo. He had spotted it, too, this fragile scrap of the past plucked from the blackness, this distant light.

A struggle unfolded in the wasted brown eyes. Whether to turn his gaze inside himself once more, to a private world that was lonely but safe. Or whether to break down the wall and reach out to a world that was painful and real.

Silence shrouded the room like an avalanche. The figure stepped closer to my body, in the grip of some profound internal power, as he battled to clutch this memory and lift it up to the sun. He raised both hands until they rested each side of my face.

'Let him touch you, Graham.'

I took a deep breath to stop myself shaking as his hands felt out the contours of my face, like the hands of a blind man. He traced the line of my lips with his fingers, before creeping up to the curves of my cheekbones. His hands were near my neck now and I found it difficult to breathe. I swallowed hard. His eyes stared deep into mine and I imagined I could see the memories there, blown like scraps of paper down a windy street.

Then the moment was gone, as mysteriously as it arrived. The eyes glazed over and saw nothing at all – the light had been snuffed out. The lonely figure settled back on the bed in the same pose as when I arrived.

'He's like a ghost,' I whispered.

The creature on the bed began to sob, very softly, with a simple pain. The tears became silent, marked only by the heaving of his shoulders. The woman in the *jilbab* looked concerned and stared across at Santo.

'We must go, Graham.'

He put his hand on my shoulder and led me from the room. As the door eased shut behind us, I heard the faint sobs once more, a hopeless grief that had worn itself out.

'Was he a friend of yours, Santo?'

'He came from my village. But no, we weren't friends.' We tunnelled our way through the dingy corridor, through one of the countless brown doors, to emerge into brilliant sunlight. A breeze splashed my skin. I sucked the cool air frantically into my lungs.

Santo lit a cigarette. 'Perhaps it's better this way.'

'What do you mean?'

'Perhaps it's better if he never comes back to our world.' He looked into my eyes. 'Wawan was his son.'

'He doesn't know?'

'Not yet. Do you mind if we walk for a while?'

I remembered my taxi and wondered if the driver was still waiting. 'If you like. But not for long.'

We stumbled past the tumbledown buildings, through wild grass and weeds, over bleached stones and bricks that jutted from the ground like bones in a desert. We reached a garden at the back of the building. A wild stretch of twisted greens that the jungle was fast reclaiming. It was hard to believe that a broken soul could be pieced back together in such a dismal place.

We sat down next to each other on a rotting wooden bench. I watched a column of ants vanish, one by one, into their nest. 'Why did you bring me here, Santo?'

'It's not only for this man. *Reformasi*. But for all the people we passed on the way here. Did you see them,

Graham? The poverty they have to endure every day of their lives?'

'I saw them.'

'I wish this man was unusual, but he isn't. There are thousands just the same as him. Broken. Discarded.' He tossed away his cigarette, barely smoked. 'Widows whose husbands have been murdered. Sisters who had to watch while their brothers were tortured. Brothers who had to watch while their sisters were raped. You can't begin to imagine.'

'I must go soon.'

'I think you're one of the good guys, Graham.' I avoided his stare by fixing my eyes on the ground. 'I think you're on our side.'

'I'm a passer-by, Santo. This isn't my fight.'

'Please, Graham. You can give us information.' He picked up a stick and poked it into the ants' nest. 'We don't have guns or bullets. That isn't the way of our struggle. We must fight them with information. With the truth.'

I kicked a small stone that lay at my feet. 'And what makes you think I have any?' I asked, with a sour burst of laughter.

'The gossip says there's another scandal soon. A much bigger one than the last.'

'The gossip is wrong.'

'That the people involved are big names. That it will discredit them for ever.' He stared hard into my eyes. 'I'm not asking you to support us. I understand you must keep your neutrality. You don't have to do anything at all, except keep us informed.'

'I've no idea what you're talking about, Santo. I'm trapped in a nightmare. Occasionally two pieces of the puzzle seem to fit together and I think it might all make some sense. But then it's an illusion again and everything's just as screwed up as before. What the hell am I supposed to know?'

156

He stared at me for a long time. 'I'll walk you to your taxi.'

The driver's face spread into a grin as we turned the corner of the building. I'd deliberately not paid him, for fear he might leave if I did, so he must have been getting scared that I wouldn't return. Santo held the door open for me.

'You're not going back to town?' I asked.

'I have some things to do first.' His voice was flat and I got the feeling he was disappointed. Whatever he'd been looking for, I hadn't delivered it. I was pretty sure I couldn't deliver it. Perhaps he believed me, perhaps he didn't.

He stopped and turned around. 'Thank you for coming, Graham. I still think you're one of the good guys.' He lit a final cigarette. 'Think about what I said. Do you promise me to do that, at least?'

There was nothing to think about, but I didn't know whether he'd accept that. I agreed to his request instead. It seemed much simpler.

'Goodbye for now, Graham. I hope we'll meet again. *Hati-hati*. This city can be dangerous.'

14

Blok M at night: a place where dreams are promised and betrayed. As the sun sinks in the evening sky, Blok M sinks with it, and the Pasaraya shoppers, with their dull, suburban greed, give way to a cast of actors slaked by more pressing thirsts. Money and sex. A colourful circus of whores, transvestites, rent boys, tricksters and pimps take to the streets – up for grabs, the closest this city ever gets to love. But it takes two to tango, and their partners in this dance – the *bule* clients – are only too keen to strip off their suits and loosen their ties before streaming into the bars to find some comfort for the night. Such a long way from home, Jakarta.

Moonbeam nightclub, one of my favourite watering holes, lay bang in the centre of this roving cabaret. I hung around the malls till they closed, drinking coffee until my nerve-ends stood on stilts, then beat a familiar path to the orange lights that flashed over Moonbeam's door. It was barely ten o'clock, way too early for punters, so the security eyed me up and down with deep suspicion. He grunted and let me through. Not once had he acknowledged me, although he surely must have recognized such a dogged client. A typical bouncer, his eyes never blinked. He did the job for fun.

The upstairs bar was empty apart from the owner, Abi, and his entourage of call girls, known poetically in

Indonesian as *kupu-kupu malam* – butterflies of the night. Most of these butterflies looked more like moths whose wings had got frayed at the edges from flapping near too many flames. But I liked these girls a lot – they were tough and looked after themselves, and there was something strangely honest about their blatant artifice. Not only that, they played a mean game of pool.

Abi stood behind the counter, arms folded, very much the proud owner. He beamed and shook my hand.

'Good evening, Mr Young. You're early tonight.'

'Early and thirsty, Abi.'

'The usual?'

'The usual.'

Two of the butterflies, Putri and Desi, alighted on barstools either side of me. They knew from past experience they couldn't interest me in sex, but they could still frisk me of cash in a wager on a game of pool.

I shook my head. 'I just want to sit here for a while.'

'You have problem, *tuan*?' Putri grinned, resting her palm on my knee. 'Maybe I make you forget all your problems.'

I laughed. She laughed, too. Mutual recognition that no deal was about to be struck.

In my early visits to Moonbeam, the girls had found it disconcerting to have this stranger around who preferred the tilt of a gin glass to their own enticing curves. I think it stung their professional pride. I'd catch them glancing my way with wounded looks, wondering why I didn't find them attractive. They quietly asked Abi if my taste ran to boys – they had lots of friends whose leanings matched mine. When this drew a blank, they asked him, in even more discreet whispers, if I was kinky in some way. Did I have some little quirk that demanded to be satisfied? Someone somewhere in this sprawling, desperate city would satisfy it.

Eventually Abi concocted a tale about a wife back home, sewing like Penelope on her blanket. I worshipped this

159

paragon of virtue and would put myself to the sword rather than cheat on her. After hearing this pious nonsense, the attitude of the girls completely changed and I became a buddy. They relaxed with me, just like they did with Abi – a big gay teddy bear of a man who fussed like a doting uncle over his girls.

Putri lit a cigarette. A local brand, so a whiff of cloves wafted over in my direction. I watched the pleasure soften her face as she sucked in the smoke and I wished for one moment I shared her addiction. Not to worry, my own addiction soon arrived in a tall glass with chunks of ice and lime. Abi could mix a G and T to die for.

He gave a wide grin. He was the kind of man who wanted all the world to be happy. 'I read in newspaper this week, Mr Young. They catch Doctor White.'

'Yes, I saw that.'

'Someone kill him.'

'So I gather.'

'I am glad. He is evil man. My girls are frightened, yes?'

'But he never –' I paused to find a tactful phrase. 'I mean, he never attacked a working girl, did he?'

'No. He like them too young for that.' His mouth twisted in disgust. 'They are little girls, just children! Perhaps he wants to be sure they are virgin, yes?'

'Do you really think that's why?'

'Ask my girls, Mr Young. For so many men, they must be a virgin.' He laughed. 'They become a virgin again and again, my girls.'

I fidgeted on my barstool and gulped down a mouthful of gin. I didn't really want this conversation.

'Now they catch Doctor White, I will tell you something secret, Mr Young. When you first come here, some of my girls think perhaps it is you.' He roared with laughter. 'Well, you arrive in Jakarta the same time, yes? And they wonder why you never want to make business.'

I felt the blood drain from my face. The smell of the room, a heady mix of flowers and liquor, reminded me of the presence I'd met in the Platinum. Aftershave and body odour.

'I don't understand, Mr Young. Why he must do such terrible things?'

'I don't know, Abi. I really don't care.'

'He can find everything he want in Jakarta. Yes, I am ashamed to say it, but young girls also, like children.' He banged his fist on the bar. 'So why he must kill them afterwards?'

'Perhaps there isn't a reason for evil.'

'You are right. I am glad he is dead.'

Fortunately, at this point a group of raucous westerners appeared at the top of the stairs, with nudges and guffaws as they loitered with intent in the doorway. They were obviously fresh in town, corporate UK on some kind of business junket.

'*Permisi*, Mr Young.' He rushed over to offer his fondest welcome to these wallets on legs.

I observed the shaking of hands as Abi turned on his considerable charm. They seemed predictable enough, these predators who had gathered at Moonbeam's oasis. Respectable citizens in their suits and ties. They showed the usual compulsion to prove themselves, a bluster that covered a snakepit of doubts, buried fears to which none of them would ever admit. The first round of drinks was guzzled down and they egged each other on with swaggering bravado. Putri and the butterflies moved in for the kill.

I'd often sit in the warm shadows at Moonbeam and watch *bules* such as these come and go, somehow conspiring to get even drunker than me. At midnight the thump of the bass from the bar downstairs rattled the floorboards, followed by the crash of cymbals and the croak of bad vocals. The action was about to start. I'd cruise down the stairway to enter a smoky world of dark-skinned women and their spectral clients, as everyone chose their next partner for the dance of death.

The girls would hone in on the punters with swift resolve and I'd feel almost sorry for the jerks. They looked so ridiculously proud of themselves, these little boys of all ages, but were nearly always way out of their depth and easy prey for such seasoned professionals. As the girls switched on the flattery, I'd watch the drunken faces light up one by one. And, for a few short hours, every little boy became the handsome prince in a fairy tale.

I guessed I liked Moonbeam because it dished up nightlife like it should be – debauched, but never too dangerous. A roller-coaster joyride where nobody was likely to get a glass smashed in his face.

Desi, far from a classic beauty but the canniest of the girls, had already managed to isolate one of the boys from the rest of his gang. Just like in those wildlife documentaries on TV, she had chosen the youngest and the frailest in the herd. She eased him across the room and perched him on the barstool next to mine. Judging by the stench of beer from his body, I figured he'd been boozing all day long.

'Great place,' he beamed, with a vacuous smile.

'Guess so.'

'Where you from?'

'England.'

'No kidding! Hey, I'm from Aldershot!'

'Well, I suppose someone has to be.'

A flash of anger blazed through the drunken eyes. Maybe the people who came from Aldershot were proud of the place. But luckily he was so drunk that he soon forgot that he was supposed to protect the honour of his fine home town. The inane grin returned.

'Nowhere like this back in England, uh?' he slurred.

'No. Everyone's far too busy at Homebase.'

Desi whispered in his ear and giggled. She slunk around to stand behind him and began to remove his tie. He cackled with nervous laughter as he slouched on his bar-stool. He wasn't sure whether to panic and run back to his mates, or to call them all over so they could watch.

'So, how long you staying here?' he asked, trying to cover up his nervousness.

'I live here.'

'No shit! You lucky bastard!'

'Lots of people wouldn't agree.'

Desi undid the top two buttons of his plain white shirt. 'Now you look more relaxed.'

He went to grab her around the waist, but his courage failed him at the last minute. 'This seems a hot place. Is it always like this?'

'Pretty much.'

'Whew!'

Desi lit two cigarettes and placed one between the boy's mesmerized lips. He was out of his depth and hopelessly confused. A grin filled his face, like a kid with a mouthful of jelly babies, but his eyes kept glancing nervously towards his mates, to check they hadn't abandoned him. The sweet shop could be a pretty scary place.

'Hey, can I have another drink?' he shouted over to Abi.

Desi picked up the empty glass so that Abi could see, slipped round to the other side of the bar and poured another beer.

'Hey! You're a barmaid here, yeah?'

I laughed. 'Oh, you have lots of talents, don't you, Desi?'

She curled the tip of her tongue and ran it along her top lip. 'Lots.'

After pouring herself a vodka, she handed the boy his beer. 'I'm sorry, no credit here.' He gaped at her like a fish. 'You must pay now,' she explained.

'Oh.' He spread open his wallet and fumbled with a wad

of grey, fifty-thousand notes. A suicidal amount of cash for a tourist in Blok M at night. The pile of notes almost tumbled to the floor. He tried again. For a second time, the wallet nearly slipped from his grasp. Desi had seen quite enough and leant over to take it from his hands.

'Hey!' he shouted.

'Don't worry,' I reassured him. 'They're honest enough here.'

She took out one of the fifty-thousand notes and held it in the air, conspicuously, so that the boy could see he wasn't being robbed. 'This is enough,' she said, and placed the wallet back in his hand.

How English he suddenly seemed, as a frown of suspicion creased his soft brow. 'Relax,' I said. 'No one's going to cheat you here.'

He gave me a questioning look. I think he felt some kind of trust in me because I was also a white man. 'It's the going rate,' I confirmed.

Desi draped her arms around him and nibbled at his ear.

'Hey, cut that out, will you?' he barked. 'I don't go in for all that kind of stuff.'

I could see him getting more and more tense as his evening span out of control. He was just a kid. Twenty-five years old at most. There was something depressingly clean cut about him, as he sat there in his white shirt, with his short, blond hair and his baby-smooth chin. Not so much innocent as empty headed. If I saw him on the street, I might mistake him for a Mormon.

I spoke a few words to Desi – in Indonesian, to make sure he wouldn't understand – to explain that English men were generally rather chewy meat, better casseroled than stir-fried. Give him some time, I said. He's just a boy. I suggested she beat a tactical retreat until he felt more at ease with his unaccustomed freedom.

I'd read the situation right. Once Desi moved away and

the pressure was off, his shoulders slumped with a heartfelt sigh. He leant over towards me.

'Can I ask you something?'

'Go ahead.'

'Why you sitting over here on your own?'

'Enjoying a drink, that's all.'

'Guess you've had most of them already, uh, if you live here?' When I didn't reply, he leant even more closely and whispered in my ear, 'These girls are prostitutes, right?'

I laughed and bit my lip. 'Right.'

'So how much do I pay one of them?'

'It's up to you.'

'No, really. I want to know.'

'I'm not the person to ask. I've never been with any of them.'

He snorted and raised his eyebrows. He didn't believe me.

'OK. Start at a third of what they ask. Settle for a half. That's the normal rule of thumb for bartering here.'

'I've never done it with a whore before,' he said, staring glumly into his empty glass.

'There's a first time for everything.'

He signalled over for another beer. 'Are they clean?'

'Abi sells condoms.'

'Not much fun then, is it? Like swimming in a mackintosh.' He seemed to think this was the height of wit, and burst into a silly giggle.

'You don't have to go with one of them, you know.'

'What do you mean?'

'I mean it's not compulsory.'

'What – miss a chance like this? Are you crazy?'

I almost said a lot of things. I almost asked him who he was doing it for – himself or his mates. I almost told him about all the times I'd seen tourists just like him, busting a gut to convince themselves they were having fun, when they'd have been far happier watching some mindless crap

165

on TV in their hotel room. I almost said, 'Why bother?' I ordered another G and T instead.

'You really never been with one of these whores?'

I shook my head.

'Ah – you're kidding me!'

'Scout's honour.'

'Why? You a shirtlifter?' His drunken mood swung violently again and a nasty edge cut into his voice.

I took a swig of my gin and leant on the bar. 'Oh, do what the hell you like, OK? You started this conversation.'

'So why you never go with them?' I said nothing. 'No, really. I'd like to know.'

'Because I'm a shirtlifter,' I whispered, in a Boris Karloff voice. 'Who likes little blond Mormons with sea-blue eyes.'

By this point, he was utterly bemused and hadn't a clue what to say. Not only were the prostitutes pushy here, but the white guys were wildly unpredictable. 'Huh – you're full of shit!' he finally spat out.

'Well, at least I know it.' He suddenly looked vulnerable again and I couldn't help but feel sorry for him. 'Relax, I'm not a shirtlifter, OK? Your cute little cherry is safe.'

'So why don't you go with them?'

'What's it to you? Look, why don't you just go and get laid and leave me alone? It's as easy as falling over.'

I spotted Putri on the other side of the bar, her arms swathed around a mass of middle-aged blubber in a suit. She was listening so attentively to what I imagined were his pearls of wisdom, or perhaps his corny jokes, gazing into his eyes like he was some kind of hero. These girls had to work so damned hard for their money.

'You know what?' my drinking companion said, with a sneer, as his mood lurched towards violence once more. 'I think you're weird.'

'Probably.'

'You got a wife here?'

'Divorced.'

'So what's wrong with you? Can't you get it up any more?'

My own morose mood was swinging wildly now as well. 'And how about you, Little Boy Blue? Are you in wedded bliss?'

He didn't need to answer. The flash of guilt that streaked across his face said it all. 'You leave my wife out of this, OK?'

I polished off my gin and tonic and gave a sigh. 'Why do it? You've got a nice little starter home in Aldershot. You've got a nice little starter wife. Then you come here on some company jaunt and you go AWOL.' I lifted my hand and waved in Abi's direction, signalling for the boy's glass to be refilled. 'Do you really think it's worth it? What are you going to get out of this except a dose of the clap?'

'Hey, Brian! What the fuck you doing over here?' A smoothie in his early thirties was sauntering our way. He was the kind of guy who poured half a bottle of aftershave over himself and imagined it made him classy. He looked me up and down. The instant loathing was mutual.

'Who's your friend?' he asked.

'He lives here.'

'Well, good for him. Why you wasting your time talking to this guy when there's all this pussy around?'

'Want to hear something really weird? This guy never gives them one.'

'That's his funeral. You see that one, the one in black who was over here before? She's gagging for it, kid. She hasn't taken her eyes off you for the past five minutes.'

The blond boy seemed to interpret this as a command and attempted to rise to his feet. He swayed back and forth and his eyes rolled, while his buddy wrapped an arm around his shoulder to hold him steady.

'If I were you, I'd go and grab that pussy before somebody else does.'

He monitored his protégé as he stumbled back to the herd. Once the youngster was safely in the ranks of the pack, the smoothie turned his attention to me. 'So what you been saying to our Brian?'

I looked at him. He wore a Pringle jumper and trousers which were much too tight.

'Nothing much. Your friend did most of the talking.'

His fingers casually flicked through sun-kissed highlights. 'He's a kid. I don't want anyone taking advantage of him.'

'Relax. I'm not interested in your friend, OK?'

'So why you been getting so pally with him? What you been telling him?'

'He asked for my advice.'

'Oh yeah? And what advice could a guy like you give him?'

'About the girls here.'

'You an expert on them, are you?'

'I come here a lot, yes. I know them all.'

'I doubt it, pal.'

'I pointed out he has a choice. He doesn't have to have sex with any of them if he doesn't want to.'

'So who are you all of a sudden, his fucking priest? Let the kid enjoy himself.'

'Doesn't it bother you?'

'Doesn't what bother me?'

'Knowing the only reason the girls go with you is the money?'

He snorted. 'I don't have any problems with that. I've been around. Bangkok, several times.'

I felt that his attempt at sophisticated cynicism lacked a certain something. Sophistication, perhaps.

'And how about the girls?' I asked.

'How about them?'

'Do you ever wonder what they feel?'

'Well, I'd imagine they feel pretty fucking grateful,

actually. How else they going to earn fifty dollars just lying on their back?' Again his fingers flounced through the blow-dried fringe. 'They want to get fucked. We want to fuck them. Where's the problem?'

'In my mind, I guess.'

'Too fucking right, pal. If you got hang-ups, that's your business. Just don't bother our Brian with them, OK?'

He lifted his drink to his lips, some ridiculous cocktail one of the girls must have bought on his behalf, complete with a bamboo umbrella. 'You live here?' I nodded. 'Take my advice, pal. Enjoy it while you can. We're a long time dead.'

A loud crash sounded from the other side of the bar. One of the tables had gone flying into the air.

Like a flash, Abi was over there, trying to calm everyone down. But before he could say much, a scuffle had broken out between a customer and one of the girls. The client, puce-faced, had grabbed hold of her wrist and was trying to prise open her fingers, to get at a bundle of notes there. She retaliated by biting his hand.

For all its hint of danger, I'd only seen trouble in Moonbeam once before. It was handled every bit as efficiently on that previous occasion.

Within seconds of the first punch being thrown, security arrived at the top of the stairs. A couple of minutes at most, and the entire English group was ejected. A few minutes later, and the tables and the chairs were sedately back in place, as if the incident had never occurred.

But the mood had altered in the room somehow. The promise of fun about to happen wasn't there any more. Or maybe the change of mood was all in my mind. I toyed with the idea of going to a different club – somewhere I'd never been before where nobody knew me and I could pretend I was a tourist. I would have loved to be a tourist right then, one of those brain-dead English bozos whose only concern is staying sober enough to get a butterfly back to his hotel.

I envied them their drunken haze. I felt implacably sober. 'I thought we might be in for a bit of excitement there, Abi.'

He busied himself washing glasses behind the bar. 'Nothing serious, Mr Young. People drink too much and lose control.'

I thought back to the other time in Moonbeam when people drank too much and lost control. Needless to say, English as well. 'I'm sorry about my compatriots,' I said. 'English people.'

'I like English people.' He nodded vigorously to prove his point.

'But we drink too much. And when we drink, we get aggressive.' I held my glass in the air. 'Any chance of another?'

My host with the most was already slicing up the lime.

'Can I ask you something, Abi?' He looked across. 'Do you ever wonder what the hell is wrong with us?'

He stifled a little smile. 'English people?'

'*Bules* in general.'

'I like *bules*, Mr Young. They pay for my rice.'

'Come on, Abi. Sometimes you must hate us.'

He regarded me carefully as he handed me my latest gin and tonic. 'Why I must hate you?'

'We come here and behave so badly. Like that lot you had to throw out just now. They'd never dream of behaving like that back home.'

'They come here on holiday. They want to relax.'

I smiled to myself. There was no way I was going to squeeze uncomplimentary remarks about my fellow Brits from Abi. He hailed from central Java, Yogyakarta, not so far down the road from Suprianto. In Javanese life, the important thing is to maintain a surface tranquillity. And if that means unpalatable truths never get spoken aloud, it's considered a price worth paying for social harmony.

Still, it makes for an intriguing game, trying to prise out

170

what people are thinking. 'Doesn't it ever depress you, Abi? What happens here? When you see what the girls have to do just to eat?'

He placed a bowl of roasted peanuts down in front of me. I think he was hoping I'd start eating them and shut up.

'It depresses me sometimes,' I said. 'We come here with our wallets stuffed full of money and we think that gives us the right to behave just as we like. It seems so sordid.'

He smiled and shook his head with his usual affability. 'What's the point of being sad, Mr Young? It's the way things are. It's our destiny.'

'Don't you ever dream of changing it? Wouldn't you like to see Indonesia change for ever?'

'You mean *reformasi*, Mr Young?'

'I guess so.'

'Of course I want *reformasi*.' He picked up a towel and began to dry the glasses. 'But I also want to eat.'

'Do you ever stop and wonder what we get out of coming here?'

'Happiness, Mr Young.'

'Did they look happy, the guys who were here before? I mean, did they really look like they were having a good time?'

'My customers are not complaining. They like it here.'

'Power. That's what I think we get out of it. These are sad little people back in England. Nobodies stuck in dead-end jobs. Then they come over here and find they're like little white gods.' I finished off my gin, but the taste was flat on my tongue. 'I think inside us we still harbour these colonial fantasies, Abi. We dream of being explorers instead of the nonentities we really are.'

Abi gratefully excused himself to go over and welcome a customer who had just arrived. A solitary individual with glasses and receding hair – a visiting lecturer, perhaps, or some kind of management consultant. An ideal client:

171

someone who would drink his beer and pay up, have sex and pay up, without throwing any punches along the way. Grateful for a little kindness so far from home.

I felt gloom; not even Abi's miraculous gin and tonics seemed able to lift my spirits. Twelve o'clock had come and gone, the witching hour. When the merry-go-round starts to whirl and all the dancers leap aboard. But instead of my usual lurch down the stairs, I was starting to worry about how I'd get home. Normally I'd just step out on the street and pick up a cab. Right now the idea seemed insane.

'You have problem, *tuan*. I can see in your face,' Putri said, sitting next to me.

'Nothing important.'

'You must not keep a problem in your heart. If you tell someone, it will go away.'

I smiled. 'Some problems aren't that easy, Putri.'

'Everyone have problems, *tuan*,' she said, with feeling.

The girls here were the closest I got to female Indonesian friends. I knew the wives of *bule* colleagues, with whom I had to make civilized conversation at tedious functions. Generally I detested them. They'd landed the ultimate prize of a rich, white husband and spent their days feigning graceful impersonations of ex-pat wives. The worst snobs I'd ever known in my life.

Putri was such an irrepressible character that I was shocked to see her eyes fill up with tears. 'I have baby, *tuan*. I work here, so he has food.' She sucked dolefully on her clove cigarette. 'But I am worried in the future. Maybe when he grow up, he will hate me. Hate his bad mother.'

Oh Putri, I wanted to say, don't go tart with a heart on me. You're tough and resilient, and you play the game on your own terms. That's why I like you and why I can't stand the local colonials dripping airs and graces. I offered her my handkerchief. She pushed my hand away, embarrassed.

'Come on, *tuan*, we play pool, yes?'

172

'You just want to take some money from me.'

'Maybe you win this time.'

'Maybe pigs will fly.'

No porcine UFOs were sighted that evening and I retired with my usual impeccable record – three games, three thrashings. I handed Putri her *rupiah*.

'Never mind, *tuan*. Maybe you are better shot with stick in pocket.' She placed her hand on my knee and ran it up my leg. 'Ah, but this stick is lonely, I think. Because you never play with it.'

Abi ambled back over, beaming a broad smile. I seemed happy once more and the surface of life was smooth. 'Same again, Mr Young?'

'Can you order me a taxi?'

'*Aduh!* You leave already?'

'Yes, I'm feeling tired.'

'Very early tonight. You have problem?'

'No, of course not,' I breezed. 'You just need to be a bit more careful these days.'

He nodded sympathetically. 'One of my customers – Greek people – he get in a taxi outside my club and they drive him into dark street and put knife in him and steal all his money.'

'Things have changed a lot round here since *krismon*.'

'Many criminals now in Jakarta. *Preman*. It is not safe.'

'Can you make sure you order a Blue Bird, Abi?' I asked, as he picked up the receiver. 'And note down the number?'

He observed me as he dialled. His finger hovered over the final digit before he put down the phone. 'Where do you live, Mr Young?'

'Ciputat.'

'Please. Use my car and driver.'

Five minutes later I was sitting in the front of Abi's dark blue Kijang beside a jocular driver who seemed delighted to inflict his broken English on a captive audience.

'Please, allow me to introduce myself,' he intoned, in a plummy accent he must have picked up from some antique language cassette. 'My name is Martius.'

He was a chatty, confident man – from his name and his manner, I guessed Batak, from Medan in the north of Sumatra. He had a wiry body, swarthy skin and a pencil moustache. While his English seemed to be limited to the clutch of formal phrases he'd gleaned from his ancient cassette, he pronounced each of these literary gems with the utmost precision.

I looked out of the window and saw that we were driving in the opposite direction from my house in Ciputat. Our progress was also painfully slow. A jolt of panic shot through my body. 'Where are you taking me?'

'Traffic jam, *tuan*. This way more quicker.'

'It's after midnight. There are no traffic jams.'

He exposed all his teeth in a broad grin. 'It is beautiful night, *tuan*. Many stars.' Then he jutted out his chin and the BBC accent returned. 'Do you mind if I ask you a question? How long have you been living here?'

The truth dawned on me and I laughed out loud with relief. There was nothing sinister going on. We were taking this convoluted route so that Martius could prolong his English lesson.

'One year,' I replied, relaxing into my seat.

When Martius didn't have one of his stock phrases to hand, his grammar collapsed. 'Oh, long time already.'

The back streets of Jakarta glided past. An ugly city. Claustrophobic. And yet, in these narrow streets far from the glinting skyscrapers, in these drab and shabby streets, Jakarta beat with a warm heart.

'*Pak* Abi say you have problem, *tuan*,' Martius reported, making no attempt at all to hide his curiosity.

'No problem.' Despite my phoney nonchalance, I could see that Martius, like Abi before him, could sense my fear.

174

'I'm just concerned about safety nowadays.'

'You right, *tuan*. Jakarta not safe now.' He shook his head and grimaced. 'But do not worry. You safe with Martius.' He patted his chest. 'I have knife.' He sprang open the glove compartment to reveal the gleaming steel weapon, the kind of fearsome blade with which a butcher might slice up a cow. He grinned across and glowed with pride.

I smiled nervously back. With relief, I saw the monument on Senayan roundabout loom into view. I knew where we were at last. 'Could we head towards my house this time, please, Martius?'

He flashed me a cheeky smile – I'd caught him out. The monument towered above us as we circled the island, a Stalinist piece of sculpture featuring an athletic male figure who strained for the sky with a plate of flames on one hand. Locals called this statue *Patung Senayan*. *Bules* called it Pizza Man.

We entered a harsher Jakarta, concrete and functional. A place built for cars, where people didn't linger on the streets.

'A white man get killed here, Mr Young.' He pointed to a building secured behind iron grilles. 'Next to car shop. They put knife inside his heart and steal his money.'

'Thank you for sharing that with me, Martius.'

Misunderstanding my irony, his face lit up with pride. 'Ah, but do not worry.' He patted the glove compartment. 'You safe with Martius!'

Pondok Indah Mal sped past. A few minutes later, Lebak Bulus bus station. One place in the city where I wouldn't want to find myself alone at night. The usual shifty faces peered out of the darkness there.

'My house near here, Mr Young.' He pointed to the left. 'One kilometre, maybe.'

'Are you married, Martius?'

'Of course.' He puffed up his chest. 'Three children now.'

I was tired by now and we seemed to have exhausted the

phrases from *BBC Beginner's English*, so we sat in silence for the journey down Ciputat Raya. Featureless and dirty, too drab to be exciting, without either danger or charm. But the landmarks were familiar and so it consoled me. Soon I would be safe at my house.

I thought I spotted the *satpam* in the shadows of his security post, but couldn't be sure. Maybe he was gambling, or conducting a secret affair with a maid. The sky above was black, but the complex was shockingly bright beneath the glaring strips of fluorescence. They flooded the square plots of lawn and made them pulse an alien shade of grey.

'This your house, Mr Young?'

'I live here, yes.'

'*Wah!*' He raised his right thumb in approval.

I gave him twenty thousand *rupiah* and got out of the car. 'Thank you very much for bringing me home, Martius. Your English is very good.'

He beamed with delight. 'Thank you, *tuan*. I drive you next time, maybe.' He held out his hand for me to shake. 'It has been a pleasure.' One last piece of BBC English. He laughed and drove away.

The gate gave its usual squeak as I eased it open. I stood in my porch and looked at the panes of stained glass they'd built into the door. Some kind of Perspex. At times I couldn't get over how tacky this place was. I guess the developers imagined they were making it cosy, just like being back home, but it all seemed rather eerie instead, even the horse-carriage lamp that glowed in the corner. This was some David Lynch film set, not a home.

I gave a little gasp. The front door was open. A tiny crack.

Had Enti forgotten to lock it? She'd never done that before. Should I turn around and make a dash for security? I had no time to consider before the door creaked open. An instruction to enter. My heartbeat quickened and I stepped inside.

15

His fingers rattled on the table like gunfire. Fifty years old, with a squat body and a square face, he leant back on the sofa in the centre of my living room, an arm stretched out, drumming on the hard black wood beside him. Behind him stood a much younger man, less than thirty, angular and lean, with flawless skin and rodent eyes that darted back and forth behind wire-rimmed spectacles.

The squat man spoke, in Javanese. He stared at me, but the eyes made no contact, as if a wall of glass stretched between us. His frame sat rigid. Only the fingers moved, beating out their war drums.

'Good evening, Mr Young. You keep late hours, I see,' the younger man translated, in a voice that cut the air like paraffin. The English accent was as clean as a knife, stripped of all emotion. Public-school crisp.

The squat man in front of him stared into my face, without blinking. I watched the words exit his mouth, in single file, as if each word first needed to request permission to leave.

The young man paused before emitting a translation in his arid voice. 'I apologize if my presence has alarmed you. As you see, I am no longer young, so I needed to rest my legs. You are doubtless tired. Please take a seat, on the chair opposite mine.'

I sat on the chair as instructed. The drumming abated.

'In the circumstances, I expect you'd appreciate a drink.'

I nodded vacantly. The young man stepped into the kitchen and proceeded to make a perfect gin and tonic, with ice and lemon. He placed it on the coffee table next to my chair before positioning himself as before, behind the squat figure.

The fingers began their savage assault on the table once more. A smile crawled from the older man's lips as he watched me lift the glass.

'Let me explain the purpose of my visit.' He paused to survey me with eyes that never seemed to blink, like a crocodile in wait below the water. 'I am concerned about the friendships you are making in my country.'

I became aware for the first time of two other figures in the room, on each side of the mock fireplace, obscured in shadow. One of them had moved very slightly, a tic of the hand, and I'd caught the twitch in the corner of my eye.

Somewhere in the complex, a dog barked.

'You are friendly towards my people. This is commend-able. But a man can be too friendly for his own good.'

I looked at the figures in the dim light of the table lamp, two identical black beetles encased in the shells of their jackets. Shadow hooded the eyes. At the base of each face, I made out the gash of thin red lips.

The fingers rattled on the dark wood. The squat man turned his glare on me, for what seemed an age. Black at the heart, these eyes, bloodshot at the edges. Eyes that could monitor as someone was tortured.

As his stare picked out my features, like a searchlight on a prison wall, the fears at the back of my mind burst to the surface. I thought about the students shot dead in Semanggi in May. About the ninja killings in Banyuwangi. The corpses washed up on a riverbank in Lampung. The mass graves scattered across Aceh and East Timor. I thought back to the riots and a country that seemed on the verge of civil war. The sporadic outbursts of violence since then, *provocateurs* fomenting unrest so the military had an excuse to step in and reinstate the *Orde Baru*. Dead bodies in piles, anonymous, discarded. I tried to repel the fear that mine might be next.

At last my captor broke the silence. His interpreter, whose bony frame must have relaxed an imperceptible fraction, shot back up to attention. The translation juddered out of his mouth like tickertape from a machine.

'You live alone, I see, Mr Young.'

I nodded.

'Not yet married?'

For the first time, I spoke. 'Divorced.' My throat was dry and the word croaked out.

'This is common in the west, I gather. I fear western people do not show sufficient patience.'

For some inexplicable reason, this comment almost caused me to smile. His radar picked up the curl of my lip. The reptile eyes narrowed in displeasure.

'But you have friends in Jakarta.'

I nodded.

'Many friends, I am informed.'

'Not so many. I've only lived here just over a year.'

The rattle of fingers on wood grew fiercer.

'Who are your friends in Jakarta, Mr Young?'

'People at work. Office colleagues.' I glanced up at the younger man to check that he had understood. He dutifully translated in the same spare voice.

'I expect you are speaking of western colleagues?'

'Yes.'

'I have no interest in your western friendships. They are no concern of mine.' The drumbeat of the fingers rolled. 'I am interested in your Indonesian friendships.'

I wasn't sure I had Indonesian friendships. Most of the people I met every day I would list as contacts, not friends.

Cocooned on the complex, I went through my life, like most ex-pats around me, detached from local people.

The glazed eyes slid from side to side behind the mask of coarse skin. He rattled his fingers and waited.

I had no idea what he wanted me to say. There were some Indonesians who worked for my NGO, mainly in supporting roles as administrators and secretaries. But I didn't want to mention them. They didn't have the protection of being foreign and if I implicated them in whatever was going on I might put them in danger.

But I had to find some kind of answer. He watched me with growing impatience. 'I sometimes have to deal with local officials,' I finally blustered.

The young man translated. The drumming grew more insistent. It was not the answer that my captor sought.

'I like to think that my gardener and my maid are like friends. And I talk to the people who live near my complex.'

'These are *kampung* people. I have no interest in *kampung* people.'

Desperate for some answer that might take off the pressure, I snatched at what I hoped might prove a trump card. 'There is a detective from the Jakarta police. Detective Suprianto.'

My interrogator let out a catarrhal snort and gave a burst of mirthless laughter. '*Bapak* Suprianto is an extremely able officer, I am sure. I have encouraging reports of his work. But you are an outsider here and should not overestimate his influence.'

He had taken my trump card seriously enough to respond to it, but it had made no dent in his confidence. He sat there, suffused with self-belief, a player who could over-trump at will.

My eyes shot once more to the figures in shadow. To the young man's shiny gaze, devoid of emotion. I felt as if I was the only thing alive in the room.

'*Bapak* Suprianto is an influential man in Indonesia.' He corrected himself with a grunt. 'In Jakarta. But however much influence a man may hold, there is always someone else who is even more powerful.'

For the first time he changed the position of his body, leaning forward in his seat to rest his hands on his knees.

'It would not be wise to rely on *Bapak* Suprianto.'

My questioner hailed from the military, I felt sure. He had the air of a soldier, even out of uniform. His batik shirt looked fresh from the box, the creases in his trousers were pristine and his black shoes gleamed, even in the faint light of the table lamp. If he had chosen not to intimidate me by wearing his khaki, I figured his visit was unofficial. Maybe he came from a rogue faction of ABRI who no longer took their orders from the official chain of command. Perhaps his loyalties lay elsewhere.

My speculation was shattered by the renewed rattle of fingers. He snapped a few words for the young man to translate. The latter almost clicked his heels in response.

'My superior would appreciate your co-operation.'

'Please tell your superior I wish to co-operate in every way possible.'

My answer was transmitted back in Javanese. The squat man pondered my words and the drumming softened. He fixed me in his stare. 'Tell me about your work in Jakarta.'

'My work?' I could see that he sensed my unease. 'I work for an NGO.'

'So I am informed. What does this work entail?'

I felt like a butterfly pinned under glass. 'I investigate irregularities.'

'Missing money, I believe.'

'Not just money. Aid in general. Things often never reach the people they're meant for. I track the process and try to ensure that they do.'

'I imagine such work requires delicate collaboration.'

'We need to liaise with other organizations, yes.'

'And discretion, of course. Sensitive information could be damaging if it fell into the wrong hands.'

The room fell silent.

'Let us return to the matter of your friendships in Indonesia.' He shifted the position of his body for only the second time, leaning back in his chair.

'What would you like to know?' I asked.

'I would like you to tell me about the friendships you have with students.'

'To the best of my knowledge, I don't have any friends who are students,' I stammered.

'You may take your time.'

My stomach turned over. I had no idea what he wanted me to say. 'Some of the people in the *kampung* may study at the local Islamic university.'

'Indeed.' The drumming slowed down. 'Let us clarify what I mean when I speak of friendships. I am not referring to close ties. These links may be merely convenient for all concerned.'

I was still perplexed and could only shake my head in silent denial. Displeasure glinted in his eyes. His words were peppered out with machine-gun ferocity.

'My superior wishes to remind you about the student in your hotel room.'

I felt a sense of relief on hearing these words. I had some idea what he wanted to know about. When I finally spoke, my throat was so dry that I coughed up some phlegm. 'I didn't know he was a student.'

The crocodile eyes thinned into slits of disbelief.

'He hardly seemed intelligent enough. His friend was a student, I knew that. In Australia.'

'Did he tell you this?'

'Yes.'

'And you believed him?'

'Of course. Why shouldn't I?'

'How many times have you met with this other student?'

'Twice.' I swallowed hard. 'That's the truth, sir. I promise.'

'What took place in these meetings?'

'Nothing. We just chatted.'

'What matters were discussed?'

'Nothing important. Music, mainly.'

'So these were just casual encounters?'

'Yes.'

'In which polite conversation was made?'

'That's right.'

For a third time he moved, leaning forward again in his chair. 'And your visit to the mental hospital?'

The wound on my arm gave a twinge of pain. How could he know so much about my every movement?

'Did you also make polite conversation there?'

'The student asked me to go. He wanted me to see someone.'

'Did you know this person?'

'No. Not to speak to.'

'It seems rather strange that you should agree to visit him, therefore.'

'I suppose it must.' I felt frozen like prey in the predatory beam of his eyes. 'I don't know why I went. I just did.'

'So innocent chat is all that transpired in these meetings?'

I cleared my throat. 'Yes.'

He sat quite still and ran his stare up and down my body. I was stiff with tension and I didn't dare move my head.

'I swear it.'

His top lip curled and he raised his right hand. The figures in black stepped forward one pace, into the light. Their shoulders stiffened. I could see the sockets of their eyes now, but the eyes within them remained hidden. These shells of human beings seemed more like insects: they lacked mammalian warmth.

183

My captor put his hand down. The shoulders relaxed.

The squat man boomed with laughter and thumped his fist on his knee. He had sucked pleasure, like juice from an orange, out of witnessing my fear. Behind him, impassive, the young man stood motionless, with a face like a sheet of blank paper. The barrage of laughter died on the squat man's lips, as abruptly as it began. My captor leant forward.

'I think I can do business with you, Mr Young. You have answered my questions most patiently. I fear many of your countrymen would not have been so amenable.'

His hands crept forward, the skin thick and leathery, like a lizard's scales. Close enough to reach over and touch me if he so wished.

'You appear to be a realistic man. I advise you to continue to be realistic.' To my relief, he maintained the fragile distance between us. 'Do you understand the implications of this advice?'

'Please tell me what you want me to do.'

The thin man translated in his expressionless voice. The squat man's face, twisted into a perpetual scowl by some inner violence, loosened on hearing my words. As he spoke, he fixed me in his bloodshot eyes.

'You will have no further contact with this student. I am satisfied that you are blameless, but you are not aware of the significance of your actions.'

The sentences followed each other from his lips like soldiers on patrol. He was used to giving orders and having them obeyed.

'You are a visitor here and may be allowed a certain licence. However, you would be wise not to overstep the mark. The fact that you are a guest here requires an under-taking on your part not to get involved in matters which are of no concern to you.'

A faint whiff of aftershave prickled my nose and distracted my thoughts. A cutting scent, with an edge of

184

metal. An improbable scent in this sealed-off cell of a room.

'In the current situation, your safety cannot be guaranteed. It might be better for all concerned if you returned to England for a while. I am sure you have family and friends who would be delighted to see you.'

The slit of the young man's mouth continued to discharge its translation. It was almost as if the metallic aroma emitted from these lips.

'This conversation will remain a secret between ourselves. Embassies do not appreciate becoming entangled in delicate situations. And I wish to stress once more that such friends as you have in Indonesia are not sufficiently powerful to guarantee your safety.'

For the first time in this frozen encounter, the squat man allowed his eyes to make real contact with mine. Something passed between us.

'I trust I have made myself quite clear.' He eased back in his seat. The distance was restored between us.

I stifled a sigh of relief. The smell of aftershave had gone.

My captor and I stared at each other in silence. A minute, perhaps, even more, while neither of us moved a muscle. But for all our stillness, some mute communication was flickering between our eyes. I hoped that mine showed compliance with his wishes; I interpreted a softening of his glare as recognition of this compliance. The drumming ceased for good.

'You may go to bed now.'

He lifted his right palm. The guards took up position on either side of the door. The young man picked up my glass, carried it into the kitchen, threw the slice of lemon into the bin, rinsed the glass with cold water and left it to drain. The squat man leant his palms on his knees and rose to his feet.

Without another word they were gone, closing the door behind them.

I turned off the light and sat alone in the dark.

16

A snapshot of a woman and two smiling kids. An ordinary snapshot, the kind that adorns a million office desks. Taken in the sunshine, on a carefree day – at the zoo perhaps, or the seaside, or a fair. The kids are clutching ice-cream cones, sporting baseball caps and grins. And the world appears a joyous world, unravaged by famine, unstalked by disease. Angels playing in paradise, watched over by a benign deity.

I'd found it in a corner of a drawer, this snapshot, beneath a pile of cast-off papers, credit card slips and junk.

Now I'd made up my mind to get out of Indonesia, I needed to decide what things to take with me. I had to travel light, so I wouldn't give the impression I was leaving for good. Then, if Suprianto's boys were waiting at immigration, I could claim I was going on holiday.

These were my children in this picture, I'd given them life. This was the woman I'd slept beside for fourteen years. Now I felt next to nothing as I looked at these faces. I forgot all about these faces for weeks at a time.

I remembered a conversation just before my ex-wife and I had separated. We didn't shout and no one shed tears – it was much too late for that. We huddled together on a bench in the garden, in the late autumn sunshine. I pulled the cork from a bottle of chilled white wine. Then we took out the scalpel and dissected what was left of our marriage.

'You're a little boy, Graham,' I could still hear her say. There was no bitterness in the voice. 'You play at life.'

In some secret corner of my heart, I recognized the truth of what she said. I filled up her glass and stared out at the garden.

'I've never had a feeling of commitment from you.'

'That's not fair.'

She shook her head gently. 'Never.'

'We've been together for fourteen years. I've never cheated on you. I've been a good father to the kids.'

'Sometimes I've wished you weren't a good father. It would have made everything easier.'

Apples lay and rotted on the soggy autumn lawn. 'Have you met someone else?'

'It's not like that.'

'Then what is it?'

'You don't know how to love someone.'

The shock I'd felt when she said this hit me just as strong, even now. It was a terrible indictment and perhaps it was true.

'You have no passion, Graham. Not even for your own children. Oh, you love us in your own way, perhaps. It's not that you don't care. But you don't really need any of us.'

'I don't show that I need you.'

She smiled faintly. 'You've never needed anyone in your life.'

The sun hung low in the sky, a burnt-out shade of orange. Early October, and the nights were drawing in.

'I've kept my loneliness hidden away for all these years,' she said. 'I even tried to hide it from myself. Lukewarm love is a cruel thing, Graham.'

A chilly wind shook the heads of the battered dahlias. I stared into my glass. 'I'm sorry.'

'You'll be happier without us. You can be free. It's what you want.'

I went to protest, but something stopped me. Deep down I knew she was right. As surely as if she'd put up a mirror and shown me my own face. Somewhere inside me I wanted to escape from them all.

'Let's go inside,' I said. 'It's getting cold.'

She looked into my eyes and I saw how much she still loved me. 'I'm sorry for you, Graham. You'll always be alone in the world.'

The snapshot lay on my desk, where a few nights before I'd spread out the newspaper clippings. For the first time in years – so long ago I couldn't remember, but I was certainly still a boy – I began to cry. I bit my bottom lip hard and sucked the tears back into my eyes.

Then I got out the scissors and cut up the snapshot, into tiny pieces, snip snip snip. I took my lousy life and cut it up.

I would take nothing at all to the airport except a razor and a change of clothes.

The tropical sun was still low in the sky when I reached the complex gate, so the *becak* drivers stood outside their pedicabs, laughing and joking. I was ready to make my final journey through the potholes to Ciputat Raya.

'Where's Agus?' I asked. I wanted to play the bargaining game with him one last time.

The tinkle of their laughter ceased abruptly. They looked across at each other. I turned my gaze on each man in turn. The bravest found the courage to speak.

'*Agus meninggal, tuan.*'

'*Meninggal?*'

'*Meninggal, tuan. Meninggal dari dunia. Mati.*' The look on their faces confirmed it. Agus was dead.

'How?'

A pause before one of them answered. '*Demam berdarah, tuan.*'

'*Demam berdarah?*' The heads nodded one by one.

188

'Dengue fever.' I whispered the words, as if they were magic, an incantation, and could weave an evil spell.

'*Kasihan. Dia orang yang sangat baik.*' Everyone agreed: Agus had been a good man. Six pairs of eyes looked down at the ground, staring into some private landscape of grief.

Or perhaps the emotion was fear. Agus, an ordinary man, just the same as them, was dead. A few days ago, he was laughing alongside them, and now he was dead. A meaningless death. A farcical death. Nothing noble at all about it, a pinprick from a mosquito. The insect could have bitten any one of them. It could have bitten me. The dice rolls.

But the show must go on, that's what they say at times like this, to keep our peckers up. And suddenly they were laughing again, the *becak* drivers, bantering over who would get my fare now that Agus wasn't around.

Was I just getting older, or was it something about Indonesia? So different from the west, where the buildings have a false permanence, as if they've stood there for centuries and nothing has changed. The jungle is lush and generous, but it houses a ruthless god. He gives life in abundance and he takes life without compassion, reclaiming his gifts. I'd come to realize that I wouldn't live for ever. I sat in the taxi and tried to banish these thoughts. I couldn't afford sad thoughts today; they would drag me down when I needed to be strong.

I had to make it into a game. I had to become a movie hero, some fearless hulk with a square jaw and a chunky name like Brad. A man of action who straddled mere life and death, unperturbed by his mortality.

I looked out of the rear window of the taxi. A black car, registration B 2683 VK, had stayed close behind for a long time, ever since I picked up the cab in Ciputat Raya. Two squat figures sat like sculptures of stone in the front seats.

I'd had no sleep in the night. I couldn't explain why I didn't ring for a cab and make for the airport as soon as my nocturnal visitors left – my brain had been numb and I hadn't been able to think straight. The mind takes freakish turns in the black heart of the night, and fears ricocheted like stray bullets around my skull. Maybe they wanted me to run, I told myself. So they could ambush me on the toll road. Kill me somewhere anonymous, far from my house. For long hours, I chased these obsessive thoughts, unravelling their thread through the maze of my mind. Only to hit the same cul-de-sac, time and time again.

Until dawn broke, and the unearthly summons of the mosques shook me to my senses. I was getting out of Indonesia. It was what everyone seemed to want.

The black car maintained the distance between us. My driver signalled to enter the feeder lane to the toll road. The black car followed suit.

'No! No!' I shouted. 'Taman Anggrek. I've changed my mind!'

The driver glared at me through his mirror. 'You don't want airport?'

'No, I've changed my mind. Mal Taman Anggrek.'

He muttered under his breath and indicated to pull back over to the left-hand lane. I looked behind. The black saloon flashed left, like a visual echo. It edged even closer.

I checked the contents of my backpack. It was just an excuse for something to do. Then I flicked through my wallet and counted up my money. Fortunately, since the riots I'd kept a lot of cash in the house so I could beat a quick retreat if things blew up again. I had money, passport, credit cards, change of clothes. What else could a square-jawed hero need? I wished to God he'd brought along a bottle of gin.

My taxi turned left to join the main highway at Slipi. Not so far from where the students got shot in May. When the black car didn't follow, but continued straight ahead, I let out a sigh so audible that the driver turned around and threw me a wary glance. I was safe for the moment. But these guys would be much too cute to have just one car on my trail, I told myself. They'd have a whole fleet of cars, and walkie-talkies, and later there'd be a thrilling climax when they sprayed the taxi with bullets from an angry chopper.

It just about kept my spirits up, mocking my own paranoia. If I turned the whole thing into a joke, it couldn't be happening.

The traffic jam below the Tomang flyover was real enough. '*Aduh!*' my driver grunted. He scowled at me in the mirror as if I were to blame.

At Taman Anggrek shopping mall, I checked my money again in the toilet. Once I'd deducted the cost of an air ticket, it didn't seem so much after all. I decided to top up my funds at an ATM – leaving my credit card freer for Singapore. The square-jawed hero never needed to consider such trivial matters, of course – he always had plenty of cash, even if he never seemed to do a day's work in his life.

I stood in the queue and sweated. The man in front of me turned round and gave me a curious stare. I caught my reflection in the door of the ATM kiosk. Even in the tinted glass my skin seemed to shine. I was so conspicuous. So white. This was how black people must feel, I mused, in the snow-white heart of middle England: not a person, but a skin colour. Visible and vulnerable.

The ATMs lined up in a corridor on the second floor of the mall, separated from the multi-storey car park by a wall of glass doors. Two men loitered by the lift in the car park, looking beefy and mean. The girl inside the kiosk was taking an age. I pushed my nose against the tinted glass and tried to see what she was doing. She seemed baffled by the technology, as if she'd never used the machine in her life; the card slid out and went straight back in and the process began all over again from scratch. The figures in the car park stared over in my direction. They stood closer to each other and lit fresh cigarettes.

'Come on, you stupid cow,' I muttered under my breath. 'How difficult can it be?'

I was under surveillance, I felt sure. These guys were straight out of Tarantino – they even held their cigarettes between thumb and forefinger. At last the little princess in the kiosk had unearthed her buried treasure and she slipped a wad of notes into her handbag, a chi-chi number in shiny black leather and gold. She caught me watching her through the tinted glass and cast me a withering glance as she stepped out of the door. I scooted in, bolting it shut behind me.

With one eye fixed on the car park, I clicked the keys with lightning speed. Soon I had my money, but where had everyone gone in those few short seconds? The corridor was suddenly deserted and I stood alone, except for the hefty figures beside the lift. I pretended to use the machine again while I waited for someone else to appear. Nobody came. For a third time I mimed tapping the keys.

At last, thank God – the lift doors juddered open. The figures tossed their stubs to the floor and lumbered inside.

I shot through the mall and out of the main exit. The air outside the building stank of petrol fumes. I beckoned to the first Blue Bird taxi waiting in line. '*Stasiun kereta api. Gambir.*'

I'd decided to ditch the airport altogether. It meant going along the toll road and the idea just scared me too much. I'd head instead for the railway station at Gambir. I figured I could catch a train to Surabaya and a plane direct from there to Singapore. I could slip out of the country in secret.

I regretted my decision as soon as I hit the station entrance. Gambir was writhing like a disturbed nest of ants.

I seemed to be the only *bule* in the whole building. Perhaps I should have changed my mind and gone back to my original plan, but at least I had to be safe there, amongst all those crowds of people. And my throat was raging for a drink.

God help any poor tourist who tries to negotiate the Javanese rail system. There are trains of all kinds on offer, from luxury expresses which float above the ground, where minions fuss over you like minor royalty, to stinking bone-rattlers where you perch on rock-hard seats surrounded by chickens and goats. Even knowing which ticket to buy is an arcane mystery. Not to worry, I was almost native now, I told myself. I knew what I was doing. I stood at the end of the shortest queue. It stretched to a mere ten people.

I reached the cashier at last. 'Surabaya, please. *Argo Bromo.*' This is the luxury express that zips along the north Java coast.

'Yogyakarta,' she replied, in a curt voice.

'Surabaya.'

'Yogyakarta.' She pointed to a sign above her head. 'Yogyakarta' was written in capital letters, with a host of smaller cities in lower case beneath. She pointed to another queue. The longest queue. 'Surabaya.'

I suddenly had what seemed like a brilliant idea. If I bought a ticket for Yogya with my credit card, I could leave a false trail of Visa transactions behind. They doubtless had the technology to check these things. So I'd throw them a red herring. Meanwhile I'd pay for my real ticket in cash. I grinned a stupid grin, feeling inordinately pleased with myself. OK, so I might not have the square jaw, but did that dumb mass of muscle have my subtle cunning?

'Yogyakarta,' I said, handing over my credit card. She looked at me, confused. 'Yogyakarta, please.'

'But you want Surabaya.'

'I've changed my mind.'

She raised her eyes to the heavens and shook her head. These crazy *bules*!

'Is it the fast train?' I asked, as she pushed the buttons on her keyboard.

'Oh, you want *Mutiara*,' she rasped, with a glare. She pushed the cancel button and started again.

'Yes, *Mutiara*. Please.'

As she struggled with the keyboard and the moments ground by, appalling memories slid back into my mind. Agus, Wawan, the corpse in the morgue. I felt like a fugitive, as if something stood at my shoulder and I could feel its breath on my neck. If I only had a drink, I could banish these awful memories. The hero jutted out his square jaw and taunted me with my inadequacy.

'You don't have money?' she asked, looking at my credit card with obvious annoyance.

'I'm sorry.'

She rummaged under her desk for a machine to process the transaction. She couldn't find one. She asked the cashier next to her, who rummaged under his desk. He couldn't find one. Finally she let out a yell that they could probably hear all the way in Yogyakarta. There was a lot of animated discussion and a great deal more rummaging, until somebody ultimately found one.

'Can I buy another ticket now? Surabaya?'

'You have ticket already. Yogyakarta.'

'I want two tickets,' I whispered. 'One to Yogya and one to Surabaya.' She stabbed her finger silently in the direction of the other queue. 'The computers must all be networked. Why can't I buy one here?'

'*That* is line for Surabaya!' she screeched, finally losing her patience entirely with this exasperating *bule*.

The man behind me leant over and placed his money on the counter. 'Excuse me!' I snapped, turning round and pushing my nose into his face. The cashier asked him where he wanted to go. 'OK, OK,' I said. 'I've got the message. That is line for Surabaya!'

I imagined the square-jawed hero and the permanently smug expression on his face. The bastard could well be smug – he never had to cope with the Indonesian rail system. Did you ever even see him buy a ticket in the movie? No, somehow he was born with the thing in his hand.

I reached the head of the queue. 'Surabaya, please.'

'Yes, *tuan*.'

'*Argo Bromo*.'

'No, *tuan*.'

'I'm sorry?'

'You cannot buy ticket for *Argo Bromo* here.'

By now I was dripping with sweat in this oven of a ticketing area where a thousand human bodies were doing nicely. 'But it says Surabaya up there.'

'But *tuan* want *Argo Bromo*.'

'That's right. The *Argo Bromo* goes to Surabaya.'

'But there is special place to buy ticket for Argo Bromo.' He responded to my glower with a nervous grin. '*Argo Bromo* is very expensive, *tuan*. Executive class. No need to wait in line. There is executive ticket office.'

'But I've already waited in line for half an hour. Can't you issue it here now?'

His eyes grew panicky as he pointed vaguely to his right. 'Special executive ticket office.'

My shoulders slumped and my legs went weak. I suddenly felt defeated, on the point of collapse. 'Where do I go?'

I flailed through an ocean of faces, a drowning man. What the hell was I still doing in Jakarta? Why hadn't I got out in May, like almost everyone else?

But I gained fresh heart when I saw a window with a hand-written sign that read '*Argo Bromo*'. And the face behind the counter seemed quite amiable.

'You must buy ticket in advance, *tuan*.'

'What?'

'At least one day before, yes?'

'I didn't do that last time.'

He eyed me suspiciously. 'You buy ticket on day of travel?'

I paused to think. 'No, I got it through my travel agent.'

'At least one day before, yes?' He told me this with such cheerfulness that I could have garrotted him. Or burst into tears.

'But I have to get to Surabaya today. I have an important meeting tomorrow morning,' I lied in desperation.

'Perhaps I can help you, *tuan*.' He smiled once more and beckoned me to take a seat. He turned to face his keyboard and thrashed out the characters one by one with his index finger. The confident smile of a moment earlier faded. 'Oh, *habis*. Sorry, *tuan*. Full.'

'Full?' The word sank from my mouth into my stomach, like a stone.

'Tomorrow morning, perhaps?'

Most of the westerners who had stayed had a reason to be in Jakarta. A wife, a husband, a lover. Money, perhaps, or ambition. I couldn't begin to explain why I was still there. It wasn't as if I believed in my work – my job was a pointless exercise with the sole rationale of making the rich, both western and Indonesian, feel less morally uncomfortable. And I certainly hadn't stayed for the culture. I couldn't even say I was putting by a nice little nest egg to take back to the UK for my retirement.

I think the simple truth was that staying put had been the easiest option.

I suddenly realized the ticket officer was waiting for me to speak. 'There's not a single seat on the whole train?' I asked.

'Very popular now. After *krismon*. Plane in dollars is too

expensive.' He looked at me. 'You must buy in advance. At least one day before.' He nodded sagely, as if my plight were proof of the wisdom of his words.

But why not stay put in Jakarta? It was the perfect city to surrender all hope. Places like Venice or Prague, with their beauty and nostalgia, might awaken dreams that I didn't want awakened, hopes that might exhaust me. In Jakarta I could get up each day and go through the motions of being alive – take on the form of a real person, if only in silhouette, like a shadow in a *wayang* play. Jakarta demanded nothing from me, which is why it was so perfect. It was the easiest place in the world to pretend to still be alive.

I tried to concentrate on buying my ticket, but I was losing all heart and it didn't seem to matter much any more. 'Can't I buy a ticket anyway? And stand all the way?'

He looked shocked and shook his head. 'It is not allowed!'

'But this is Indonesia. Everything's allowed.'

'It is not safe, *tuan*.'

'I've seen people hanging off the doors of trains like acrobats.'

He stared me in the eye. 'It is the rule.'

I'd given up on my life, like the man in the mental hospital. Even the break-up of my marriage had done nothing to ruffle my complacency. These things happen, I told myself. No big deal.

'OK. How much?'

'I'm sorry, *tuan*?'

'Can't you help me if I help you?' A standard way of initiating a bribe.

He shot upright in his chair and puffed out his chest, proud of his probity. 'No *korupsi* now, mister! Not after *reformasi*.'

When my suitcases lined the hall, I'd asked her one last time. 'You're sure you want me to leave?' She stared down at the dull beige carpet, with the stains of a dozen years. 'I'm sorry, Graham. I'm bored with you.'

I didn't blame her. I was bored with me.

I had one option left in the ticket office. The sob story. 'If I miss this meeting, I'm in big trouble with my boss,' I pleaded. 'Maybe I'll lose my job.' Indonesians are generally softhearted and throwing myself on his mercy seemed my only hope.

He looked at me with genuine pity – he was a nice guy and he really wanted to help me out. 'Maybe there is place on express train.'

'Could you check?'

'Of course, *tuan*,' he said, proudly. He banged away at the keyboard. 'Oh yes, still many seats.'

'When does it leave?'

'One hour again.'

'How long does it take?'

He peered at his computer screen. 'Nineteen hours.'

'But it's called the *express*!'

'Do you want me look at the standard train?'

'No, please. That really won't be necessary.'

'You don't want to buy ticket, *tuan*?'

I imagined nineteen hours in a sweaty box surrounded by chickens and goats. Much worse by far, by Indonesian children.

'I'll go to Yogyakarta instead.' I shook his hand and he shook his head. Why was I going to Yogya if I had a meeting in Surabaya? These crazy *bules*!

So my decoy ticket to Yogya had become my real ticket and my great escape was starting to look like something a cow might dump in the street. But I was too worn out to care and the past was weighing my heart down. There was an airport at Yogyakarta – maybe I could get to Singapore from there.

I took my ticket to the turnstile and presented it to a fat

man with hands like boxing gloves. He stamped a hole in the centre and let me pass into the station.

What little was left of my confidence was crushed completely when I arrived at the top of the stairs. A thousand people, more, spread themselves over chairs, against walls, across the floor. Mine seemed the only white face. Square-jawed hero? I was cracking into pieces inside.

It was another two hours before my train left, so I bought a newspaper and went to sit in a café. The final blow – not a single drop of alcohol in the building. Not even Bir Bintang.

'Hello, Graham.' I held my newspaper close to my face and pretended no one had spoken. The voice repeated itself. 'Hello, Graham.'

I peered over the top of the newsprint to see Santo, his head tossed back, with crazy laughter streaming from his mouth.

17

I lifted my newspaper back into the air and sheltered behind its fortress of black and white columns. The same shrill laugh rang out. Santo's presence hung over me, like a shadow on a wall. I felt compelled to speak.

'I've been told I shouldn't talk to you.'

'Do you always do what you're told?'

The muffled sounds of the café went on around us, in their mundane way. He sat down beside me. 'They can find you whenever they want to, you know. I found you, didn't I?'

He took two cans from his shoulder bag, Coke for himself and Bir Bintang for me.

'Why don't we have a drink together?'

I looked at the can and laid my newspaper on the table. He opened his Coke with a pop. 'Relax, Graham. You look like you just saw a ghost.'

Again the forced laughter. For all his desperate jokiness, its false ring was obvious. 'Hey, Mr England! Whatever happened to the stiff upper lip?'

'You don't mess around with people like these.'

'What – these guys? Tin soldiers!' He snorted and leant his head back, swigging from his can. 'I want to get to know you, Graham. This is the third time we've met and yet I feel we've never talked.'

'Do we have anything to say to each other?'

He held up the can of beer. 'You should pray to God

sometimes. Then you wouldn't be so scared of death.' He was talking brave, but I got the feeling he was just as frightened as me. There was a haunted quality about this intense young man. He kept glancing over his shoulder, like some creature in the jungle that knew it was stalked.

I snatched the can of Bintang from him and ripped it open. 'Hey, chill out!' he breezed, cracking the knuckles of his fingers one by one. 'They won't do anything to you.' He lit a cigarette and blew out the smoke. 'So, what happened last night?'

'You mean you don't know?'

'How should I know?'

'You seem to know everything else.'

'You must learn to trust people, Graham. What's wrong with you today?' He flicked his ash to the floor. 'Hey, I'm just a student, OK? Do you think I'm working for them?'

'I'd be happier if you left. I don't want to be seen talking to you.'

'We've been seen already.'

'Where?'

'I don't know. Somewhere out there, among all the faces. We're being monitored.'

'Do you really think that?'

'There is nowhere to hide,' he announced, with more manic laughter, like a trailer announcing a horror movie. 'Oh, Graham, chill out! You have the best insurance policy in the world. A western passport.'

My third encounter with Santo, and his third personality. Each one had been a performance for my benefit, a scripted role. First he'd served up the slightly loopy music fan, but I think he was too proud of his intelligence and could never quite bear to hide it. When that failed to impress, I'd been treated to his serious side – the austere idealist fighting for humanity. I watched him flick his ash to the floor and fidget on his seat. Santo Mark Three. Perhaps this version was closer to the real thing. This precarious individual staring over the edge of some inner abyss.

I had drained the can of Bintang dry. He reached into his bag and produced a second. 'It's routine stuff, you know. The visit in the night. It used to happen all the time in the days of Soeharto.' He cracked his knuckles again. 'Someone got a bit careless, spoke out against the government. So some bonehead from the army turned up at his door for a chat.'

'This wasn't a chat. It was the third degree.'

'I like that word, don't you? Bonehead. It's *lucu*.'

'Have you been drinking?'

'That's your department, Graham,' he said, with a smirk, as the smoke from his cigarette swirled around my face. 'Oh, come on, so they spelt things out in a little more detail than usual because you're a white guy. They wanted to make sure the message got through.'

'Oh, it got through all right. Loud and clear.'

'Well, everybody's happy, then.' He started to calm down a little and his speech grew less frenetic. 'It's no big deal, Graham. In my village there was a *dalang*. Have you heard of the *dalang*, the guy who works the shadow puppets in *wayang* theatre?' I nodded. 'His performances were getting too political. You know, he'd slip in these little comments about the government? So one night these –' He paused and laughed. 'These boneheads from the military came to his house. All very civilized, a nice quiet chat over *kue* and tea. The politics stopped and no one got hurt.'

'That's very reassuring.'

'That's how we do things in Java. We don't like conflict.'

'I've noticed.'

'You really are so superficial sometimes. Westerners, I mean. You see a few riots on CNN and you think we're all deranged here. You know zilch about my culture, Graham. Zilch.' He toyed with his cigarette pack, slipping it in and

202

out of the Cellophane wrapping. 'Our problem isn't some kind of bloodlust. Just the opposite. We don't know how to manage conflict, that's our problem.'

I shuffled on my seat. I could feel myself, against my will, getting dragged into this conversation.

'It's my culture, Graham. Everyone must agree all the time.' He cracked his knuckles. 'Different thoughts are dangerous. So if we have them, we must be persuaded to think the same as everyone else.'

'And what if someone refuses to think the same?'

He shook his head and smiled. 'It doesn't happen. This isn't like the west. Everyone wants to think the same.' He stubbed out his cigarette. 'Collectivism. We even have a phrase for it. *Gotong royong*. It might work OK for a village, but not for a nation state.'

He reached down to pick up my backpack, to weigh how heavy it was. 'So where you heading?' I didn't reply. 'You still don't trust me? Poor Mr England, so stressed out today. And I always thought you western guys were such big, brave heroes.'

'You watch too many movies.'

He shrieked with laughter. 'I like you, Graham. You're cool.'

'So – are you going to leave now, please?'

He continued to crack his knuckles. The sound put my teeth on edge.

'You want to hear something scary, Graham? Western people remain a mystery to me. Even after living in Oz, I don't get you guys at all.'

I glanced up at the TV screen in the corner. Shots of the latest disturbances, riots in Kalimantan. This country was falling apart at the seams. 'What don't you get?'

'You make fun of your leaders and don't show them respect. I mean, you guys are cruel with your satire. We couldn't do that here. Not only because we'd be scared to.

It would just *feel* wrong inside.' He took a fresh cigarette from his pack and placed it, unlit, in his mouth. 'Yet you're terrified of something as natural as death. Can I ask you something, Graham? Do you have a God?'

'What do you think?'

'In Australia, someone died in the house right next to mine. A young guy, about my age. Went through the windscreen in a car crash – the sort of crazy thing that might happen to anyone. Now in Indonesia all the neighbours would gather around to show their respect. I'm not kidding – the whole neighbourhood would be there. But in Sydney – wow, it was just so weird! Everyone pretended it was like any other day. And the family of the dead guy, they hid themselves away somewhere. You know, as if it was their fault? As if they were ashamed because they were the ones who brought death to the street.'

'Why did they kill your friend?'

'You mean Wawan?' I nodded. 'To frighten you, I guess.'

I blanched. 'That can't be the only reason, surely?'

'He spoke up for *reformasi*. But he was nowhere near smart enough. Wawan didn't know how to play the game.'

'I thought *reformasi* was official now. I thought everyone spoke up for it.'

He finally struck a match and lit the cigarette. 'Oh, they say this, of course, every one of them. But lots of people at the top don't want *reformasi*. They're scared of what they've done in the past and what might happen if the people get justice. Some of them are just greedy. They still want more. And maybe a few of them really believe. I mean, believe inside their hearts. That if there's *reformasi*, Indonesia will be broken.'

'Believe it enough to kill someone?'

A blast of sour laughter shook his whole body. 'You think they killed just one? Hundreds, Graham. In Aceh, in Timor. I've lost so many colleagues. A close friend tortured to death. Here, in Jakarta. Then the body disappeared. We couldn't even bury him and give his family a decent funeral.'

I suddenly remembered the bloodshot eyes of my visitor the previous night. 'Look, Santo. I don't think it's good for either of us if we're seen talking together.'

He smiled indulgently. 'Oh, Graham! What do you think will happen? They're not going to kill you, are they? If they wanted to kill you, believe me, you'd be dead by now. Last night, in your house. It would have been so easy. They kill you, smash up your house, steal a few things. Everyone would think it was burglars. They give the *satpam* some money to make up a story, they give the police some money to find evidence.' He placed his hand on my shoulder, very lightly. 'Nothing's going to happen to you.'

The second can of Bintang was drained of liquid. I squeezed it flat and laid it out on the table.

'You don't believe me?' He shot up from his seat. 'OK, let's go prove it! Come on, let's take a walk around the station.'

'What?'

'You know, *jalan jalan.*'

'You're crazy, Santo.'

'Do we hide away in this corner because the bad guys are out there? They can come for us in here, you know. If they want to kill us, they can kill us. As simple as that – whenever they want to.' The neurotic edge had vanished from his voice, and instead there was a steely resolve. 'We must show them they don't scare us.'

'I thought that was the whole idea. I thought they meant to scare us.'

'OK, Graham, it's up to you.' He shrugged his shoulders. 'But I haven't got any more beer. If you want some more, we have to go out and get it.'

'Nowhere in the station sells it.'

'We can get it here, if we know where to go.' He seemed

quite miffed when I declined his offer and stayed put in my seat. 'What's the matter?' he asked. 'Are you scared you're going to die?'

'Aren't you?'

'We belong to Allah. He can take us whenever he chooses.'

I didn't quite believe this show of nonchalance. Oh, I believed he was sincere in his religious beliefs. I'd known enough devout Indonesians to suspend my western cynicism on that score. But there was something else I couldn't quite place. He was scared for some reason, and I could sense it.

'Poor Graham,' he said. 'You don't know how to behave in a country where you must stay silent. How to obey with your face but fight in your heart.'

'No. Maybe I don't.'

'I guess we have to be brave, too. Indonesians, I mean. We must say to ourselves, it is God's will if I die today.'

'God's will,' I repeated, in a bitter echo. I picked up an empty beer can and crushed it even flatter.

'One thing I noticed about the west. Everyone is so protected there. Here, in Indonesia, life is cheap.' I remembered Agus, and the smell of the canvas of his *becak* as it bumped down the road. 'I'm not sure where I picked up that phrase,' he pondered to himself. 'From some B-movie, I guess.'

'Why are these people interested in you, Santo?'

He appeared not to have heard my question, though I felt pretty sure he had.

'We must play a game here,' he said. 'We must challenge them softly. It's like the guy in the circus who has to walk the rope.' He lit another cigarette. 'We must show respect for everyone, even the shadows who are watching us now. Because some of these shadows are our friends. They must play the game as well. They must show one feeling on the face, but keep a different one locked in the heart.'

206

'Why are they interested in you?' I repeated, more forcefully.

'I'm a student.'

'There are thousands of students. What makes you so special?'

He looked rather shifty and gave a little laugh. 'So you still don't trust me? Yes, who knows? Maybe I'm one of the bad guys after all. I want to lure you downstairs so you're an easy target for their guns. Or I'm a secret agent and in my pocket I have poison to slip in your Bintang.' The eyes looked me up and down with cool disdain. 'Life isn't so dramatic, Graham. *You* watch too many movies.'

'Then why are you so edgy?'

'Edgy?'

'You're scared, Santo. I can see it.'

He ignored me and took hold of my arm. 'What's the problem, Mr England? Can't I buy you a beer? Even if I'm one of the bad guys?'

I stood at the top of the stairs and felt thousands of pairs of eyes pore into me. Yet I had a fresh spring in my step. The prospect of alcohol had given my flagging spirits a miraculous lift.

'I guess you don't get many too white guys in Gambir?' I asked.

'Only backpackers.' He patted my beer gut. 'Not middle-aged business types like you.'

Santo seemed much jollier, too – delighted with the attention we attracted. Not for the snob value of being seen out promenading with a *bule*; he was much too cute for that. It amused him, perhaps, to watch his people gape in awe at this overweight white vision. I think it consolidated a sense of his own superiority.

As we made our way down the concrete stairway, he puffed on his cigarette, dramatically, like an actor. 'We walk around Gambir and we know they are watching us. Our shadows. We wonder who they are and where they are. But they're wondering, too. They're wondering what we're talking about. We have our secrets as well. And our secrets bother them.'

'Wait here, Graham.' He walked over to a youth selling cigarettes from a box on a string around his neck, the kind usherettes carry in cinemas. After a few furtive whispers, I was beckoned over. 'Would you like beer or something stronger?'

'What else is there?'

'Have you ever tried *arak*?'

'Once. And I lived to tell the tale.'

'Would you like some?'

'I don't think I can cope with it neat right now.'

'Neat?'

A moment of delight – I'd found another hole in his English. I loved it when this happened. He always looked quickly away, as if he were terribly bored. But he could never quite hide how much it bugged him.

'Yes, neat. Without any mixer,' I explained, patiently.

'I have mixer,' he snapped. He pointed to his bag. 'What do you want? Coke? Sprite?'

'We don't have any glasses.'

'No problem.' He raised his eyebrows. 'Well?'

'OK, why not?'

I went for my wallet, but he brushed it aside with his hand. 'I don't want any money from you, Graham. I don't want anything from you at all.'

He slipped a note into the boy's cupped palm. The fist tightened immediately and the boy laid his box by Santo's feet before scampering away. 'What do you think, Graham?' Santo joked, as he squatted on the floor and examined its contents. 'Where are the bad guys? How about him, maybe? He looks a mean dude to me.'

'I don't think this is funny, Santo.'

He shook with woozy laughter. 'No? I think it's hilarious.' He opened his packet and offered me a cigarette. 'So, do you trust me yet? Am I one of the good guys?'

'I don't smoke.'

'That's right.' He removed a Lucky Strike from the pack. 'Do you mind?'

'Why ask me now? You never asked me before.'

He lit his cigarette, got to his feet and leant on my shoulder. 'This is difficult for everyone, Graham. I don't know who the good guys are any more than you do. The history of my country happens in whispers. Even I'm not sure which way someone will jump in the end.'

'Are you trying to tell me you don't know what's going on?'

'I haven't a clue.' He giggled. 'I'm not proud to say this, Graham, because I'm speaking about my own people. But Javanese people are the best liars in the world.'

The boy returned and picked up his box of snacks and cigarettes. Santo edged up close to him and a bottle of colourless liquid changed hands, followed by a plastic cup in shocking pink. Santo crouched down to face the wall, opened the bottle with a clandestine twist, ran a little *arak* into the cup and topped it up with Coke.

'We must do this discreetly. Drinking alcohol is not allowed in here.' He slipped me the cup. Such a discreet colour.

I took a quick slug of the purple-black liquid. Even the cloying sweetness of the Coke couldn't hide the force of the *arak* as it hit the back of my throat. It tasted like shit. But for me, right then, it could have been champagne.

'That's Javanese people,' Santo explained, as we started to walk. 'Nobody says what he feels in his heart. He says what he thinks you want to hear.'

'It makes for a pleasant society.'

'But sometimes we need to be honest, Graham. About important things.'

I'd drained the pink cup dry and stared at the stain left behind by the Coke. I glanced up and caught him watching me, with something horribly close to pity in his eyes. Even so, I didn't get a very strong sense of disapproval. I don't think he cared enough for that.

In any case, he was now consumed by a more ponderous mood. 'The Dutch came here and colonized us, so we had to be silent and smile. Then the Japanese came, and the same things happened. And then, even when we got independence, we found we weren't free. Our own government this time.'

We had finished our grand tour of the lower floor sights: a prayer room and some stinking toilets. 'Shall we go back upstairs?' I suggested, keen to get back to the café now I had my booze.

But at the top of the stairs, Santo veered off in the opposite direction. He perched on a ledge of concrete overlooking the taxi rank. The station felt cooler here, open to the outside world, and much less claustrophobic. The oily smell of petrol fumes drifted up from below and made my head ache.

'Are there things you can't tell your own people, Graham? Other westerners, I mean?' He poured a second *arak* and Coke in a matter-of-fact way, too wrapped up in his thoughts by now for exaggerated shows of secrecy. 'I have a feeling inside me which I never dare speak to my own people. I can only say it to you, because you're a *bule*.'

As I listened to his words, my head began to spin. The *arak* was taking effect. But the feeling was nasty and harsh. Not at all soft-focus.

'Sometimes I wonder if my culture is wrong. Sometimes I wonder if the reason we've never had freedom is because we don't demand it.' All his earlier mania had gone. He was

210

grim and sincere. 'Freedom lies in our minds, Graham. And it's so deep in my culture to kneel before the big man and smile. How can we ever be free if we're not brave enough to be honest?'

'Don't you think *bules* tell lies?'

'You don't have the eyes for it.' He shook his head sadly. 'I wish my people were the same as you. Maybe next year, if we have elections.'

'Who were the men who came to my house last night?'

'I don't know. Some branch of the military, I guess.'

'Why are they interested in me?'

'I don't know.'

'Why did Suprianto tell me the dead man was Doctor White? Why involve me at all?'

'I don't know, Graham.'

'Bullshit! You're the same as everyone else, Santo. That's what I get from the lot of you. "I don't know." Everyone in this country's full of that crap.'

'And if I do know, why should I tell you? Why should I trust you? What have you been saying to Suprianto? What have you been telling the military?'

'Why does everyone seem to think I've got this mysterious information? I don't know anything, Santo. It's like there's fragments of glass all over the floor and none of them fit together.'

He roared with laughter. 'Welcome to Indonesia, Graham.' With chilling speed, he cut his laughter short. 'I can tell you what I think if you like. Then it's up to you whether you believe me.'

'So?'

'I think Doctor White was getting jittery about *reformasi*.'

'What do you mean?'

'Maybe the people he's buying off won't be so important in the future. Maybe they'll be replaced by honest people. People he can't buy off.' He paused to peer into my eyes – to see if I believed him, I think. 'So he decided it was time to arrange his own death. An official death, with all the correct paperwork. That's where you came in. You provided the evidence.'

'Who gives a shit about evidence here?'

'That's just where you're wrong, Graham. In a country where no one trusts people, bits of paper become very important. Because bits of paper don't tell lies.' He lit another cigarette and sucked the smoke deep into his lungs. 'So Doctor White is dead and the case is closed. And Graham Young, who tracks down corruption for an NGO, makes the perfect witness.'

'But why would these people protect Doctor White? He's butchering their own children.'

He snorted, incredulously. 'Dollars, Graham. Dollars! What else? What else matters in this godless world?' He stared into my face. 'I don't drive a flashy car like *Pak* Suprianto.'

My hands started shaking. 'Is there any more *arak*, please?'

'Indonesia is a weird place, right?' he asked, spotting my tremble. He took the cup from my hands and mixed another *arak* and Coke. 'Good guys, bad guys, all mixed up. And no one's sure which way to jump.'

I snatched the cup from him. 'We spend all our time trying to piece the fragments together,' I muttered to myself. 'There's a picture in them somewhere, if only we can find it.' I knocked back the *arak*. 'Only there never was a picture in the first place. We just imagine it's there.'

'Sometimes I hate the west, Graham. But if I'm honest, I love it, too. It's like a beautiful woman dancing in front of me and she calls me to join in her dance. Oh yes, she's beautiful, but her heart is wicked.' He chewed moodily on his cigarette. 'My people don't think enough. Ask them what they want. *Reformasi*. It's so easy to say. But it's only a word. We have no ideas, we only copy what you do in the west.'

I felt uneasily close to him now, as the breeze drifted in from the world outside and stroked us both. We felt almost like brothers. Maybe the whole thing was calculated and he'd worked for this moment ever since he arrived. But no, I think I believed him. I believed he was being sincere at last.

'I watched you in Australia,' he spat. 'Westerners. You don't deserve your freedom. It's something precious and you tread it in the mud. I'm afraid this will be my people, if they get *reformasi*. They will also forget their God.'

He balanced the bottle of *arak* on the concrete ledge. As it rested there, I could make out I'd drunk halfway down the faded label. 'So where's your God, Graham? In that bottle?'

A new tone entered his voice, holy and joyless. 'Oh, you're good at talking in the west. Good at telling us what is right for Indonesia. Like the IMF. They act like they're God, the IMF, telling us what to do. Have you seen the director, a German guy? He's always coming here, giving us lectures, like naughty children who need to be smacked.' He wiped the spittle from his lips with the back of his hand. 'But my people have never built gas chambers. Fifty years ago, that's all. And now they come here and lecture us about democracy.' He held the bottle up to the light. 'The wonderful west.'

Lines creased his forehead and scraped beneath his eyes. The stigmata of a beaten young man. Within those eyes, I imagined, I saw the beginning of tears.

'I want to love my country, Graham. But I can't any more.'

He tossed me what was left of the bottle of *arak*. 'Maybe I've stopped believing in *reformasi*. Maybe I don't think the west has anything to offer. There's just my God now. I believe in my God, that's all.'

Two policemen appeared at the top of the staircase,

hastening our way. The younger of the officers broke into a trot.

Santo bolted to his feet, leapt on the ledge and bounded to the concrete below. People scattered in all directions through the muddle of taxis and cars. He hit the ground hard and struggled to drag himself away. His ankle looked broken.

The officer raised his gun and fired three shots. I watched each bullet strike Santo in the back. He slumped to the ground. Blood seeped into his T-shirt and stained it violent red. His body twitched instinctively, like a fish with a hook in its throat, or a slaughtered animal hung up to bleed dry. Seconds later, the convulsions ceased and he lay there, quite still.

18

Bodies hurtled down the concrete flight of steps, screaming. I just hoped the police couldn't get a clear shot at me among this tangle of skin. But I was taller than everyone else and stood out above the crowd. A simple target for a bullet in the back of the head.

A woman stumbled, feet lost their grip, and it seemed all the bodies would crumple in a heap and crush each other to death. But hands stretched out and grabbed the fallen, yanking them upright again. By some miracle, the death crush never came.

Behind me, the screams grew more frenzied. The flood of human bodies swelled forward, irresistible. I'd forgotten my silly mind games about being a hero. I was an animal now, gripped by mindless panic, scrambling to get out alive.

No time to take stock at the foot of the stairs, as the crowd swept me on towards the turnstile. The man with big hands was trying in vain to calm people down and squeeze them through in orderly fashion. Two new policemen arrived on the scene. They pushed the man with big hands to one side and took control.

I rode the sea of bodies as it surged towards them. Like driftwood in a storm, tossed this way and that, powerless to resist. And all the time, somewhere behind me, the military police. Guns in hand. I tried to make myself invisible by squeezing my head into the pit of my chest. But I could never be invisible. Not with this luminous skin. One of the officers at the turnstile had already spotted me. He prodded his partner and pointed a finger in my direction.

Arms and legs lurched through the turnstile ahead of me. My time came. I heard the creak of the machinery, I felt the metal against my thigh and I was through. An arm's length from the police. I kept my eyes fixed on the floor and waited for the hand on my shoulder. Someone spoke, but I couldn't make out what he said above the screams of the crowd. I was careful not to look up and meet his eye.

The hand on my shoulder never came.

A moment later, I was free. On the other side of the turnstile with space ahead of me. It loomed above me and around me, this space, like an empty cathedral. No time to let go and sigh, I had to keep moving. If I turned to the left, I might find a taxi to get me away from Gambir. But that would take me straight past Santo's bloodstained body. I couldn't face it and turned to the right instead.

A little group of people had sought refuge in a gap between a food stall and the station wall. '*Hati-hati*, mister,' a man in a McDonald's baseball cap yelled out from behind the stall. '*Ada polisi*. With gun, mister.' He held out two fingers and mimed the action of firing a pistol.

A baby was screaming and children sobbed. A mother cowered in the shadows behind the stall, her baby in her arms, while her two young children clung miserably to the folds of her dress. An elderly woman with skin etched by years in the sun turned her face to a darkening sky. Huddled beside her, a yuppie in a suit and tie, his body crouched over, hissing into his mobile. If I joined this group, I could put their lives at risk. But they might offer me some kind of insurance. I might not get shot in front of so many witnesses.

Only a clutch of buses remained in the station entrance – I guessed the other drivers had panicked and fled. The few that remained were besieged with human bodies, like ants besetting scraps of food. A new bus pulled in, empty, and the man in the baseball cap rushed out, frantically waving to get the driver's attention. The bus headed our way and the man leapt on board. A moment later, the little group behind the stall scurried out from the shadows to join him on the bus. I looked around, alone. No police in sight.

I decided to latch on to this group. But my moment's hesitation had cost me dearly, for the bus was already overwhelmed by a swarm of fresh bodies. Voices yelled out in Indonesian, too fast and frantic for me to understand. '*Ada anak! Ada anak!*' I heard someone scream, and somehow the mass of bodies parted to let on two families with small children. The man in the cap did his best to keep the gap open for an old man with a walking stick, but the pathway vanished as people surged back and scrapped in a free-for-all for a place on the bus. Survival of the fittest, the law of the jungle.

The driver, his face bloodless with fear, just wanted to get the hell out of there. He revved the engine and inched the bus forward. 'Mister, mister!' the man in the baseball cap called out. He clung to the edge of the open door with the fingers of one hand and held out the other for me to take. I grabbed his fingers and tried to scramble on board as the bus pulled away. The sudden lurch made me lose my grip and I almost fell, but he held on tight and I was left hanging, flapping like a flag in the wind. Some passengers tugged at my T-shirt and hauled me inside.

Sweat poured down my back as I tried to squeeze further inside the bus. At last I felt sure I couldn't be targeted, swallowed by this mound of hot bodies. I peeped through the forest of arms to note that a couple of new police had arrived on the scene. I couldn't quite shake off the feeling that they were hunting for me.

The foot stayed on the accelerator as we hit a snarl of bad-tempered buses in a fight to be first out of the station.

I'd seen this kind of madness often enough in Jakarta, where no one would give an inch until eventually nothing could move, in any direction. Our driver thrust his face out of the window and hurled a string of abuse at a rival who had stolen that vital two inches ahead of us.

By now every single bus driver had his hand jammed on the horn and his foot on the accelerator. The stench of petrol was so overwhelming that I needed to concentrate just to stop myself being sick. Children wept, a baby wailed. One man spoke a prayer aloud. The bus crawled forward a few more precious feet.

'The police go crazy, mister,' the man in the baseball cap shouted across to me. 'Shoot out, with pistol.'

'Yes, crazy.'

'Why, mister? Why they must always kill people?'

'You tell me.'

'*Gila!*' He shook his head. A few of the braver passengers made noises of agreement – the whole thing was crazy – while the rest looked away and pretended that no one had spoken.

All hell was suddenly let loose as our driver and a rival traded insults. They squared up to each other behind their open windows. They talked a good fight, like boxers at the weigh-in, and a real fight looked on the cards as they worked themselves into a frenzy. One tense stand-off later, our driver proved the victor in this battle of nerves and we crept ever closer to the main road.

'Where are you going, mister?' the man in the cap asked.

'I don't really know.'

'Me also, I don't know. New York, maybe.' He laughed. 'More safer, yes?'

At last the driver intruded the nose of our vehicle into the long line of traffic on the main road. The whole bus heaved a sigh of relief and a woman burst into tears. The man in prayer seemed to be thanking God for deliverance, while even the baby's wail took on a softer note. Gambir could no longer be seen and the relief was palpable.

But we weren't travelling very fast or very far, for this was central Jakarta in the middle of the day, and the bus jolted down the road in staccato fashion. When we built up a little speed, a breeze blew in through the window and splashed my brow. But it was gone as soon as it came and left me feeling even more stifled. Sweat streamed into my eyes and made them sting.

A fresh mood had swept over the bus and everyone seemed desperate to speak. The noise was suddenly deafening. Colour flooded back into the driver's cheeks and he became almost genial. But by now I was sweating so badly that I couldn't relax into the new mood – I didn't have time. If I didn't get off the bus right away, I knew I'd pass out. I looked through the window to try to see where we were. Still walking distance from Gambir, probably, but I couldn't bear the heat any longer. I banged on the roof of the bus with the side of my fist.

'You go, mister?' the man in the baseball cap asked, with a look of regret. I think he'd rather enjoyed taking care of me. '*Hati-hati*,' he shouted, as I reeled off the bus. A few of the other passengers echoed his advice.

My luck was in – an empty taxi followed straight behind. It wasn't a Blue Bird, but I was too desperate to care. I flagged the driver down.

'Soekarno-Hatta,' I gasped, flinging myself into the back seat.

The driver leant his arm on the back of his seat and turned casually around. He sat there and sized me up with relish. 'Long way, mister. *Jauh*.' He stretched the diphthong in the Indonesian word to underline its meaning. I knew a demand for a ridiculous fare would follow. I wouldn't even bother asking him to use the meter – it would be *rusak*.

'How much?'

'*Seratus ribu, tuan.* One hundred thousand.' The English was suddenly perfect. He dangled his arm across the steering wheel and slithered into a smile. The bastard could smell my panic.

'You must be joking!'

'One hundred thousand.'

Stories went the rounds that some taxi drivers charged a thousand US dollars to take terrified *bules* to the airport in May. Looking at this toad and the smirk on his face, I could believe it.

Then I asked myself if any of this mattered. I'd just watched someone die.

'OK, a hundred. Just go! *Cepat!*'

I checked that the window was closed and the door was locked. My shirt, awash with sweat, clung to the skin of my back with the feel of raw liver. I leant forward in my seat. 'Don't you have AC? *Pakai AC?*'

'*Rusak*, mister.'

Oh, who the fuck cared? I was safe, that was what mattered, with a sauna thrown in at no extra cost. I lay back in my seat with a sigh. For a few blissful moments I sat there, floating on my solitude. All I could hear were the crackles of the taxi radio and the muted sounds of the city through the tinted glass.

My respite was short lived. As if my mind had grown addicted to anxiety and could no longer rest at peace, it conjured up a new set of nightmares. I rapidly took stock. I still had my passport, my wallet. They could easily have been lifted during the chaos. On my trawl through my pockets, I even found the *arak*, just over a third of a bottle. I twisted it open and gulped down a mouthful, spluttering aloud. If only I could find that soft-focus feeling.

We reached the bleak little kiosks at the start of the toll road and the driver turned around and asked for the toll fee. Once we'd swapped the bustling streets for a bare expanse of concrete, I felt safe to open the window and enjoy the blast of air. Motoring along the toll road, weaving in and out of traffic, at last I got some kind of feeling I was heading for freedom. The force of the wind seemed to blow through my mind, scattering my fears like autumn leaves, until only stark winter trees remained. Suddenly everything seemed straightforward and I couldn't understand why I'd made it all so complicated. Only one course of action made any kind of sense – buy a ticket to any city on the globe and get out of Indonesia.

I looked out of the window and got a flashback of Santo's body on the concrete. Face turned towards me, mouth gaping open. I saw the pattern of his blood as it seeped into his T-shirt: red and white, like the Indonesian flag. I hadn't liked him very much, I guess – he was cocksure and mercurial and I never quite managed to trust him. But he'd been smart and provocative, and now he was dead. There'd be a column in the paper tomorrow: a report of a drug dealer shot dead while resisting arrest. Or maybe there'd be nothing at all, even in this age of *reformasi*. I heard his voice once again in my mind, as clear as if he sat beside me in the car. 'So, you still don't trust me, Graham? Yes, who knows, maybe I'm one of the bad guys.'

I was jolted from these memories when a black car trailing behind us slammed on its horn. Two slabs of muscle with animal snouts sat grim-faced in the front. Maybe they had orders to take me out and I would die here, alone, on this anonymous stretch of concrete. 'They would have done it last night,' I said to myself, recalling Santo's words. It gave me little consolation. Not even a neat slug of *arak* had much effect. I barely spluttered as it hit my throat.

Still the black car stayed close, almost kissing our bumper. The figures in the front didn't move, expressionless faces and hooded eyes, like undertakers. We reached the point where the toll road splits – fork left for the airport, straight

221

ahead for Ancol theme park. My taxi indicated left. The black car sped straight on. I laughed out loud, with a manic ring, and took another swig of *arak*. The driver watched me through his mirror. A few minutes later, I was hurrying through the doors at Soekarno-Hatta.

For once the girl in the ticket office looked just like they do in the ads, with her serene smile and her sparkling eyes. 'Yes, can I help you?' The voice was soothing and seductive: it belonged in some dark, soft, secluded place, not in an airport. I longed to run my fingers through her hair. I felt unbearably lonely.

I told her where I wanted to go. Her fingers skipped with accuracy over her keyboard and the lilting voice changed to tones of dull efficiency. 'I'm terribly sorry, sir, but our flights to Singapore are fully booked. Would you care to go on standby?'

'Where else is there?' I blabbered. I told myself to calm down or I'd arouse suspicion. I tried to cover my tracks. 'I'm only free for a few days,' I said. 'I don't want to waste time. Where else can I go?'

'We have a flight to Bangkok at seventeen twenty.'

'Bangkok's fine.'

She didn't seem fazed by my rapid change of mind. 'Will that be one way, sir?' I nodded. 'A return is almost the same price. You can always buy an open return if you're not sure when you'll come back.'

I gazed at her neck as she stroked the computer keys. How long it had been since I had felt the need for a woman. I wanted to talk to her for longer, I wanted to flirt. But her face had hardened and she suddenly looked rather severe. I could have begged her to soften up again.

'A return, then,' was all I eventually said.

This seemed too easy. It was like being back in the west. Two minutes later, I was checking the details on the ticket in my hand.

Check-in at Soekarno-Hatta gives a totally false impression of Jakarta city. It doesn't have the chaos or the dirt. I might have been taking a plane from a wealthy provincial capital in Europe, a city like Zurich or Milan. I became aware that I was walking faster than everyone else, even the other *bules*, and told myself to calm down. Life was normal here. Today was a day like any other. And it would all be the same tomorrow, because airports never change. People come and go, planes take off and land, yet airports exist in a zone outside time, rootless and static, too unruffled to be real.

I stared up at the TV screens. The flight to Bangkok was already checking in. Soon I'd be on the other side of immigration.

Four people queued ahead of me at the check-in desk. I tried not to fidget as I watched tourists struggle with wayward trolleys across the gleaming floor. So much of this business had been spent waiting. For the police to arrive, for Suprianto to answer my questions. And every time I waited, having to struggle to conquer my restless heart inside. Perhaps this was what being a hero was really about. Not getting a gun and mowing down the bad guys, but forcing the heart to be calm when it was riddled with fears, finding the courage to stand still when every fibre in your body longed badly to flee.

And now yet more waiting. Three people still ahead of me.

It was a showcase for Indonesia, Soekarno-Hatta, proof to all the world that Jakarta was every bit as chic and cosmopolitan as Singapore. Even the Indonesians here had the air of westerners. Taking an international flight was an everyday thing, so they had that slightly bored quality about them as they went about their business. They draped themselves over chairs, or fussed over their luggage, or held tête-à-têtes on their handphones. The only difference between the Indonesians and the *bules* in this affluent world seemed to be that the former dressed with more style. Nobody dresses down in Java. Not a single pair of shorts or back-to-front baseball cap.

How normal it seemed. How calm. And how hard to believe that Gambir had happened an hour ago.

Two people still ahead of me.

Yes, check-in at Soekarno-Hatta was a world of elegance and privilege, a million miles from downtown Jakarta. How different from arrivals. I remembered landing in Jakarta, my first trip out of Europe. Stepping naïvely through the airport doors, to be assailed by dubious taxi drivers and hotel couriers and money changers and all the other sharks who preyed on virginal tourists. I'd wanted to turn around and go straight back home.

The girl at the check-in desk gave me her regulation smile. A yellow boarding card, Gate D8, a window seat, 32F. I made the small walk to the counter to pay fiscal, an airport tax which residents are charged each time they leave the country. One last spell of waiting. The woman ahead of me was twenty thousand *rupiah* short. She refused to believe it. It was counted out in front of her. She still refused to believe it. It was counted out again. Finally she counted it herself with mind-numbing slowness before she conceded and handed over the extra banknote.

Someone tapped me on the shoulder. I turned round to see two men in dark-blue jackets. Immaculately turned out, like high-class waiters.

'We have car, sir.'

'I'm sorry?'

He opened his jacket just enough for me to spot the handle of a gun.

19

If I ran or shouted for help, it seemed unlikely they'd stuff a bullet in me. The airport was too busy, with too many *bules* milling around – surely they wouldn't kill me in front of them all? But I was dealing with basic machines, programmed to follow orders and prod a gun in my back. If I forced them to make a decision, perhaps these machines would malfunction. Perhaps the circuiting would go haywire and they'd start blasting out.

I'd found an excuse for doing nothing. It seemed to be my forte. But for God's sake, I told myself, you have to do something – and do it damn quick. The more detached I became from the other *bules*, the greater the danger I was in. They frog-marched me to the exit, where one of them was whispering furtively to a security guard. Money changed hands and a deal was struck.

I was escorted through glass doors to the outside world, where nearly every face was Indonesian. I still had a chance to get out of this if I made a dash for the taxis or shouted for help. I did nothing. Numb inside, unable to move, a robot or a zombie. Under a spell, as if the stride of their footsteps beat out some kind of magic, a hypnotic cadence that made my mind blank.

They snaked their way through a labyrinth of motorcars and led me to a black saloon. There was no one in sight now to summon for help, *bule* or local. One of the hands held the rear door open, gesturing that I should enter.

I stared silently into their eyes in the futile hope that they might let me go. Nothing came back. Negotiation was out of the question. If I stepped inside the black saloon, I might never come out alive.

The door of the car behind us swung open. Suprianto stepped out.

They clearly recognized him, but seemed surprised to see him there. He gave a perfunctory nod and held out his hand. The three of them huddled together a short distance away, speaking in whispers, although no one was around to hear them except me, and I couldn't have understood their Javanese. I watched the detective's hands as they fluttered – Suprianto was nervous. Normally they were firm and still, like tree roots, but today they were a flux of tiny movements. The two men towered beside him, inanimate objects, like chunks of black rock jutting out of the earth.

Eventually Suprianto spoke. 'Get in the car, Mr Young.'

'What's going to happen to me?'

'Don't ask questions. Always you ask questions. I'm trying to help you.'

Our eyes met, and for the first time neither of us tried to conceal our true feelings. In my face, I imagined, he saw a mix of contempt and disappointment. In his eyes, I thought, I saw guilt.

'Why did you not leave Indonesia like I told you?'

'Told me?'

'At the zoo.'

'How was I supposed to know what you meant?'

One of the figures in dark blue seemed to decide we had said quite enough. He shoved me in the direction of the car.

'We must be silent now,' Suprianto advised. 'Perhaps they do not trust me if we speak. I am on your side.'

Inside the car smelt heady with cigarettes. Suprianto sat beside me on the rear seat and took a handkerchief from his pocket. He folded it several times, into a thin, white strip of cloth. 'You must wear this, Mr Young.' He placed the blindfold around my eyes and secured it at the back. 'It is better that we do not speak again. They don't know English and perhaps they are suspicious.'

I wondered if this was the end, a bullet and oblivion. I heard a click. The key turned in the ignition and the engine ran. I caught a whiff of petrol, but it was instantly gone, as the motor ticked over and we pulled away.

Cradled in the soft seat, rocked by the purr of the engine, I felt as if my body had ceased to exist. Then my heart began to pound in my chest and the thumping in my ears made them fit to burst. I was choking, gasping for air. I felt a hand squeeze my shoulder, gently, like a lover's touch. The hand patted my back with the same soft concern. I spluttered and coughed and gulped in mouthfuls of air. I could breathe again at last.

I had to keep myself active, to block out the panic. I had to occupy my mind. So I began to imagine the progress of our vehicle, as if I had eyes. This seemed quite impossible at first. I was a blind man in my new universe and there was nothing in the darkness for my senses to grasp. Just a single sound – the drone of the engine. Two musty smells – tobacco and leather.

Adrift in my darkness, I turned to the only thing I had left: my sense of touch. The leather seat beneath me felt cool and smooth, like snakeskin. Then I ran my fingers along my denim jeans – much more textured, with a gratifying coarseness. My cotton T-shirt, soaked in sweat, was less pleasurable to my fingers. It felt heavy, like a muggy afternoon.

I was learning to read my new world, with the helplessness of a baby. Even if I had no eyes, I could bring this world to life.

And then, in the solitude of my dark cave, an inspirational

moment. Simple and unspoiled, like fresh air, or sunlight. A match scratched the side of a box and the whiff of fresh tobacco filled the air. A smell that plunged into my lungs, blew open my brain, kicked it alive.

We were travelling along the toll road, I knew for sure, because our progress was so smooth and we never changed speed. Suddenly a fresh sound trespassed on my benighted world. A series of taps I couldn't place at first, which didn't seem to make sense, until I recognized rain. Moments later, the heavens had opened and the noise was a thunderous crash that seemed to block out every other sound. But no – that was wrong. If I listened very carefully, I could make out the splash of tyres through water and the scrape of the windscreen wipers. It grew chilly inside the car.

We slowed down and stopped. When we pulled away once more, I knew we'd left the toll road and were driving through the city streets, for the car juddered forward in a set of stops and starts. I could make out some fresh sounds beneath the lashing rain: car horns blaring, the screech of brakes, snatches of music, Indonesian voices. Human sounds. Comforting, banal.

We slowed down and pulled to a halt. I heard the creak of a gate and the car edged a few feet forward. The engine came to a stop.

'You must wait here, Mr Young.'

Three doors opened in quick succession and closed quietly shut. I was alone in the car. The darkness, the pounding rain, and a fresh smell drifted in from the world outside – the bottle-green fragrance of rain-drenched leaves. It felt cloying now, and damp, my universe of darkness, so I spoke softly to myself, just to hear my own voice, a sound, any sound. Then, from some forgotten corner of my mind, a memory unfolded. A picture from such a long time ago, as bright as if my eyes were looking at it now. A map of the USA in a childhood encyclopedia, the rectangular states slotted neatly into each other like bricks in a wall, in vivid blocks of colour, reds and purples and greens.

Could I remember the name of every state? I began alphabetically, speaking each one aloud. Alaska, Alabama, Arkansas. I couldn't think of a B. Colorado, Connecticut, Delaware. By the time I reached Z, I boasted thirty-four states. Nevada, thirty-five. Illinois, thirty-six. Missouri – I wasn't sure if that was just the river, or the name of the state as well.

It didn't matter, for the sound of approaching footsteps cut short my puzzle. Three doors opened and closed; I assumed the same three people sat back in the car alongside me. It was hot again by now and I was sweating hard and my throat was dry. The engine started up. I cleared my throat but I didn't speak. I knew words couldn't help me.

Memories blew through my mind like scraps of paper in the wind, things I hadn't realized I still remembered. The morning at infant school when I painted a field and used too much green paint, so my favourite teacher got angry and shouted at me. How I moped for days and told my parents I'd never go back. Many years later, in the head-master's office with its musty air, as if the windows were never opened. He sat and rapped his finger on the desk, threatening me with expulsion for petting with a girl in the changing rooms. The resentment I felt for getting all the flak when she was the one who'd made most of the running. The day I rushed home in excitement, hoisting the silver cup I'd won in a school debate. How my father got angry, threw it against the wall and slammed out of the door.

I don't know why I should remember these bad times, because in truth my life had been untroubled. I was bright as a button at school and good at sports, I cruised through university in second gear, got a job full of promise and a set of rapid promotions. Soon I had a detached house in that boring blob of suburbia that adheres to the city of London, plus a beautiful wife and two mop-haired kids who could have been cloned for a Corn Flakes ad. It was easy to be a success in England, I mused, as long as you knew your place and were content with mediocrity. It was a game everyone played, and everyone seemed happy as long as nothing really changed. I wondered if all the other guys in suits and ties felt the same as me, as if they wore borrowed clothes.

I suppose my life hit the skids on the day my wife filed for divorce. Or at least this marked the official moment, when the worms inside the cake chewed through the icing. But there'd always been a nagging discontent inside, some vague, intangible longing I'd never addressed. Maybe this secret need had driven me to Jakarta.

What was I searching for? Some kind of faith, perhaps. Oh, I was smart and ironic, and I showed the whole world just how blasé I could be. But it comes pretty cheap, that kind of cynicism. Like the green fields of England, it stretches empty into the distance. Believing in something takes courage – whether it's your family, your country, or your God.

The car was cool and the rain was slowing down. I'd grown fond of my world of darkness; I didn't need eyes. I was preparing myself to die.

My mind went back to a summer's day in the garden of the house of my childhood. I was four years old, maybe five. It was one of those sleepy summer days when the sun beats down from a perfect blue sky, when insects hum and butterflies dance and ice-cream vans chime in the distance, and which perhaps exist in our memory only, as our dream of what a summer's day should be. My mother called me from the house and emerged with a jug of homemade lemonade. I ran to her side and buried my face in her billowing dress, white with summer flowers as dazzling as buttercups. I could feel her beside me now and smell that dress – a pure, sunny smell that took my mind away. I sipped iced lemonade as she ran her fingers through my hair.

I felt fingers at the back of my neck and the blindfold fell from my eyes. I squinted in the grey light of a rainy day. We were back in the car park at Soekarno-Hatta.

As I blinked to adjust to the daylight, Suprianto held open the door and helped me out of the car. The men in the front seats stared forward, without speaking. We had parked a short distance from Suprianto's BMW, so he placed his hand on my shoulder and guided me through the car park in the steady rain. Neither of us looked behind.

'Where are we going?' I asked, as his key turned in the ignition and we pulled away.

'To my house.'

I turned around to see if the two men were following.

'Am I safe now?'

'It may take a long time today. The traffic is bad.'

We reached the toll road. Everything had become unreal – the driving rain, the cars, the man in the kiosk who smiled and took our money, the straight grey lanes of the toll road stretching ahead. I felt outside my body, just like at the zoo, only this time it didn't scare me. It didn't matter any more if I wasn't real.

'Who were those men?'

'Try to relax, Mr Young. You have had much stress.'

'Where did they take me?'

'Please, I am tired of your questions. Western people. You are good to talk but not so good to listen.'

'And I'm tired of your games. Why can't you say what you mean instead of making everything into a puzzle?'

'I may have saved your life, Mr Young.'

'Am I supposed to say thank you?'

'I worry I am too late. Already they take you.'

'Who were those men?'

'You need not know. I have made an agreement with their boss.'

'That's comforting to know. Is he that goon from the military?'

'Do not ask me any more questions. No, you must not! It is important that you do not know about these people. I persuade them you are innocent, you know nothing that can hurt them.' He stared across. 'You must leave Indonesia.'

The skyline of the Golden Triangle lay obscured by sheets of grey rain. 'I can manage that.'

'My country is unstable at the moment. Things are happening which no one understands. Secret things. It is a mystery, like 1965, when the communists make revolution.'

'You like your mysteries, don't you, Detective Suprianto?'

'Still people argue what really happened then, Mr Young. Clever people – doctors and professors.'

'And will they argue about *reformasi* in thirty years time? About why it never happened?'

'Perhaps my people not ready for it.'

'And perhaps the people at the top want to make sure they never have the chance.'

Neither of us felt inclined to develop the argument – it didn't seem to matter a great deal. I stared through the window at the rain. The sky and the earth seemed to merge into each other, a huge wall of grey. I felt like a figure from a computer game, some shadow in a simulated universe. The world wasn't real, I wasn't flesh and blood, and my body wouldn't be mangled if the car crashed.

We exited the toll road near Jalan Arteri and passed the beggars beneath the flyover.

'Why are we going to your house?' I asked. 'If you want me out of Indonesia, why not leave me at Soekarno-Hatta?'

'It isn't finished yet.'

'What isn't finished?'

232

'You will see.'

I looked wearily out of the window. Another of Suprianto's mysteries.

We turned into Metro Pondok Indah and the Citibank building flashed by on our right. 'We are nearly at my house now.'

'You live in Pondok Indah?'

He gave a snicker of embarrassment. 'It is not a palace, Mr Young. My house is only small.'

We turned right at the traffic island, heading towards Jakarta International School, just a stone's throw from the Hotel Platinum where this strange dream had begun. A few moments later, the BMW pulled to a halt outside an impressive white building. OK, so it wasn't quite a palace, Detective Suprianto, but I wouldn't call it small. The policeman sounded his horn and a houseboy sprinted into the yard to open the gate.

Suprianto tossed a cigarette stub into the street and wound up his window. 'It is difficult between us now, Mr Young. You think I am a bad person.'

A middle-aged woman appeared in the doorway to greet us. Her head was draped in a diaphanous scarf that hung over her shoulders and covered the length of her arms. A tight sarong in yellow and green clung to her slender body, stretching almost to her feet. I'd got so used to Indonesians in jeans and Hard Rock T-shirts that she might as well have been in fancy dress.

'This is my wife, Mr Young.'

She bowed her head in deference and cupped my right hand between her palms. Softly spoken, modestly dressed – the stereotyped Javanese lady. *'Ma'afkan saya, tuan. Saya tidak bisa bicara Bahasa Inggris.'*

Two children ran out to join us: a girl of about fourteen and a boy maybe five years younger. The girl offered me a handshake, western style, and greeted me in confident

233

English. The boy hid behind his mother and clung to her sarong, peeping out from time to time.

We lingered in the doorway for a few minutes, smiling and saying the right things. But nothing could hide the tension which hung over the house. The setting seemed unreal, like an architect's model, while the characters in this drama were as stiff as a mechanical orchestra. Everyone was simply going through the motions.

Suprianto eventually led me into the guest room. It had a vaguely colonial air, with its ornately carved wooden furniture and its white marble floor. I expected to be seated here and offered tea, but instead I was guided beyond, into the part of the house usually reserved for the family. An honour indeed. I felt intrigued. He led me up the stairs to a wooden door.

'This is my study, Mr Young,' he said, with undisguised pride. 'Please, go in. I have something I want very much to show you.'

20

Suprianto's study gave the impression of never being soiled by the drudgery of everyday life. The odds and ends of messy reality stopped dead at the door. This was a place to contemplate, to set the mind to higher things. It stood beyond time, like the library in an ancient, rambling house, the scene where the murder gets committed in an antediluvian whodunit.

He gestured towards a solid chair at a writing desk. 'Forgive me, Mr Young. I will be back soon.' The door closed behind him.

I ran my eye along the titles on the bookshelves. The spines of the older books were difficult to read, for the room had just one source of light, a corner window overlooking the front of the house, and the grey air of a rainy afternoon enveloped the study. The titles were neatly stacked along the shelves, while weightier tomes were secured behind glass doors in bulky cabinets. Even from the other side of the glass, they exuded their seriousness. A cabinet devoted to criminology and law, a second to Islamic philosophy and thought, a third to the art and culture of the Indonesian archipelago. All very worthy stuff.

Then I spotted the detective paperbacks secreted in a corner – Chandler, Spillane, Simenon in English translation, plus a row of Agatha Christie. The forensic triumphs of Haircool Parrot.

'Ah, you find my detective novels, Mr Young.'

I jumped out of my skin. I hadn't heard him come back into the room.

'Is this a full set of Christie?' I asked.

He nodded, proudly. 'In English. I read so slow, because they are difficult for me. But every book I have already finished.' He knelt down and took out a paperback copy of *Death in the Clouds*. The cover, protected like all the others by a sheet of transparent plastic, bore a drawing of a giant wasp attacking a plane. 'This is my favourite, I think.'

Then he shook his head sadly. 'But life is not a detective story,' he sighed, as he slid the book back into its slot. 'Life is not tidy.' He signalled towards the chair once more. 'Please, Mr Young. Sit down.'

He switched on a reading lamp, which cast a creamy circle of light over the dark brown wood. There was a gentle knock at the door. His wife came in, closely followed by a maid, who placed a wooden tray on top of the desk. In the centre of the tray, a silver teapot and two china cups.

'For one last time, Mr Young, we take tea together.'

The heads of his children bobbed out from the left-hand side of the door. The girl, far bolder, gave me a little wave, while her brother stayed hidden, peeping from time to time when he plucked up the courage.

'*Silahkan*,' his wife invited me, pointing to the teapot and bowing her head. She ushered the children away and edged out of the room, closing the door behind her.

'My wife is a good Javanese woman. I am very lucky.' Emotion glistened in his deep brown eyes. 'I would not like one of these modern women, always asking for money and presents.' With a courteous smile and a lift of the hand, he poured tea into both of the cups. 'My wife still follows the Javanese ways.'

Nestled in his hand, the china cup seemed delicate: so delicate that I almost felt afraid to take hold of it. From the road outside the front gate, car brakes suddenly screeched.

'But my children, Mr Young! They do not care about my culture.' He watched me closely as I took my first sip of tea. As I'd expected, it was disgustingly sweet. 'Dewi is only interested in the boy bands, yes? For Udin, it is football. He is crazy for Manchester United.' I made no polite effort to seem interested in his waffle. 'Everyone tells me my children will change when they get older. But perhaps it is too late by then. I say to them, you must learn about your culture, it is where you come from. But they only want to know about western things.'

'Look, I appreciate the tea and this is all very nice and civilized,' I said. 'But I'm bored with this game, Suprianto. Just tell me what happens next.'

'Straight to the point. So western.' He gave a tense little laugh. 'But sometimes western people want everything too instant, Mr Young. They are not patient. Sometimes we can only sit and wait.'

He nodded enigmatically, as if privy to some deeper wisdom. I let him enjoy his moment of mystery and glanced up at a picture on the wall. A seascape of a sailing ship, tossed on a heaving grey sea. It was the only thing in the room that didn't exude calm. It seemed utterly out of place.

He went over to a bookcase and knelt down to take out a book. 'I would like to show you something very special, Mr Young. You are the first person to whom I show this.' His hands trembled as he placed the book in the soft pool of light. 'Not even my wife.'

He indicated that I might touch it. The cover bore the title, *My First English Primer*.

'In my village when I was a boy, there was an old man from Holland. We called him *Bapak* Jakob. Because this is a name from a local song for children.'

I took the book in both hands and lifted it up to the light. The paper cover, smoky purple letters on a pale grey background, had frayed at the edges and was torn along the spine. Beneath this ragged skin, the hardback was plain and beige.

'He was kind and wise, *Bapak* Jakob. Like a father to my village. It didn't matter to us that he was Dutch people.' He went over to the window and stared wistfully out. 'I was always his favourite, Mr Young, I don't know why. Many hours he spent with me, to teach me things, about Europe and the world. Then one day he must leave, go back to Holland. The day before he leave, he came to my house and give me this book. "You must study every day," he told me. "You must work very hard to improve your English. Because I will come back to Indonesia one day and we can speak English together." I was sad because I know I will never see him again. He was very sick, Mr Young. He was going home to die.'

As I opened the book to the first page, Suprianto recited from memory.

'Mr Jones wakes up at six o'clock. He goes to the bathroom and has his bath. He eats his breakfast in the dining room. Mr Jones works in London. He catches the train every day at eight o'clock.'

Word perfect. As he spoke, I studied the sketch in the book, with Mr Jones on the platform awaiting his train. The fingers of the station clock above his head pointed exactly to eight. He held an umbrella in his hand and he wore a bowler hat.

'Mr Jones works in a bank. He is a bank manager. He starts work every day at nine o'clock.'

A second sketch showed Mr Jones busy working at his desk. A plaque in front of him read 'Mr Jones, Manager'. Now that he had taken off his bowler hat, we could see he was bald.

'When I was a boy, I used to look at my book every night. Before sleeping, Mr Young. I had a secret dream in my heart that I must hide from everyone. One day I will be same with Mr Jones.' He sighed as the memories flooded back. 'Oh, his life is so busy and so discipline. Always he leaves for work at eight o'clock and always he gets home at half past five.' The expression on his face changed abruptly, becoming grave. 'I could not imagine a life like this. In my village in Java. It was not easy to dream there.'

I became aware of the silence that filled the room. Soft like a cushion or a blanket, soft and suffocating. Something like love.

'But because of Mr Jones, I have a dream. One day I will be rich, Mr Young, I know this in my heart. I will be rich and happy. I will have a beautiful, smiling family – same with Mr Jones.'

He left the window and approached the desk, leaning over my shoulder to slide his fingers beneath the page. He turned to the next with the utmost care.

Once more he was word perfect. 'Mrs Jones is a housewife. She goes to the shops every day to buy food. She cooks the family dinner at seven o'clock.' He shook his head. 'So perfect their life seemed to me, Mr Young. So simple and elegant.'

The sketch above the text showed the family at their evening meal. A formal occasion. Mr Jones sat at the head of the table with a glass of wine, Mrs Jones held a serving spoon in the air, while well-behaved brother and sister waited patiently for their food. The clock on the wall read seven o'clock exactly.

'But one day I get very bad trouble with my mother, Mr Young. I want to look like Mr Jones, so I take some flour from the kitchen and put on my face. To make it white, yes? I was only a child. But when my mother saw me she became very angry, she shouted at me, "Why you do this stupid thing? Why you must look like a white man?" And then she started to cry. All night long she cry.'

Outside the window, evening was drawing in. The soft grey shadows inside the room were deepening to charcoal.

'All night I stayed awake, because I knew it was my fault, she was crying because of me. But I could not understand why.' He bit his lip and laughed. 'Now I am a man, of course, I understand. My mother cried all night because she thinks I am ashamed of her, ashamed of my brown skin.'

Three blasts on a car horn sounded from outside the front gate. Suprianto shot up straight. 'I must go. Please, I will not be long.'

I leafed through the yellowed pages of the book and the everyday routine of the family Jones – Johnny helping his dad to polish the car, while his sister Lucy busied herself in the kitchen. I seemed to recall a book like this when I learnt French at school, except the family was called Dupont. I turned to the front to find the date of publication: 1952. I did a quick bit of mental arithmetic; the book was probably old-fashioned even when Suprianto first used it. On the inside cover, I found a signature in a flowing, confident hand. 'Remember me, *Bapak* Jakob'.

But I wasn't interested in the book, I was just keeping myself busy; my mind was on Suprianto and what was making him so agitated. When the outside gate creaked open, I could sit still no longer. I walked over to the window and stood to one side, from where I felt I couldn't be seen. Peeping out, I saw a navy-blue Kijang reverse into the driveway. I gripped the wrought-iron grille in front of the window as I felt a nervous flutter in my chest.

A young policeman in uniform stepped out of the Kijang. Suprianto walked over to speak to him: explaining something, or giving him orders. The detective's wife and his children emerged from the house, followed by the houseboy who was struggling with two green suitcases. Suprianto hugged his children and kissed them both on the brow. Then he turned to his wife, looked into her eyes and

240

squeezed her hand, leaning over to kiss her gently on the cheek. The boy started crying. Suprianto wiped his son's eyes and patted him on the back.

Then everyone seemed to freeze in the light of the lamp by the gate. The human beings became puppets, acting out a script that had been written long ago. A moment later, the detective's family took up their positions in the rear of the car.

The rain had almost stopped, but the sky was black and more seemed sure to follow. Suprianto addressed the officer one last time, checking that his orders had been understood, before the young man stepped into the driving seat. The houseboy pushed open the heavy grey gate and the Kijang inched out.

I heard the front door swing shut. Suprianto came back into the study, walked straight to the window and stared out, distracted. 'My garden is too dark, Mr Young. I must put another light, there in the corner.'

'I heard a car.'

He gripped the wrought-iron grille so hard that his knuckles grew pale. 'My family went on holiday.'

He drew the curtain shut. This seemed to help him to gather his thoughts and he picked up the conversation exactly where he had left it, as if there had been no interruption. 'What do you think of my book, Mr Young?'

I cast him a weary glance. 'I had one like it at school.'

'This book is the most important in my life. Except for the holy Qur'an, of course. Indonesian people do not like books, Mr Young. They are lazy for reading.'

He bent over to light a cigarette. 'Forgive me. I know I should not smoke inside the house. My wife does not like this.'

The match lit his face from below, picking out his cheekbones and masking his eyes, until his head resembled a skull.

'It's your house,' I said. 'Do what you like.'

'But because of this book, I studied hard at school. I was not lazy.'

He moved closer and gazed into my eyes, desperate that I listen to his meanderings. But I thought of Santo's dead body and I remembered all the times when the policeman had evaded my frantic questions. He didn't deserve my attention. I ignored him and stared down at the desk, refusing to meet his eye.

He ploughed on with his memories all the same. 'Many years later, my dream came true, Mr Young. I must go to the west for six months, in order to study your police methods. I was grown up now, not a child any more, but I couldn't sleep at night. *Wah*, I was so excited! I was going to England – Detective Suprianto from a village in Java!' He looked down at the floor and his voice went quiet. 'But when I got to the west, it was nothing at all like my dreams.'

'Because the people didn't have umbrellas and bowler hats?'

He laughed politely, before looking up and pausing to make sure he had my attention. 'Mr Jones did not really exist.'

He stood back at the window, clutching the wrought-iron grille. 'Yes, I was stupid, Mr Young. I know that now. A stupid young man with stupid dreams. But I lost those dreams in the west. I lost them for ever.' The smoke from his cigarette swirled upwards and faded in mid-air like last night's dreams.

Drops of fresh rain began to spatter the window. Against my wishes, I was starting to feel some sympathy for him.

'When I came back to Indonesia, I could not believe any more. So many bad people I must meet with in the west. Even police colleagues. They make love with a woman who is not their wife. They take money, same with police in Indonesia.' He frowned and bit his lip. 'They did not want me in England, Mr Young. I was not good enough because of my brown skin. A hundred times every day, they make sure I know this.'

'That was a long time ago. I hope things would be different now.'

He took three short puffs of his cigarette, as if stabbing himself in the mouth. 'Do you want to know something, Mr Young? I wish now that I never went to the west.'

'Who had Santo killed, Detective Suprianto?'

This stopped him in his tracks and he stared across.

'The student. Who had him killed?'

'What does it matter now?' He broke his stare and turned away. 'He is dead.'

'I'm supposed to listen to your stories and feel sorry for you. Feel sorry about your broken dreams. We all have to live with broken dreams, Suprianto. How about the student? I'd say his dreams were pretty broken, wouldn't you?'

'You would not make a good detective, Mr Young. You try to solve the mystery before you know the facts. And for you, from the west, they are always so simple, yes? Facts.'

He walked over to the seascape that hung on the wall. 'I bought this in Cambridge. My souvenir from England.' He beckoned that I should join him in front of the picture. 'Come and look close, Mr Young.' I could see at once that it wasn't a painting at all, but a giant jigsaw puzzle in a wooden frame.

'More than two thousands pieces. A detective must be logical, he must put the pieces together and make a picture. This is why I went to England.' He gestured towards the jigsaw with a dismissive flick of his hand. 'But it is only a game. I know that now. Like my novels with the clever detective.'

He nodded towards the chair. 'Please, Mr Young. Sit down. I want to tell you about this student.'

I sat at the desk as he requested. The corners of the room, barely touched by the table lamp's buttery glow, were swallowed up in darkness.

'To you this student is a hero, perhaps. Like me and Mr Jones. But when I went to England, I saw the truth and not my dreams any more. And if you know inside the heart of this student, Mr Young, he is not such a hero.'

'He was honest with me. Which is more than you've been.'

'Oh, he is honest, perhaps. Yes, he is honest to tell you what he wants you to know. And did he tell you that his father is from the military?' I picked up my teacup to try to disguise my shock. 'You are surprised to hear this, yes? His father is a general, Mr Young. And did he tell you that he send his friend to Bali and know all the time that his friend will die there? His friend who loves him like a brother and thinks he is a great man?'

'You're lying.'

He smashed his fist hard against the wall and let out a howl. 'Why didn't you leave, Mr Young?'

He turned towards the window so that his face was hidden from my view, but I saw how his body was shuddering as he struggled to get a grip on his feelings. He breathed long and deep and hard, clinging to the wrought-iron grille, until he willed his emotions back under his control. 'It is dark very early today. There is so much rain this week.'

He opened the window and threw his cigarette stub into the yard. A mosque was calling the faithful to evening prayer. 'Can it sometimes be too late to change, Mr Young? Too late for *reformasi*?'

'It's just talk, Suprianto. *Reformasi*. It's an empty word.'

'For you in the west, perhaps. It is just a game you play. Because there is so much freedom in the air that you forget to stop and smell it.' A peal of thunder rumbled in the distance. 'And when you look at people who must struggle for their freedom, you don't understand. You don't understand, so you judge us.'

'Did you tell me the truth? Did Santo really send his friend to his death?'

'Who knows what is inside a man's heart? We have a saying in Indonesia, Mr Young. You can measure how deep is the sea, but you can never measure how deep is the human heart.'

I gave an ironic little laugh. 'I thought you'd be an expert on that by now.'

He closed the window and drew the curtains tight. 'It is almost night. He will arrive soon.'

'The soldier who came to my house?'

He shook his head. 'Doctor White.'

'Then it's true he's still alive?'

'Did the student tell you this?'

'Yes. The student. Santo.'

'He seems to know everything, this student. What else did he tell you?' I stared in his direction but said nothing. 'Did he tell you I have instructions?'

'Instructions?'

He looked into my eyes. 'My instructions are very clear, Mr Young. You are never to leave this house alive.'

21

I sat at the desk, Suprianto stood at the window. The evening shadow that draped the room softly thickened to black. The table lamp cast a lonely ring of light around the grey and purple book. It glowed like a lone candle shining in a landscape at night. It felt valiant and futile: the only light in the world.

We fell silent for a long time.

Finally, the detective turned to face me. 'You haven't drunk your tea, Mr Young. It is cold.'

'So, what am I supposed to do when I meet Doctor White? Congratulate him on his recovery?'

'You are angry with me. I know this.'

He walked towards me, his head bowed like a naughty child. After pondering for a moment, he sat down beside me and took my hand. 'We must work together now.'

I pulled my hand free of his grip. 'We have no need to be polite to each other any more.'

'I will not allow this thing to happen, Mr Young. Already there is too much blood.' The call of the mosque sounded faintly through the window. He looked into my eyes. 'I will save your life.'

I gave a sarcastic laugh. 'Be careful. It can be dangerous being a hero.'

Once more he took my hand, wrapping it in his own and squeezing my fingers.

'You are tired,' he said. 'Tomorrow you will not feel like this.'

'I don't imagine I'll feel much at all. We can't make bargains with death.'

He breathed in deeply. 'Nor with God.'

I wrenched my fingers free for a second time. 'What a strange life you must have, Detective Suprianto. Seeing death so often in your work. Does it ever become normal?'

He shook his head.

'And do you ever stop being frightened of it?'

'Death does not frighten me, Mr Young. Only my God.'

He walked across to the window and hunched over to light a cigarette. The match glowed like a terrible secret in his hand. 'All my life I wanted to be a policeman. Even when I was a little boy, this was my only wish.'

'We have a saying in English. Be careful what you wish for – it might come true.'

He snuffed out the match and his face was swallowed in darkness. 'Every day in my job I must meet with bad people. Perhaps something slipped under the skin and into my soul.'

He went back to stare out of the window. 'Before I went to the west, I could fight it, Mr Young. I was strong enough to tell myself, these things will change one day. My country will grow up and my people will not be bad any more.' Rain tapped on the windowpane like the fingers of a ghost. 'But then I went to England. For a boy like me, from the *kampung*, this life was like paradise on earth. I couldn't understand. These people had wonderful lives, but it did not make them good.'

He dragged listlessly on his cigarette. The glow etched out his face, like a candle inside a pumpkin at halloween.

'I guess paradise is always somewhere else,' I said.

'When I came back to Indonesia, I tried to blame the west at first. It was a godless place. But then I looked around me

247

and I saw the same thing. My own people. Their lives became better and they grew more selfish. Snobbish and cruel. Why can't people be good, Mr Young? When there is no reason to be bad any more?'

'Maybe you should ask your friend.'

'My friend?'

'Doctor White. Maybe he can explain evil. He seems to know the territory.' The detective flushed and stared down at the floor. I felt a cruel pleasure at his unhappiness. 'Or perhaps you should ask yourself. You don't buy a house like this on a policeman's salary.'

'Do you think it is because I am greedy?' He lifted his chin. 'I have my family, Mr Young. I am ashamed if they must live in a house which is less than one of my officers.'

'So it's pride, is that all?'

'Oh, it is easy for you to be so critic. A man must take care of his family in Indonesia, or people gossip.'

'And that's worth letting a little girl die for? A little girl like your daughter?' I must have touched a raw nerve, for he could no longer look in my face and began to pace around the room. 'And how about the father whose little girl was killed? I bet he took care of his family, too. Before he lost his mind.'

'Do you know with this father, Mr Young? I mean, know what is true? He sold her for sex, his own daughter. Fourteen years old. That is my country. His family had no money and no food. So he made a deal with the man in Hotel Platinum. There are many *bules* who like sex with young girls, yes?'

He stood back at the window, clutching the black grille. 'This is why he is sick in his soul now. Because he sell his own daughter for half a million rupiah. And she is dead.'

'There are lots of ways of selling your daughter, Detective Suprianto. How about you?'

I was digging deep, pressing ever closer to the bare nerve.

Even in the darkness, with his back towards me, I could sense his rage. And above all, his guilt.

'When she gets older and learns about life, do you think she'll believe that all this came from the wage of an honest cop? Perhaps she'll hate you for being corrupt. But I doubt it. She'll have soaked in your corruption and become just the same. The next generation to bleed this poor country dry.'

He turned to face me, his hands clenched into fists. At that moment, I felt, he was capable of killing me himself. Somehow he managed to suck all his rage back inside. But the effort hurt, and tears welled up at the back of his eyes.

'Do you think I want my life like this? When I put on my uniform and I feel so proud in my heart? I am still proud, Mr Young. Even now. I am a good policeman and I am proud to get this case. Perhaps Detective Suprianto can catch this devil. I work so hard, I put the pieces together, like my jigsaw puzzle. Until one day my superior call me into his office. You must not solve this case, he said to me. The man you are hunting has important connections. He knows dangerous people. If you don't stop, it will be dangerous for you. For your family. It is better if an arrangement is reached. If you help them, they will help you.'

A cat let out an unholy screech in the garden. 'We must learn to embrace evil,' I whispered.

'I don't understand, Mr Young.'

The rain pounded on the window. '"For what shall it profit a man, if he shall gain the whole world, and lose his own soul?" Do you understand that, Detective Suprianto?'

I fancied I saw a tear run down his face. 'I understand, Mr Young.'

'But we all sell our souls in the end,' I said. 'That's the tragedy of being alive. Even Mr Jones. He probably got to be manager by stabbing his friend in the back.'

'We can change, Mr Young. If we ask for God's help.'

'Do you think so?'

'He can make us clean again.'

'But you don't really believe that in your heart, do you?'

'I believe it, yes.'

'Then why are you scared?'

'In Islam, at the end of the holy month of Ramadhan, there is Idul Fitri. This is the day when we say to our family and friends, "*Mohon ma'af lahir dan batin.*" Please forgive me for my sins and for my sinfulness. We ask each other for forgiveness and then we are clean again. Allah washes us pure and makes us as innocent as children.'

'I don't believe in fairy tales, Suprianto.'

He struck a match. The light scratched out the lines in his hands. They looked like the hands of a much older man.

'I tremble before my God, Mr Young. In my heart there are so many sins and one day I must face him.' He moved close beside me and bared his palms. 'Can we pretend it is Idul Fitri, Mr Young? Can I ask your forgiveness?'

A car pulled up outside the gate and sounded its horn.

'It's too late, Detective Suprianto.'

'No, Mr Young. With God's help, there can always be *reformasi*.'

'What right do I have to forgive anyone? I've sold my soul, the same as the rest of the world. Oh, I haven't traded it in for money, perhaps. I haven't buried it beneath possessions. But I've sold it slowly, piece by piece. I've rented it out to apathy and cynicism.'

The gate creaked open, the car pulled into the driveway and the engine stopped. The front door of the house eased open and footsteps padded up the stairs. Suprianto took a gun from a drawer in the desk. 'Look towards the window, Mr Young.'

I stared at him, defying him to shoot.

'Please.'

250

I smiled in his direction with something like pity in my eyes. His fingers held the gun, but I was in control. A rap came at the door. I faced the window as requested.

The detective called out and I heard the study door open. My nostrils immediately twitched at the prickly scent of an aftershave, a fragrance that seemed sweet at first, a blend of honeysuckle and rose, but which left behind a bitterness, a blast of decay, like the stench of rotting flowers. I heard the legs of a chair as they were scraped across the floor, then the door clicked shut again. Suprianto faced into the room, studying the scene behind me. Eventually he seemed satisfied and indicated that I could turn back around.

A presence skulked in the corner, the top half of its body obscured in shadow. The legs were crossed above the knee and an arm rested casually across the wing of the chair. The cut of the trousers was stylish and the black shoes shone. I couldn't make out the face. On the middle finger of the white left hand, a thick gold ring. A green stone gleamed, like some evil eye, in the centre.

'So, Detective Suprianto,' I said, with a quiet smile. 'I think they call this the endgame.'

I had no idea what set off my fearless new mood. I was trapped in a nightmare, so I could dare to defy logic and challenge the gods – it was my dream now, so I didn't need to be afraid. My buoyant frame of mind seemed to disconcert the detective. He turned round to face the window once more and pulled open the curtain to stare out at the rain, his shoulders slumped. For the first time since I'd met him, he seemed a beaten man, ragged and tired.

He spoke out to the presence in the corner, although he couldn't find the courage to turn and face him. 'Things are different now. There will be no more killing.' But the quaver in his voice betrayed his lack of faith, like an unconvincing actor who could only mouth the words.

The presence in the corner gave a snigger.

'I don't think he believes you, Detective Suprianto.'

'I guarantee Mr Young will leave Indonesia. I will drive him to the airport myself. He knows nothing that can harm you.'

In the corner of the room, the position of the white hands changed. The green gem in the ring caught the light and glinted like an eagle's eye. Rain hammered on the window behind Suprianto.

'It is different if I am single, Mr Young. But I could not let them hurt my family.'

'Who are you talking to, Detective? Me, or your God?'

'I think to myself, what is it they want? Only my silence.' He staggered over to the desk and stared, pleading, into my eyes. 'We do not plan to do evil, Mr Young. It is something little, like a mosquito – it bites in the middle of the night. It slips under the skin.' Raindrops rattled against the window like a thousand tiny stones. 'We come into this world as pure as children. But every day some more of the mud clings to us.'

A peal of thunder rumbled outside. 'Then one morning we look in the mirror and we do not see our own face.'

The scent of dead flowers now filled the room, heavy and funereal, all their sweetness gone. I stared across at Suprianto. 'I don't know which one of us is more damned,' I said. 'You, with your jealous God who plagues you and scourges you. Or me, alone, face to face with oblivion.'

The blood drained from his face. 'God will help you, Mr Young. If you ask for his mercy.'

'God? There is no God, Suprianto. There's only oblivion. So we spend our lives just running. Sometimes we run away from it, sometimes we hurtle towards it. We can never decide if it's beautiful or terrible.'

A huge clap of thunder shook the house to its foundations. The detective stood opposite me at the desk and spoke out to the presence in the corner, a fresh determination in his voice. 'I have made an agreement with important people. You must leave Indonesia. You do not have their support any more.' As he spoke, his shoulders rose and the tremble vanished from his voice. 'You must be out of the country by tonight. They will guarantee your safety if you leave.'

Once more in the corner, the white hand moved, and the green gem caught the light and gleamed.

Lightning bleached the room and I glimpsed Doctor White, a skeletal face frozen in the lurid blue flash. Cold and refined, with short blond hair and ice-blue eyes, a face that might have belonged to any one of the thousand *bules* I passed each day in the mall. A fraction later, blackness swallowed the face.

'It is over, Mr Young. I go to the man in the military and we make an agreement. I am frightened because he is powerful and I am not his equal, and perhaps he will think I have dangerous thinking. But if no one is brave, there will never be *reformasi*.'

I burst into laughter. It all seemed so ridiculous. 'Oh, Detective Suprianto! After all these years of selling your soul, how could you be so naïve?' A surge of warmth swept through my heart, almost a kind of love. 'Do you really think you can embrace this evil? Involve it in deals?'

The legs changed position in the corner of the room. Doctor White was getting edgy.

'I know with this man in the military, Mr Young. I have guarantee.'

'What do you think that's worth? You'd have been better to persuade him that Doctor White has become a danger to them. They might have deserted him then.' I pointed towards the window. 'They're probably waiting outside in the rain, to kill us both.'

'No. This man is a hard man, yes, but he loves his country. He is a man of honour. He will keep his word.'

The presence in the corner began to chuckle, with the indulgent disregard that the master can feel for the slave. Centuries of scorn reverberated in the hard laughter: the smell of rubber plantations, the sweat on the bodies who toiled there. Once more the presence felt safe.

Suprianto walked over and opened the window, to toss his half-smoked cigarette to the ground. Through the blast of the storm, I could make out the call of the mosque, strong and steady. 'I have done you wrong and perhaps you hate me, Mr Young. If you cannot forgive me, please try not to think badly of my people.' He closed the window and drew the curtain, blocking out the mosque and softening the wail of the storm. 'With God's help, we can change.'

He sat opposite me at the desk and peered into my eyes. 'I have faith in the mercy of my God, Mr Young. I believe he can make me like a child again.' He laid the gun across the palms of both his hands, then placed it carefully on top of the book in the pool of light, midway between us.

I looked deep into his eyes. It was like staring into a well, at the bottom where water lay glistening. A sky full of stars lay reflected in that bright black mirror and one of those stars was collapsing.

'It is a sin in my religion to take life, Mr Young.' He stared down at the gun and then back into my eyes. 'My heart is weighed down already with too many sins.'

I caught a rush of movement in the corner of my eye. I snatched the gun and fired. Three times I fired, in rapid succession, before the room went into slow motion. I seemed to watch each bullet as it came out of the gun and left a tiny puff of smoke behind. The presence lurched in my direction and then crumpled. The pale skin gleamed as it lay on the floor. One of the bullets had pierced the forehead, in the evil third eye.

Exhilaration scorched through my soul as I watched the thin line of blood trickle from the corner of the mouth. I felt like a god; I kept life and death. I had sucked the dark strength from the stone on Doctor White's finger and rendered it a lifeless pebble.

Suprianto sat helpless before me, making his peace with eternity. I looked into his face. He had the eyes of a child. If he wanted me to kill him, I could do it.

Thunder rumbled outside, much farther away. The flesh on the floor suddenly shed its eerie glow and became just a human body once more. The room grew familiar, an ordinary study, and Suprianto reverted to being an ordinary policeman. My strange exhilaration had burnt itself out.

I placed the gun back on the table, in the circle of light, on top of the language primer.

'You must leave now, Mr Young.'

Suprianto called out and the young officer rushed in, brandishing his gun. The detective held up his palms to calm down the young man, before rattling out some sentences in Javanese. He took a handkerchief from his pocket, the cloth which a few hours ago had been my blindfold, picked up the gun and wiped it clean.

'My officer will drive you to the airport and see you safe on your plane.' He opened the drawer of the desk and produced a large envelope. 'Do not worry, everything is arranged.' He gave a little laugh. 'Paperwork. Always more paperwork.'

He handed the envelope to the officer and patted him on the shoulder. 'What do you think of him, Mr Young? He is a fine young officer, yes? *Aduh!* How do you say it in English?'

For one last time I watched Suprianto wrestle to drag an English idiom from his memory. And for one last time, I saw the swell of pride when he won this battle. 'A credit to the force, yes? A credit to the force. People like him are the future of Indonesia.'

The officer stood to attention and blushed at this heartfelt praise.

'Please, Mr Young, take this.' He handed me the language primer. 'I am a man now, not a boy. I do not need it. And when you remember us in England, do not think badly of my people.'

I followed the young officer, step by step, down the flight of stairs. I knew it was coming, in my heart I was waiting for the sound, but still it shocked me. One last bullet from behind the closed door.

I saw the young man shudder, but he kept his eyes fixed ahead as he guided me to the car. 'I will take you to Soekarno-Hatta, *tuan*.'

I sat in the passenger seat and stared out at Jakarta, glistening like a black diamond after the rain. No, I won't think badly of your people when I remember them, Detective Suprianto. I won't even think badly of Jakarta.

I placed the language primer in my pocket. There I found the bottle of *arak*, enough for one more drink. I wound down the window and tossed it away.

How beautiful the rain smelt, how fresh and clean. Maybe it was too late by now to start a new life. Perhaps I was running away one more time and when I woke up tomorrow, nothing would have changed. Perhaps I was too old to change and it was too late.

I hoped it was never too late.

We reached Senayan roundabout and the statue of Pizza Man. Draped across his bare chest, a bright red banner flapped in the cool night breeze. In the centre of the banner, in large black letters, I read a single word.

'*Reformasi!*'